THE Caretaker

THE *Caretaker*

C.P. HARRIS

Photographer: Rafagcatala
www.instagram.com/rafagcatala_13/?hl=en
Developmental Editing & Proofreading by Anette King
Editing by Shauna Stevenson at Ink Machine Editing
Proofreading by Lori Parks & Teresa Smith
Formatting by Allusion Publishing
www.allusionpublishing.com
Beta Readers: Mihaela Zollinger, Vikki Elliott, and Irish T Hill.

AUTHOR'S NOTE

The Caretaker is book 3 in the Infidelity series. Themes include amnesia, cheating (not between the MCs), second chances, and hurt/comfort. The Caretaker deals with the death of a spouse, the off-page death of a child, and grief. All of which are addressed throughout the story. There are also brief mentions of fertility issues. As always, I encourage readers to put their safety above their curiosity.

"It is what the heart remembers that matters most."
~H Pierre

CHAPTER 1

Noon

"HALEY COVE TAVERN." I read the sign above the stone facade multiple times but it meant nothing to me. I waited for a memory to come barreling through my brain, because between the receipt in my pocket and the way my body hummed with anxious energy, this place—this quaint town—*should* mean something to me. But...nothing.

"Fuck!" I bashed the heels of my palms against the steering wheel repeatedly before gripping and jerking it in an attempt to rip it from the dashboard. To provide some semblance of control, even if it was only an illusion; even if the only thing I could control was the destruction of something.

My phone chirped with an incoming text, snapping me out of my daily rage ritual. Rage. I was *consumed* with it.

Heaving out a breath, I continued to stare beyond the manic swishing of the windshield wipers doing little to combat the heavy snowfall. I drowned out the sound of the whirring engine, of the heat blasting through the air vents, of the oxygen pumping at a fast clip in and out of my lungs. It all faded away as I concentrated on remembering—to no avail.

The phone rang this time, and I screamed until my voice gave out, until a couple stumbling arm-in-arm to their Uber were startled out of their drunken stupors. I hadn't realized I'd begun thrashing in my seat, or that the truck now rocked with my movements. This had been my last hope, and it was slipping away from me.

I yanked my hat off, my shaggy hair falling to my shoulders as I dragged aching hands down my overgrown beard. I was a wreck, and I didn't care. I'd lost my wife, the only person who my love still burned bright for, and no matter how hard I tried, I couldn't get my life back on track. I was beginning to not care, beginning to entertain no longer being here, no longer existing, and that scared me the most.

Sometimes I wished I didn't remember Stacey so vividly, if only so I could have a moment of peace from the pain of missing her. Not even in my sleep did I get a break. Her love haunted me there too. In some ways I was grateful for the unending dream. It conjured up this overwhelming feeling of love that saw me gasping awake in a cold sweat, and helped to keep that love front and center during the long months of rehabilitation and grief.

The scene never changed. She and I passionately entangled, our bodies writhing on top of an unkempt bed. The lovemaking was untamed, almost violent, sweat licking down her spine as I wrapped her long hair around my fist.

I could never quite make out her face, but the wild emotion that filled my heart and soul during those sleeping hours made one thing pretty clear: I would forever love my wife, with all of me. So I clung to that one dream with every useless scrap of my life.

Another chirp, and I knew without looking that it was Leland doing his weekly check-in. If I didn't reply, he'd keep trying to reach me. He used to be my best friend. Insisted he still was. Claimed we'd reconnected after having grown apart nearly a decade prior when I left Seattle for New York. The reconnecting years were gone for me, though. Lost amongst the two most recent years of memories that the accident had wiped away from me. Our history was incomplete on my end, which left me less enthusiastic about him than he was about me since the accident.

Not even Stacey had escaped what I couldn't recall from that time period. Those years were completely gone. Not a hint of them remained.

I desperately wanted that time back, wanted every moment I'd spent loving her during those years back. It was what brought me to Haley Cove. I refused to believe I'd driven hours to the tip of New York state for nothing.

Cutting the heat off, I pressed my sweaty forehead to the steering wheel and focused on my breathing, like my therapist said I should whenever I sensed a panic attack on the horizon. It was the only good tip she'd given me before I fired her. None of them knew how to help me. Not her, and not the others before her.

Only once I'd calmed, could I check my text messages.

Leland: *Are you okay?*

Leland: *Hello?*

Leland: *Dammit, Noon. Just let me know you're okay.*

Me: *I'm fine. Stop treating me like a fucking child.*

I hit send, and his response came in immediately, as if he'd been watching the screen for my reply.

Leland: *I'm sorry. Just worried about you.*

He cared, and that triggered my guilt, because all I seemed to do was make him pay for giving a damn about me. Sometimes my guilt weighed just as much as my grief. In moments like this it overshadowed it. I didn't know whether to be thankful for the reprieve or to be upset by the momentary distraction from my sorrow.

Leland stubbornly refused to give up on me, though, no matter how much I pushed him away. There were enough photos taken of us together to prove he wasn't lying about any of it, but the truth didn't matter if I couldn't feel it, if I couldn't see it in my mind's eye. The man standing beside him in those photos wasn't me. Not the version of me I'd been living for the past nine months, if what I'd been doing could even be called living.

Tucking my phone into my pocket and grabbing my satchel, I exited the truck and headed inside the tavern.

The interior of the building was reminiscent of an earlier time, much like what I'd gleaned so far from the town. I had my pick of seats at the bar—business looked slow tonight—but opted for one of the creaky leather and wood booths near the back instead.

Pulling my camera from my bag, I snapped a few photos of the place to look over later if nothing jogged my memory now.

"What can I get for you?" a bubbly waitress asked, withdrawing a notepad and pen from the apron tied at her waist. Her name tag read Liz.

"I'll take whatever you have on tap," I said, my voice scratchy from all the screaming I'd done.

"Anything to eat?"

I lowered my camera to the table and quickly scanned the menu slotted between the condiments and napkin holder. "Burger and fries. Medium well," I answered, waiting for her to scribble it down. "Can I ask you how long you've worked here?"

"It's been two years today," she said with pride.

"Have you seen me here before? Would've been nine months ago to be exact. Actually, hang on a sec." I pulled the folder I'd brought with me from my satchel, flipping past Stacey's photos and withdrawing one of me. "This is how I look on a good day." I hadn't had a good day in a while. "Do you recognize this man?" I surely didn't. That man had a fresh shave and wore a smile that said he was ready to take on the world.

She gave me an odd look, probably not getting why it mattered whether or not she'd seen me in there before or why I couldn't confirm that information for myself.

"I was in a car accident. I'm having trouble recalling things that happened in the past, but I recently came across this receipt in some of my things that were salvaged from the crash." I fished the tattered piece of paper from my pocket and held it out to her. "It proves I was here the night before the accident. I don't remember ever stepping foot in this town, though."

"I've never seen you before," she said, studying both the photo and the receipt, "but we're the closest restaurant off the highway and tend to get a lot of foot traffic in here because of it. Especially on weekends. Kind of makes it hard to remember faces."

"Thanks," I said, slumping in my seat.

"Maybe Trisha remembers," she said, pity in her eyes. She called Trisha over, but she'd barely glanced at the image before confirming that she'd never seen me before either.

I showed them both a photo of Stacey, feeling desperate now. "Do you recognize this woman? She wouldn't have been here with me that day, but maybe we visited Haley Cove together some other time."

Liz's brows furrowed in concentration. Trisha didn't even try to hide her boredom. I withdrew another photo. This one was a close-up of her.

"Here's a better one," I said, but Liz shook her head. Trisha shrugged.

"Maybe she came in before I started working here," Trisha drawled, grinding away at her bubble gum.

"Maybe," I replied, feeling drained of energy and hope. "Thanks anyway."

"Yeah, sure," she said flatly, leaving me alone with Liz.

"I'll get your order in," Liz said, tapping her pen against the pad of paper before sauntering off.

Frustrated, I shoved the photos and the receipt into my bag, then closed my eyes and focused on my breathing again. Once centered, I picked up the camera, preparing to take a few more pictures but deciding to review what I'd taken of the tavern so far first.

Zooming in on the woodwork along the bar top, and the exit sign above the back door, I meticulously went through each shot. Studies showed that the most innocuous things could trigger an amnesiac's memory. Maybe I tripped and fell under the restroom sign when I was here last. Maybe I banged my knee under the bar top. Willing to do anything to regain what I'd lost, I refused to take anything for granted.

I scrolled to the last photo I'd taken and nearly fumbled the camera. My pulse quickened in unison with my spine straightening, and I swung my head up to find the booth on the other side of the tavern now empty. I frantically scanned the place, but the man who'd been sitting there was gone, only an empty wine glass and cash for the bill remained.

My breaths came in harsh, shallow puffs as I re-examined the photo with building hysteria. A blinding pain shot through my skull as I fought to latch on to...to *something*. I scooted out of the booth, turning in place, eyes flickering everywhere in desperate search of him.

I rushed for the entrance, almost knocking a server down in the process. "Sorry," I said absently, ignoring the cautious stares everyone now aimed at me.

"Sir?" my waitress called. I vaguely registered her holding my drink as I tore through the door, coatless, the air billowing from my parted lips forming tiny clouds. The blustering wind cut through my shirt, and the icy snow pelted my face and neck as I searched the parking lot.

He couldn't have driven off that fast. *How many cars were here when I arrived?* I didn't know, hadn't thought to count. Why hadn't I counted? I counted now, but the total of four cars, three vans, and my truck meant nothing to me when I didn't know how many there were to begin with. *How many were here?* I spun in place, gripping the sides of my pounding head. How many? How many!?

Sprinting back inside, I grabbed Trisha by the elbow as she passed. "Th-the guy who was sitting over there. D-did you see him leave?" I stammered, too far gone to care about the flash of fear in her eyes.

The restrooms. I hadn't checked the restrooms. I released her before she could answer, hurrying to the rear of the tavern where the flashing restroom sign taunted me. Turning the corner, I collided with the man from the photo, and my headache escalated to a teeth-grinding migraine.

Cornflower-blue eyes that were already too wide for his smooth, angular face, widened farther. They glistened, like maybe he'd been crying, and suddenly my problems became secondary to his.

"Are you alright?" I asked, forcing my panting breaths to slow while looking him over for signs of injury. He no longer wore his hair in a topknot, like he had in the picture. It now flowed down his back and shoulders, as though he'd yanked the blond tendrils free of their restraints.

"No. I'm not." His voice was gentle and a tad breathless.

"No. I'm not."

Those three words set off an alarm in me, and my blood rocketed through my veins as I tried to make sense of it. He slid his hands from mine. I hadn't realized I'd been holding them. *Shit.* I had to get myself under control.

He stood there waiting as I did, his own control seeming to hang in the balance while he continued to stare at me. He appeared more stable than I did. He was a deer caught in headlights, frozen by the moment, while my mind flailed with my confusion.

"Have we...have we met before?" I asked, once able to speak. I tracked his every twitch, his lazy blinks, the rosy color rising in his cheeks. I followed the motion of his tongue swiping across his wine-stained lips. He was androgynous, beautiful, meek in a way that somehow complemented him, and the screeching in my brain grew louder.

"No," he whispered, almost as if it pained him too. "I'd remember someone like you."

My shoulders sagged. Maybe the familiarity I'd felt came from his pain, which shot from those watery eyes to connect with mine. He was hurting, possibly even as much as I was, and perhaps that was what I'd recognized in the photo.

His gaze swept all the way to my feet before rising again, and I became painfully aware of my disheveled state. At nearly seven feet tall and broader than most men, the wild hair and beard only made me more intimidating, gruesome even. And while he was taller than the average male height, I still loomed over him and was at least twice his size. I'd unintentionally cornered him, so I backed up a bit, fighting to form a smile I didn't feel to put him at ease.

"I'm sorry," I said. "You just seem familiar to me."

He tucked his hair behind his ears, pulling himself together. "Familiar?" His delicate but husky tone was inquisitive. "How so?"

"I don't know," I admitted, roughly combing my fingers through my hair until my hands intertwined at my nape. "None of this makes sense," I said under my breath.

"What doesn't?" he asked, his irises swimming within an ocean. I wondered if those were actual tears or if he always looked like he was on the verge of them. I wanted to hold him, to assure him that everything would be okay. The strange urge to do so baffled me.

"This place, life, you," I replied sharply, my agitation directed inward.

"What about it doesn't make sense?" He genuinely seemed to care about my answer. He'd taken a few cautious steps forward, eliminating the space I'd given him.

"Nothing." I shook my head to clear it. "It's not your problem. Again, I'm sorry for barreling down on you."

We were supposed to go our separate ways now, but neither of us moved, and when I tried to move my feet they wouldn't budge. I couldn't take my eyes off of him. It appeared as though he was struggling to do the same, and for the first time since waking up in a hospital bed to the news that I'd lost my wife, I felt something other than sorrow and fury.

I felt seen and understood, like whatever pained me pained him, but that couldn't be. Unless what we were feeling wasn't as complicated as I was making it out to be. He didn't need to have lost years of his life to a brain injury. He didn't need to have lost the love of his life either. Maybe what connected us was something universal, an emotion brought on by any number of life's various atrocities. Despair.

"Are you alone?" I asked. I knew the answer. I'd seen from the picture, and the solitary drink on his table, that he'd been here by himself. What I really wanted to know was if he was alone in general, alone in this world, or if there was someone he could turn to once he left here. According to his own words and the crushing look on his face, he wasn't okay, and I wanted him to be.

"Yes," he said, almost gut-wrenchingly so. "I'm alone."

"Me too." Amnesia was lonely and isolating, especially when surrounded by people eager for you to remember. The pressure made it worse. But this beautiful stranger didn't know me, didn't have anything to gain from me remembering. I felt a need to hang on to that for a while longer.

"Are you a local?" I asked.

"Ah, yeah, you can say that."

"I was involved in an accident that left me unable to recall some important details of my life," I said, keeping it simple. "I was here before. In this town, this tavern. Nine months ago, to be exact. It's likely that I was here for more than just one night. I know you said you don't recognize me, but I would have looked different then. Would you mind stopping by my table and looking at a few photos? It's right over there." I pointed out my booth just as my waitress dropped off my food. My drink had likely gone warm by now.

"And what if I still don't recognize you? Or better yet, what if I do? What happens then?" he asked, his expression concerned.

"I...don't know." I'd assumed I would show up and my memories would magically return. They hadn't, and so what good would someone recognizing me do? Where would I go from there?

"I know I was here, and not only because I have the receipt to prove it. I can *feel* it. I guess if someone recognizes me it might spark a memory for them of a conversation we might have had, things I might have said. Things that could help me remember or lead me to my next destination out here. It's a long shot, but it's the only shot I've got right now. This town matters to me, and I need to know why. Why was I here the night before losing the best thing that's ever happened to me?" I'd asked that more to myself, and felt the odd need to apologize for it when he braced a hand on the wall next to him. Had he lost someone too?

"Okay." He swallowed. "I'll see what I can do."

"Thank you." I led the way to my table.

Pushing my food and beer aside, I reached into my satchel again. "How long have you lived in Haley Cove?" I asked as he settled in across from me. Living in Haley Cove didn't mean he'd have been in this tavern on the day I visited. I'd honestly have better luck badgering the rest of the staff. But maybe he'd seen me somewhere else in town. I doubted I'd come all this way just to eat.

"Permanently? Almost a year. I used to live in New Jersey. Willowbrook to be exact."

"Willowbrook," I repeated, hand stalling on the folder.

"Have you been there before?" His tone was careful.

"No, I don't think so," I said, unsure of why the town name caught my attention in the first place. I lined the pictures up in front of him. He took his time looking at mine, which I appreciated. It showed he was taking this seriously, and not brushing me off the way Trisha had.

My optimism flared when his finger traced my smile, like maybe it had triggered a memory for him. He barely glanced at Stacey's photo before shoving both back in my direction.

"Sorry, I've never seen either of you."

"Are you sure?" I implored.

"I'm positive. Who is she?"

"My wife." I closed the folder, exhaustion taking its toll on me. "She didn't survive the accident." I gripped the two wedding bands and the diamond engagement ring dangling from the gold chain I wore. My band was a replica. The original was absent from my finger when I woke up in the hospital. Likely removed before I'd been rushed into surgery. No one could account for it. They'd had to sedate me after I'd noticed it was missing. Stacey's rings were sitting on her bedside table when I got home. She hated sleeping in jewelry and had probably forgotten to put them back on before leaving. It wouldn't have been the first time.

I let go of the rings that hung close to my heart and glanced up to find him staring at them, a broken expression overtaking his face. Did he lose his wife? Or husband? He didn't wear a ring on his hand, so maybe a lover?

"Sorry for your loss."

It was a sentiment I'd heard one too many times, but I didn't hate it when he said it. Our gazes locked and held, and a senseless sort of longing filled me. I attributed it to Stacey, to missing her.

"She was pregnant," I whispered.

"Did you say *pregnant*?" he breathed, like maybe he hadn't heard me correctly. He'd leaned forward in his seat.

"Yeah. I had my wife and my opportunity at being a father taken from me in one fell swoop."

"H-how far along was she?"

"Roughly twelve weeks is what I was told."

He fell back as if the news were a blow, mouth slightly agape. I took his shock as sympathy. My gaze fell to his hands, which now gripped the edge of the table so tight they'd paled. I hadn't wanted to invade his privacy with intrusive questions, even though I seemed to have no issue revealing my own problems to him. I couldn't sit there and not care, though. Not ask. Not when it was clear that I wasn't the only one at the table suffering.

"Hey," I whispered, laying a hand on top of his. At the contact, his eyes snapped to mine, the devastation there matched the reflection I saw in the mirror every day.

"Did you lose someone?" I asked, pulling my hand back, the air around me becoming easier to breathe with the action.

"Yes." He'd said it so low it was no more than a hiss. "Someone who made me feel like I could do anything, be anything. So I understand what it's like to wish you could get back the person you loved and lost."

"Did your person die too?"

"No, he didn't, but it feels like it sometimes."

"Maybe you should try and find him." I would've given anything to have an opportunity to find Stacey. I would've paid any price to know she was alive and well, and that the only thing keeping us apart was the physical distance between us. I would've hunted her down and never let her go again.

"Yeah," he said, sounding unconvinced. "Maybe."

We gazed at each other, that string of familiarity at the back of my skull tugging wildly.

"Are the last couple years before the accident all you've lost?"

"No, but it's the only part of my life I've lost so completely. It's the only part of my life with her that I've lost at all."

"Oh," was all he said.

I leaned my forearms on the table, my fingers pressing into my forehead. "My estranged childhood friend Leland came back into my life during that time, and he brought with him his partner, Franklin, and Franklin's sons, Jasper and Cole. Apparently, we'd all become one big happy family, except I don't remember reconnecting with Leland, and I don't remember Franklin or his sons at all. Well, that's not entirely true. I remember Franklin. I lived in Seattle up until a decade ago. We'd met a couple times before I left for New York, but not under the best of circumstances, and we definitely weren't friends. But now I'm supposed to care about him."

I looked up, expecting to find him bored, to get some indication that he was ready to escape me. The opposite held true. He was listening, truly listening like he had nowhere else to be but right there with me, and I didn't even know his name.

"Keep going," he said, and so I did, because God knew I needed to. Needed to not feel so alone. And maybe he needed the distraction that listening to my problems provided. It helped to know that I may be helping him in return.

"My childhood years aren't forgotten completely. Best way to describe it is waking up after a night of excessive drinking. Most of what happened is a blur. You have to rely on the people around you to recount the events. Some of what they say you remember clearly, some of it's a distorted haze that you kind of remember. The rest is news to me. Thankfully, I have the years spent with my wife. All but those last two."

He nodded as though he understood me. "And that's the missing time you want back."

"It's the priority, yes. My wife is the priority."

"Not to minimize what you lost," he started, "or *who* you lost..." His voice gave out then, and he turned away, only turning back once he'd regained his composure. "Not to minimize any of it," he began again, "but shouldn't the time spent with the people still here be your priority?"

The question didn't offend me. Not when his tone was gentle and searching, like perhaps he'd had to ask himself the same question a time or two and hadn't known how to answer it. Did he have friends or family that he'd neglected because he couldn't get over the person he'd lost? Could we really be that similar?

"Not when it feels like my heart is still out there somewhere," I said. Because it wasn't with me, not really. It was with Stacey, with the time I'd get back, come hell or high water. Hopefully, my answer inspired him to not give up on his person too.

"I think my wife led me here, and I need to know why. I need to remember. Nothing else matters until I do."

"Do your friends know you're here?"

"No. Most days I don't even answer their calls. I avoid my sister as well. It's easier with her. We live on opposite coasts. I'm angry and resentful and confused, and I want to be left alone to wallow in that. They all want me to be the person I used to be for them, but all I want to be is who I used to be for *her*," I stressed, emotion clogging my throat.

"I've got this well of love in my chest, robbing me of breath most days, and sustaining me on the other days. I don't know what to do with it. I don't want my memories returned to me because I can't live without them. I want every second of what I lost back because I can't live without her, and I want to remember every moment of the life we had together. Even the last seven hundred and thirty days of it. It's what my heart wants."

"That can't be easy," he said, voice strained.

I scoffed. "Which part? The having to fend off the people in my life? The people whose eyes fill with hope every time I walk through their door, or every time they barge through mine, only for that hope to be snuffed out when they realize I'm still not the happy-go-lucky version of myself. Not the man they once knew. Or the never-ending obsession with someone who's no longer here? An obsession that I'm sometimes not even sure belongs to her—" I shut myself up, wishing I could take the words back. I'd never voiced that last part out loud. To be honest, I'd never had words for the feeling until then. There was a vast and all-consuming hole inside of me that I attributed to her being gone because...what else could it be? "Which part is the hard part?" I asked him, anger and shame now replacing dejection.

"All of it," he said, his big blue eyes filled with compassion. The validation took my breath away, leaving me deflated and having to reinforce my forearms against the table to keep from crashing face-first onto it.

I returned to the topic of my friends and family, leaving my bewildering admission behind. "I'm just so sick of everyone trying to remind me of everything like it's their goddamned duty to fix me," I said, and he nodded again, as if he understood that too. I believed that nod. It had been a while since I believed anything, but I believed that. I believed...*him*.

"It confuses me, makes me defensive. It doesn't help, even

though it should. I just want to remember. I want to feel something other than lost."

"That sounds reasonable to me."

"Thank you," I breathed, because he was the first person to tell me that since I woke up in this new reality of mine. "Sorry to dump all this on you. You're obviously going through something of your own."

"It's fine," he said, dismissing my apology.

"I'm Noon, by the way. Noon Waters."

He hesitated before saying, "My name's Solace." He watched me from beneath lowered lashes, as if waiting for something.

"Solace," I said, tasting it, thinking about the comfort he'd given me without even knowing it. "It suits you."

Twin crimson blotches appeared on his pale cheeks, and he pointed one long, elegant finger to the camera on the table. "Photographer?"

"Not my official job title, but it feels right." I shrugged, holding up the bulky piece of equipment. "It was on display in the window of an electronics store I passed on a morning walk. Had a panic attack after spotting it. Figured it must have meant something. A clue, maybe. So I bought it. Turns out I'm good at it."

Solace smiled, this half grin that was both shy and alluring. Everything in me said he was oblivious to the latter. It registered in me as a fact, one that made me uncomfortable because of how vehemently I knew it. I wanted to stay in the presence of this seemingly guileless man. My own smile shook from the force it took to maintain it.

"What's your official job title?" he asked, those shimmering eyes lighter now that we'd moved on to a simpler topic.

"I freelance in property and estate management. Or at least I used to. I haven't worked since the accident." I hadn't done much but grieve and lock myself away from the world. Thankfully, I could financially afford to continue to do so for the foreseeable future.

"What if you never figure out why you were here? What if you never get all your memories back? Is that a possibility?" Solace asked.

"Yes," I said with a defeated sigh. "It's a strong possibility. The head trauma I suffered was that severe." I unconsciously sought out the scar tissue hidden by my hair.

"What then?" he asked for the second time, a hint of his melancholy returning. I found myself wanting to do anything I could to make it vanish again, because while he was lovely like this, sad and broken and in desperate need of care, he looked otherworldly when happy, even if I'd only caught a glimpse of it through his boyish grin.

I gave him an answer I'd never contemplated before because I'd never looked that far into the future. Not when so much darkness had blinded me to the road ahead. "Then I'll have to settle for making new memories. I'll have to *try* to," I corrected, because it wouldn't be easy, if at all possible. A sudden spark ignited behind those majestic eyes of his. "I booked a room at an inn across town."

That surprised him. "How long will you be in Haley Cove for?"

"I don't know. A few weeks. As long as it takes."

Liz returned, noting the untouched food with a frown. "Can I get you anything else?"

"No, I'm fine. Thanks."

She turned to Solace. "How about you?"

"No, thanks," he said. "I'm heading out."

"I'll take the check and a to-go box," I told her, seeing no reason to linger any longer now that he'd be leaving. I snapped a few more photos of the tavern while he watched me, his expression thoughtful.

He pulled a pen from his pocket, stealing a napkin from the small stack near my plate. "Here's my address and phone number in case you need a tour guide. Or someone to talk to," he added.

"Your address? I could be a serial killer."

Solace chuckled, the sound throaty and warm. "Well, you certainly look like one," he joked. "But I have a feeling you're harmless." He stood, gaze going to the coat rack near the entrance. "Cell service can be spotty up here, especially when the snow is this bad." He jerked his chin to the napkin I now held. "Use either to find me, if you want or need to."

There was nothing duplicitous about him that I could sense or see. It was clear he had demons he wasn't willing to share, but his intentions felt pure.

"Okay," I said, already planning to take him up on his offer. And for the first time in nine months, I felt like maybe there was something to live for.

And with that, Solace was gone, but he'd left something behind.

Hope. Solace had given me hope.

CHAPTER 2

Solace

Twelve Months Ago
Then

PATRICK HATED MY sentimental nature. He said I used nostalgia as an excuse to not move past traumatic events, so maybe today wasn't the best day to dig through Gavin's vinyl collection—the one I couldn't seem to part with for sentimental reasons—in search of one of his favorites. Patrick was sure to see my actions as passive aggressive, but it wasn't. It was Gavin's birthday, and I had every right to miss him.

I powered up the old record player, dusting off the needle before setting it on the most important album ever created in the history of creating albums—per Gavin. Lowering the volume, I peered toward the stairs, waiting for my husband to come charging down in annoyance...or outright fury.

Sighing with relief when that didn't happen, I dragged myself over to the media console to run fingers over the framed photo of my older brother Gavin—Gav as we preferred to call him. I couldn't bear to look at the photo next to his, so I flipped it face down, then retook my seat on the bay window bench, tucking my feet under me.

Gavin's favorite song from the album came on, and the irony of it never failed to take my breath away. He would bellow the lyrics at the top of his lungs, and wouldn't stop until everyone else joined in. Well, until I joined in. The song had always made Patrick uncomfortable.

I allowed myself a few tears, then brushed them away with the sleeve of my sweater as I glanced toward the stairs again. Patrick said I cried too much, that I felt too much. He used to love that about me. He'd said it made me emotionally open and mature. Now he slung around terms like "too sensitive" and "too dramatic," using them as weapons to hurt me. If only I could manage being cold and distant, an artform he'd mastered.

I traced a G into the condensation building on the window, then used a flattened palm to wipe it away. Leaving it there wouldn't have gone over well.

The snow flurries coming down barely accumulated along the front yard, but the weatherman predicted we'd be hit with a storm soon. I'd have to stock up on supplies before then, since I'd be here alone while Patrick spent the next three months on a humanitarian mission with Doctors Beyond Borders. He'd be gone by morning.

"You're not dressed," he snapped, startling me. I twisted around to see him waiting at the bottom of the landing, mask in hand.

"Dressed?" I eyed his tuxedo in confusion, setting my feet on the floor.

"I assumed you were using the guest bedroom when I didn't see you getting ready upstairs." He stormed over to the record player and ripped the plug from the outlet. The music stopped abruptly, leaving me alone with his enduring anger.

"The hospital charity ball," I whispered, closing my eyes. "I'm sorry. It won't take me long to get ready." I stood, but he stopped me with a raised hand.

"It's fine. I'm already running late. I'll just go alone." He pulled his Venetian mask over his head, reaching into the closet for his coat. "I do everything else alone."

As low blows went, this one fell well below the equator, hitting me in the gut, right where he'd taken aim. I found it hard to leave the house for long periods at a time, but he knew it was because I felt closest to Gavin here.

"I can meet you there," I said. We lived in the quiet town of Willowbrook. A suburban area less than an hour away from the heart of New York City. "It won't take me long to get there."

"Don't bother," he replied, not even looking at me as he wrapped his scarf around his neck. I ran my teeth over my bottom lip, crossing my arms and debating if this was worth a fight. "And don't bother waiting up," he added, gripping the doorknob. "I'll be late."

I *always* waited up for him. Couldn't sleep without him. He knew that too, but he was in the business of constantly punishing me.

"You'll be gone for months. Can't you at least come home at a decent hour to spend some time with me?"

"Well, I thought we'd be spending time with each other at tonight's masquerade ball."

"When's the last time you held me, Patrick?"

The random question caught him off guard. "Where did that come from?"

I thrived on affection, and not having it felt like drowning, like my own body was failing me.

"You deny me love, knowing how much I need it, and you won't let me love you in return, knowing I need that just as much—even though it seems that you couldn't care less," I said bitterly. I'd come to realize that love deprivation was Patrick's own form of passive aggression.

"Don't be ridiculous, Solace. And what does this have to do with anything?" His hand tightened on the doorknob, the only indication that he wasn't unaffected by my accusation.

"Why didn't you remind me about the charity ball? I was sitting down here all day. Would it have been that hard to simply remind me?"

"You didn't want to be reminded. You love to forget, to not pay attention to things." His expression dared me to ask what he meant by that.

I bit down on the inside of my cheek to redirect the ache that had its sights on my heart. "When did seeing me in pain stop hurting you, Patrick?"

"I can't do this right now." He opened the door.

"Then when? Tell me when would be a good time to actually talk about this."

Patrick turned slowly, the door still open. I tucked my balled fists under my arms, shivering from the cold.

"Do you even miss him?" I asked, voice giving out on the last word.

His gaze drifted to the picture frame still standing.

"He's my best friend. Of course I miss him."

"Don't be deliberately obtuse," I spat. "Do you even know what today is?"

His Adam's apple bobbed, the first real sign of any emotion besides detachment or simmering rage.

"It's his birthday," I whispered, slowly inching toward him, not wanting to scare off the sadness in his eyes.

"It's been nearly a year, Solace."

"So I should forget about it? Get over it? Like you have?" I'd drawn close enough to touch him. A few inches more and I'd be close enough to kiss him, to use my body to apologize since my words were never enough.

"Stop," he gritted out, and I was unsure if he meant stop speaking or stop approaching him. I ignored him, still closing the distance and still talking.

"How have you managed to get over him? Tell me. Fucking *teach me*," I begged, those tears that disgusted him so much now running rampant down my face.

"I have my packed suitcase in the car. I'll get a hotel room near the airport tonight—"

"Do you even love him, Patrick?"

"Enough," he ordered, backing away until he was flush against the now wide-open door, snowflakes blowing in on the late afternoon wind. "Not another word."

"Do you?" I asked. "D-do you love him?"

"*Loved*," he snarled, dark eyes hard again beneath his silver mask. "It's *loved*. I don't get to *love* him anymore, because he's gone." The *because of you* went unsaid, but oftentimes silence spoke louder than words. It was the things left unsaid that destroyed people, and he'd left the silent blame hanging mid-air between us, effectively destroying me, something he did with surgical precision.

I stumbled back, and he left, the door meeting the frame with a slam. Seconds later, the car engine roared and tires crunched over the salted drive as he backed away and blasted down the street.

On autopilot, I plugged the record player back in and started the song from the beginning. Staring unblinkingly out the window, I let my tears run unchecked as I mused about how much Gavin loved the snow.

♦ ♦ ♦

Two hours later I'd convinced myself that Patrick was right about me. Maybe I was too fragile, too needy. Maybe I had been grieving for far too long. I'd worked myself into an overthinking mess until I believed everything was my fault, because of course it was. I needed to stop worrying about my needs and for once be there for him, following his lead, learning by his example. And so I showered, slipped into my tux, and knotted my hair at my nape before donning my mask. At least it hid the puffiness around my eyes.

I arrived at the museum three hours late, but the party was in full swing with no signs of ending anytime soon. I kept close to the perimeter of the room as I scanned the crowd for Patrick. Many people danced in their ballgowns and tailored suits, others laughed and conversed in dim corners, and some admired the artwork plastered along the walls. It all felt very sophisticated and over the top, right down to the red carpet stationed outside. I was out of my element but did my best not to show it.

I'd been about to ask someone if they'd seen Dr. Patrick Cunningham, but then I spotted him across the room. He wore that private sly smile of his that I hadn't seen in a while. The one that said he was up to no good. When was the last time I'd seen that mischievous smile? It had to have been my thirty-third birthday. Right before he'd slathered cake frosting on my face, then proceeded to lick me clean before taking me right there on the kitchen floor. That was more than a year ago.

I took a moment to admire it, to miss it, to join in with one of my own. What remained of my world came tumbling down when I followed the direction of his secret smile.

A slender woman in a yellow dress danced with a man who stood at least a head taller than everyone in the room. His hands were positioned on her waist, his eyes closed, nose buried in her golden hair as they swayed to the intimate song. Her cheek rested on his chest, but whereas he seemed completely enraptured by her, she only had eyes for my husband. A chill skated down my spine.

The song ended, something more lively taking its place, and she accepted a kiss from her dance partner before pointing in the vicinity of the restrooms and excusing herself.

Patrick set his champagne flute down before discreetly weaving his way through the crowd to follow her. His trajectory would take him right past me, and I should've thought about hiding, but the suffocating pain made it impossible to move. It didn't matter anyway, because his fixation on her made it easy for him to breeze right by me without even noticing.

The dark-haired man she'd been dancing with now sat at a table conversing with the couple seated across from him. One of them must have said something amusing because he tossed his head back, laughing with his whole body, as if all was right in his world. I found myself envying his ignorance, because at least he wasn't now forced to choose between two options when either of them would ruin him. Didn't matter if I left now and told myself it was nothing or if I followed Patrick in order to prove that theory wrong. Either way, he'd damaged what was left of me.

The restrooms weren't single occupant or gender neutral, so they clearly hadn't gone in there. I kept moving, venturing past a velvet rope with a metal stanchion in front of it holding a sign that read "Museum Personnel Only."

It was dark on this side of the museum, the music fading the farther I crept. I rounded corner after corner, peeked into every exhibition space I passed, willing my heart to slow so I could hear something other than my own blood pounding in my ears.

I was beginning to think I'd imagined things, was seconds away from heading back to the ball to find Patrick. He'd likely stepped outside for fresh air, I told myself. Or maybe he'd gone into another restroom. There had to be more than one. But then the murmuring of voices reached me from a private room at the end of the last hall. The door had been left ajar. I recognized one of the voices as belonging to my husband, and the spinning in my head ensued.

"I hated seeing his hands on you," Patrick said.

"But I only had eyes for you," a woman replied.

"Knowing that brought a smile to my face," he said softly. "Are you going to tell him tonight?"

"No," she answered. "I was thinking..." She trailed off. "Maybe we should wait until we get back. It seems cruel to drop this on them right before running off for three months."

I propped a hand against the wall to keep from falling, my other hand clutching my abdomen.

"You're right," Patrick whispered. "Of course you are. I'm just ready to start my life with you. I can't take the hiding anymore. I can't take not waking up to you anymore, knowing that you're waking up next to someone else."

"I know," she said. "Me either."

"We'll have the next three months together, and although it won't be the most glamorous three months, I plan on having my hands on you every chance I get," Patrick said passionately. "No more passing each other in the halls of the hospital with no more than a polite nod. No more sneaking away between rounds, no more fucking you in random hotels or in the back of my car like you're some whore." He sounded disgusted by it, but she giggled.

"Well, I kinda like being your whore."

"Thank the heavens." He exhaled, and she giggled louder. Patrick shushed her.

"I love you," he professed, his awed tone unfamiliar to me.

"Show me," she demanded, and the sound of lips and bodies coming together followed. The echo of a zipper lowering rang out, and I backed away, both arms now banded around my stomach, holding me together.

I made it back to the velvet rope without passing out from the pain, but if it weren't for operating all day on an empty stomach, I would've retched right there. I stopped, panting, anger forcing its way through the self-pity and the ache of betrayal wrapping around me. How could he do this to me?

Without thinking, I marched back to that room, shoving the door so hard it rebounded off the wall behind it.

She yelped, dropping her legs from around his hips. Patrick muttered a curse, releasing her wrists from where he'd had them pinned against the wall.

"What the—" Patrick's words came to a halt as his eyes landed on me in abject horror. The woman spun away to fix her dress as his now shriveling cock hung out of his pants. "S-solace," he stammered.

"What have you done?" I asked, unsure of how I managed to utter that much. He hadn't worn a condom, and the implications of that, the carelessness, the disrespect. The resulting wound nearly took me to my knees.

"I-I can explain," he said, tucking himself back in.

"Don't bother," I seethed, vision blurring. "How long?"

The woman now had her clothes situated but kept her back to me, as if hoping I'd forget she was there. Patrick then shoved the figurative knife a little deeper into my chest when he shifted to block her from my view. To protect her from this.

"I didn't want it to come out like this," he said. "I wanted to—"

"You wanted to make me feel like shit just a bit longer, right?" Everything in me shook, every organ writhing in pain. "Secretly blame me for a few more years? Hold your love hostage a little longer?"

"That isn't true, and you aren't the only one hurting—"

"Shut up!" I shook from head to toe. "How long?" There was nowhere for either of them to go, not without getting past me first. Patrick raised his hands in front of him, as if telling me to calm down, but he didn't answer.

"Before or after Gavin?" I croaked, realizing there was still more of me to destroy. If the affair had begun after Gavin died, I didn't think I would survive this confrontation. Because maybe I could've handled knowing he'd continued on with an affair already in motion. Maybe I could've come to terms with the fact that he may have already been in love with her. I could've lived with that more. As desperate as it sounded, I could have convinced myself that staying with her afterward was out of his hands because they were in love by that point.

But if he'd started up the affair *after* Gavin's death... If he'd made the choice to accept comfort for his grief from someone else when for the last year I'd been *begging* him on fucking hands and knees to take comfort in me, to help *me*... No, I wouldn't survive that at all.

"After," he whispered. "Not long after."

I sagged, my arms shooting out to grip either side of the doorframe. She turned to me then, streaks of mascara racing to her jawline, lips trembling.

"We never meant to hurt—"

One look from me and her words died in her throat. Patrick reached a hand back for her, as if wanting to show his solidarity.

"Why?" I cried. "Why do you hate me so much?" I knew why, but my heart still wanted to hear it. My heart still hoped he'd say it wasn't true.

"I couldn't turn to you," he said, and for once in God knew how long, something besides rage and blame stared back at me. Something I yearned for so long to see, to help him through. Sorrow. "I couldn't," he repeated softly.

"So you turned to *her*. You gave *her* all of your kindness, and brought your anger and coldness home to me." My legs gave out, and Patrick lunged for me. I stumbled back into the wall to evade his help. "Don't touch me!" I shouted, and they both jumped.

"Don't touch me, don't follow me, and don't bother coming home."

"Sola—"

"Swear it!" I demanded, forbidding my tears to fall. He would never see me cry over him again. "Say you will not follow me home tonight," I gritted out, because I was weak enough to fall prey to any excuse he might come up with, weak enough to believe more of his lies. "Promise me."

"I-I promise."

I dragged my pummeled body down hallway after hallway, ripping my bow tie and mask away as I went. Everything felt stifling, even my skin.

Beyond the velvet rope again, eyes firmly on the exit, I didn't see the huge man in front of me until we'd collided.

He grabbed hold of me before I hit the floor, and after a few acrobatic movements and a spin to ensure neither one of us fell to the marble, he apologized for knocking the wind out of me.

"Are you okay?" he asked, true concern shining in those sparkling emerald eyes. In my shattered state, I realized it was the man who'd been dancing with my husband's mistress. One look at his ring finger told me she was more than just his date. "Hey," he whispered, clasping my chin and raising my head, his grip surprisingly gentle. "Are you alright?"

I couldn't remember the last time anyone asked me that, and I wanted to weep when his thumb grazed my fallen teardrop. "No," I breathed. "I'm not."

Our gazes latched together, his seeming to ask if there was anything he could do for me, and mine said there wasn't anything anyone could do.

"Are you here alone?" he asked. "Can I get you a cab—"

"Noon?" someone said from behind me. *She* said from behind me.

I removed my cold hand from his warm one, and my ache deepened. I hadn't even noticed I'd been holding it. He peered over his shoulder, his attention going to his wife. I couldn't see her beyond his broad back, chances were she couldn't see me either.

"I have to go," I panted, unable to face her again.

"Wait—" he tried, but I was already gone.

To my surprising disappointment, Patrick didn't chase behind me. He didn't text, and he didn't call. And for once, he'd chosen to keep his promise. He never came home.

CHAPTER 3

Noon

Now

KEEPING WITH THE aesthetic of Haley Cove, I expected Solace to live in a small cottage emitting smoke through a stone chimney because burning wood would be the only way to keep the old-fashioned home warm. What I got was a dilapidated farm on the outskirts of town with a modernized barn house at its center. I assumed the rest of the property was a work in progress.

After easing to a stop at the end of the post-and-rail fenced driveway, I snapped a succession of photos, capturing the grandeur of the house and the snow-covered evergreens surrounding it.

I lowered the camera, letting it rest against my chest, the strap pulling taut at my nape. Aside from Stacey, my camera was the one thing I could hold on to, and it rarely left my side—or neck.

Solace stepped outside, tugging the lapels of his oversized cardigan across his chest to fight off the winter chill. The wind tossed his loose hair around, and he squinted through the thick strands to see me through the windshield I sat behind.

Not wanting him to get sick or freeze to death, I cut the truck's engine, intending to get out. Suddenly self-conscious about my unkempt hair, I paused to glance in the mirror. I'd shaved the beard off after deciding to take Solace up on his offer to show me around, but there was little I could do about my hair. It didn't behave itself the way Solace's hair did. It curled in some spots and hung limp in others. I'd tied it back as best I could before leaving the bed and breakfast that afternoon. Finding a barber made it onto my priority list for the first time in months. Nine months, to be exact.

"You didn't tell me you had your own country out here," I said, meeting up with him at the door. I'd called him after spending the whole night replaying our conversation from the tavern yesterday afternoon. He didn't hesitate to invite me over, saying we could get started on seeing the town today, if I liked. I liked that idea very much; too much, if I were being honest.

"This is your phone number?" he'd asked after answering my call with a delayed and distrusting hello.

"Yeah, why?" I'd asked in return.

"Nothing. I just...didn't recognize it."

My phone hadn't survived the accident. Months later, when Leland threatened to show up at my door unannounced every day if I didn't replace it, I'd made sure to get a new number. I didn't want any work-related calls, any well-wisher calls, or any calls from people who were unknown to me. So I understood the hesitancy in answering a number you didn't recognize.

"Save it," I'd told him. Doing so felt like taking a big leap. I never wanted anyone to call me, but suddenly I looked forward to the idea.

"Saved," he'd said, the word little more than a wisp of air.

I found Solace refreshing. He didn't know the old me and had no expectations of me ever being that person again. I needed that. And it didn't hurt that he was a great listener and also kind.

"It belonged to my grandfather." He stepped aside and gestured for me to enter ahead of him. He took my coat, hanging it in the closet as I kicked off my wet boots.

"This is incredible," I breathed, descending into the sunken living room, the obvious centerpiece of the home. He had a fire going in the massive hearth, and the sun shone through the wall of windows that ran adjacent to it. "I didn't see any animals."

"It hasn't been a working farm for some time," he said from behind me. "At one point I considered adding stables to the property. Get a few horses. Now, I'm not so sure."

The interior had been decorated with warmth in mind, from the mink-colored sheepskin rug in front of the fireplace, to the matching armchairs perched across from the couch. Grays, browns, and several variations of beige mixed throughout, making the place feel inviting. It felt like home.

"What changed your mind?" I asked, dragging a hand along the back of the couch, drawn to it. All of a sudden, I wanted to stretch out on it and sleep for days. How long had it been since I'd slept for more than a few hours at a time?

"Mostly a loss of passion," Solace answered. "Also seemed like a lot for one person."

"No family?" I headed toward the two photos on the mantel.

"None close by," he said, coming up next to me.

"Who's this?" I picked up the first frame.

"That's my brother, Gavin. I call him Gav. He's in the military. Special Ops. Doesn't come home often. He's an adrenaline junkie and would rather be in the field."

I set the photo down and moved on to the next one. "And this little guy?" The boy in the photo had curly, auburn hair. He gripped a vinyl record to his chest, Christmas wrapping paper littered around him.

Solace sighed, taking the picture frame from me. He held it like it was his most prized possession. "That's my son, also named Gavin. He died a couple years ago. He was six." He set the frame back exactly as it was, making minor adjustments until it was right.

"I'm sorry," I said. The firelight did wonders for the thin, watery shimmer that seemed to never recede from his eyes. It was just enough to illuminate the bold coloring of his irises, to add a shine to them. To hypnotize an onlooker. But not so much as to make him appear needlessly weepy.

"Why?" he asked. "It wasn't your fault. It was mine." He strode off before I could formulate another apology, changing the topic before my heart had adjusted to the painful news he'd delivered. "Make yourself comfortable." He ascended from the living room. "I was about to make us tea before you showed up."

"Do you have chamomile?"

He glanced over his shoulder, wearing a look I couldn't quite put my finger on. "Sure do," he said before rounding a corner and disappearing out of view.

I turned to the photo of young Gavin again, huffing a laugh at his smile with the front two teeth missing. He didn't resemble Solace or the uncle he shared a name with. Maybe he looked like his mother, or maybe he'd been adopted. Solace didn't wear a wedding band, and he'd all but said he lived alone. "What happened?" I whispered to the photo. "And why does your father blame himself for it?"

I wanted to take that blame from him, take that pain and every other moment of agony he may have experienced in this lifetime and carry it for him. I shook the thought from my head. I didn't even know him, yet the want lingered in my chest.

His reaction when I'd mentioned Stacey being pregnant made sense now. I'd opened up a wound for him. I lowered my head, fighting against the urge to run into the kitchen and apologize again.

I sat on the couch and stifled a groan, then a yawn. It should've been a crime for anything to be this comfortable. Setting my camera on the coffee table, I snuggled into the mountain of pillows, convincing myself it wouldn't hurt to close my eyes until Solace returned with our tea. I knew it was the worst idea I'd ever come up with as soon as my eyelids lowered and something warm and soothing yanked me down into an abyss.

◆ ◆ ◆

I woke with a gasp, shooting upright and frantically taking in my surroundings. *Where the hell am I?*

"You're safe," said a tender voice, calming me. I blinked the rest of the sleep away, seeing Solace sitting in one of the cozy armchairs across from me. "Bad dream?"

"Yeah." I screwed my eyes shut. "The accident. Or *an* accident, I should say." I didn't remember the actual crash. "Truck horns blaring, bright lights blinding me, and broken glass everywhere. The usual nightmare fanfare." I flopped back, about to ask where we should start with our town tour, but stiffened when I noticed the full moon beyond the windows. I shot up again, whipping my head toward Solace, who had a stack of magazines spread out on the coffee table and his lap. "How long have I been asleep?"

He checked the time on his phone before removing the black-rimmed glasses he wore. "It's eight o'clock."

"Six hours?" I asked in surprise. "You let me sleep for six whole hours?"

"Yeah, I let you drool too," he said. I brought my fingers to the corners of my mouth. They were dry. He cracked a wicked grin.

"Liar." I grinned in return. "I can't believe I slept that long, and that you let me."

"You obviously needed it. And I'm sure you'd have done the same for me if our roles were reversed and I needed the rest."

"I would have," I said. "But we've wasted a whole day."

"We'll get another one tomorrow."

A few days ago, a comment like that would have upset me. I knew because Leland said something similar to me and it had set me off. No one understood the anxiety of an amnesiac; the lack of trust we had for the world around us. No one understood how it felt to not have the full picture of your life, to be missing important parts of it. There was a constant urgency to get it back. It hummed in my blood and shook my bones. That urgency never left, was always at the forefront of my mind. It screamed *now, now, now*! Except...it didn't scream that at this moment. At this moment I believed Solace. I believed that we could put it off for tomorrow. And for once I wanted to, if only so I could remain seated across from him. So I didn't have to leave this place—his home—that felt so much like my home too.

"Okay," I said. "Tomorrow."

Solace nudged a thermos in my direction. I had the lid unscrewed and chamomile tea flooding my throat before he could explain that it might not be hot after all this time.

"Hot, warm, cold...it doesn't matter," I said, coming up for air.

"Have you always loved tea?" he asked with a hint of amusement.

"No. Franklin is a tea connoisseur. He's Leland's partner," I stopped to remind him.

"I know. I remember everything you've ever said to me, Noon."

I dropped my gaze, swallowing down my reaction to his words, to the passion I must have imagined them infused with. To the "ever" that seemed out of place but perfect all the same. "He, ah, was tasked to babysit me one day, early on, before I could manage taking care of myself. He made me a cup of tea. The first sip ended with me in tears. It felt more familiar than anything else at the time. I've never had it taste quite like this, though. Did you add milk?"

"Yeah," he said after staring at me for a beat. "It's my grandfather's secret recipe. My son loved it too."

I wanted to know more about his son, but I wanted to avoid bringing up painful memories for him even more. "What's with the magazines?" I asked instead.

"I used to model. Feels like forever ago. Was thinking of maybe getting back into it. Thought I'd see what's popular these days. See if I still have what it takes."

I snorted. "What, good looks? You've got that in spades." I froze with the thermos cup to my lips. "Sorry," I said, lowering it. "My filter seems to be locked up in the same place my memories are."

"Or maybe you just don't have a filter," he said, as if that was okay. That was how I felt around him—*okay.*

"Maybe," I agreed.

"I'd need to reach out to my previous agent. See if she'll take me on again. First I have to update my portfolio," he mused, slipping his glasses back on. They transformed him from elegantly handsome to studious and quirky, adorable even. I cleared my throat, but it did little to clear the sudden spark of attraction or the subsequent confusion and guilt behind it.

Solace went back to flipping through the magazines as I finished off my lukewarm tea. An idea hit me.

"I could take the photos for you. If you're okay with that." I pointed to my camera when he peered up at me questioningly. "I know a thing or two about taking pictures."

"Editorial photos are a different beast."

I quirked a brow. "Is that a challenge?"

He tucked his hair behind his ear, blushing, and I wondered what about this exchange would make him nervous or embarrassed. Solace shook his head. "I couldn't ask you to do that."

"You didn't ask, and it's the least I can do after storming into your life with all my crazy. You show me the town, and I'll help you build your portfolio. Deal?"

He bit down on his bottom lip, and I had to look away or risk thoughts that might violate my vows. Reality came into sharp focus as soon as those words filled my head. *Stacey is gone.* Even if the love was here to stay.

"Deal," he said, stopping my grief in its tracks, preventing it from taking a solid hold of me. "Speaking of tours, want to see the rest of the house?"

"I'd love to." I stood, stretching and staring at the couch. "I still can't believe I slept for six hours. I never sleep that long."

"It's the couch," Solace said. "It has that effect on people."

"People?" I asked, then realized the answer was none of my business. "Sorry. Guess I'm a bit possessive of her already. I might have to take it off your hands when I head back to the city." That didn't amuse him like I thought it would. I wondered if it was the prospect of losing the couch, or the mention of me leaving, that had brought about his frown. Likely the couch. It probably held sentimental value to him.

"Let's start with the kitchen," he said before padding off in that direction.

He'd managed to achieve both a rustic and modern theme with the kitchen decor, the pantry's barn door keeping with the exterior's motif. Solace didn't explain things as we went, just allowed me to take in every nook and cranny as he observed me.

"Wow." I stood back to absorb the scope of the arched, wrought iron and glass doors that led out back. They were as tall as the ceiling, and as expansive as the darkness beyond them. "Impressive."

"We can take a drive around the rest of the property tomorrow, if you're up for it," Solace said, and I turned my attention from what I couldn't see in the distance—even if it called to me—to his reflection through the glass door.

He leaned casually against the teakwood and marble island, the baggy cerulean cardigan he'd worn since this afternoon slipping off one shoulder to reveal the smooth, milky skin there beneath the thin strap of his fitted tank. His stomach muscles pushed against the ribbed fabric.

"I'd like that," I said, fighting back the terror attempting to rattle my limbs.

We made our way to the second floor, then past a narrow set of stairs that likely led to the attic. "What's up there?"

"That's where I keep Gavin's things." His steps continued toward the only room he hadn't shown me yet.

Solace stopped at his open bedroom door, motioning for me to go in.

I appreciated the height of the archways and doorframes throughout the house. It wasn't often that I didn't have to bend before walking through one.

The color scheme aligned with the rest of the house, but the walls were paneled, and the fireplace in the sitting area rivaled the one in the living room. I rubbed at the back of my neck, smoothing down the hairs that rose to attention there.

"What's wrong?" Solace asked, still standing in the doorway as though he didn't want to get in the way of my exploration.

"Nothing," I answered, because it didn't make sense for anything to be wrong.

In a handful of strides, my long legs carried me over to the gargantuan canopy bed. Everything in this house was exaggerated in size, including the high ceilings. Solace's bedroom was no different. It felt good to walk with my shoulders back. To not have to make myself small in order to fit inside my surroundings.

I fingered the gray linen curtains hanging from the iron railings to pool on the carpeted floor. "This is...beautiful," I said, instead of "familiar," because it wasn't familiar, couldn't be, and I didn't want to scare him off with my apparent insanity.

"Thank you," he whispered.

A fresh headache began to take shape, and sweat coated the palm I still held to my nape. "I should go," I said abruptly. "It's getting late, and I've taken up enough of your day."

"I don't mind," he assured me, but I was already moving past him for the stairs, and lacing my boots by the time he met me at the door.

"I'll give you a call tomorrow," I said.

"Yeah. Okay," he replied, sounding disappointed. "If you can't get me by phone, just show up. I'll be here." He pulled my coat from the closet, and I took it with a murmured thanks as I opened the front door.

"Your camera," he said, dashing for the coffee table. I never forgot my camera. Never.

"Thanks," I said again, accepting it from him. The pain in my skull escalated when I stepped outside, the intensity increasing the closer I got to my truck. By the time I opened the driver side door, the hyperventilation had reached level ten. *What the fuck is wrong with me?*

Snow crunched on the ground behind me, and Solace's voice cut through the panic racking my body. "Hey," he said, turning me to face him with a hand on my shoulder. "Are you okay?"

I peered at the house, then the snow-covered drive that would lead me away from it, then back to the house again. I squeezed my eyes shut, willing myself to calm the fuck down. Solace waited patiently, giving me room as I stripped out of my coat, flinging it into the truck, then bracing my hands on my knees.

"Breathe," he whispered from beside me, rubbing soothing circles on my back. He leaned forward until his face was only inches from mine, until his warm breath hit my cheek. "Breathe."

I listened, focusing on the timbre of his voice, twisting my head toward his doe eyes. There was no judgment there, no fear, only a desire to help. It took a while, but I got myself in order and straightened. "I'm okay now," I promised, and Solace surveyed me for signs of the opposite. "You must think I'm crazy." I began pacing a tight circle with my hands on my hips.

"I would never think that," he said, his cheeks and nose red from the cold. "Never."

My gaze went back to the long drive, and I started up the breathing exercises again. "I-I just...want...this to end," I gasped between deep inhales and exhales. Solace worried his lip between his teeth, and the need to apologize overwhelmed me. "I'm sorry. I shouldn't have dragged you into this."

"Has anyone ever told you that you apologize a lot?"

I huffed a laugh. "Feels like I've been on an apology tour for the better part of the year."

"You don't need to be sorry, Noon. Not with me." We locked gazes for two, three, maybe a dozen heartbeats, and by the time he slid his warm palm into my cold and clammy one, the headache was gone.

"Stay," he whispered.

Stay.

Stay.

Stay.

The word tugged and tugged, drugging me, and I nodded in a daze. Solace closed my truck door and led me inside by the hand, unlacing my boots before helping me out of them, then leading me to the stairs.

"Do you mind if I sleep down here?" I asked, pulling him to a stop. Solace looked to the couch, then back at me.

"Not at all. I'll get you a blanket and something to sleep in." He returned with a t-shirt and sweats that surprisingly happened to fit me. Maybe they belonged to his brother, or to the-one-who-got-away. The man he'd said made him feel like he could do anything, be anything. I wanted to ask him about it, but I'd had enough strange reactions for one day.

I sighed as I got comfortable and stared into the fire, wondering how I could possibly be so tired after the long nap I'd had in this very spot.

"You don't have to stay down here with me," I said as he curled up in the armchair with a book. He'd changed clothes too, his joggers gripping his toned legs, his t-shirt not quite hitting his slim waist.

"I don't mind." Worry lines creased his forehead. "I'll head up once you're asleep."

I didn't want to be alone, so I didn't argue. That night, I didn't dream about car crashes. I didn't dream about my wife either. For the first time, under the protection of Solace and his watchful eyes, I dreamt of nothing at all. For the first time, I felt at peace.

CHAPTER 4

Solace

Then

IT'D BEEN ALMOST a week since the charity ball, and I hadn't heard a word from Patrick. Granted, he was in a third-world country doing important work—with *her*—but he hadn't even made an effort to contact me. Hadn't stayed behind to deal with this, to deal with us.

I couldn't sleep, because the pain went beyond something I could sleep through, beyond something I could even breathe through. It had surpassed excruciating.

All that was left to do now was die from a broken heart, if that were possible. At least I'd get to be with Gavin again. Did I even deserve a place in heaven for what I'd let happen to him?

My skull ached, like someone had taken a hammer to it. Side effects from my hangover, or so I'd thought. Took me a moment to realize that the pounding filling my head wasn't from my migraine. Someone was beating down my front door.

I rolled over, ignoring the headache and the summoning to the door. The ringing of the doorbell came next.

Other than moving when absolutely necessary, I'd remained in the fetal position in the center of our bed, a bottle of vodka pressed to my mouth or crushed against my chest at all times. Now, my bones protested at having to do more than accommodate the small movements needed to do those things.

Empty liquor bottles crashed to the floor as I inched my way off the bed, feeling along the wall until I reached, then opened, the bedroom door. "Damn it," I muttered, shielding my eyes when sunlight hit me from all angles. The blackout curtains were drawn closed in the bedroom, screwing up my sense of time and now causing a momentary impairment of my vision.

The pounding and the ringing grew in intensity as my eyes adjusted, and at any second I expected a fist to break through the wooden door.

With every step, the current state of my life came back to me, and my weakened body gave out before I reached the landing. I fell to my knees, palms catching me before my face hit the floor.

Gavin.

I dry heaved.

Patrick.

I heaved again, almost sinking back into my vortex of grief if it weren't for the urgency of the knocking on the door, the sound tethering me to the present.

Affair.

I gripped the banister, focusing on the chiming of the doorbell, dragging myself to my feet before swaying and stumbling back into the wall.

Alone.

"C-coming," I panted, my shallow breaths disturbing the strands of hair dangling across my face. By the time I got to the door, I needed a minute to refuel, to build up the strength required to unlock it. My limbs were jittery, the acid in my stomach burning its way up my throat, so I pressed my forehead against the cool surface, taking the time I needed.

The banging resumed, forcing my head back. I was in rough shape, and I didn't stop to think about who awaited me on the other side of the door. I needed them to stop, to go away so I could get back to my misery.

I swung the door open in time to see a tall, broad figure marching toward a pickup truck. He spun my way, unholy anger lighting up his green eyes as recognition hit him. Those beautiful gem-like eyes that had been full of compassion at the charity ball, now narrowed on me.

He strode my way, fists balled. "*You*," he sneered, as if he thought I was the other half in his wife's affair. I slumped against the doorframe, welcoming those enormous fists to put an end to me.

He grabbed me up by the collar of my robe, hauling his arm back with a snarl. My eyes connected with his then, because I wanted to see it all. His rage, his agony, his payback for what happened to him. I wanted to see my pain in someone else, wanted to see my anger and jealousy and fear reflected back at me. I wanted to not feel so damn alone.

His labored breathing faltered as he peered deeper into my eyes. Winter air pumped past his full, parted lips in puffs of smoke before being snatched away by the wind. "You," he said breathlessly, his sneer slipping away, the coldness in his eyes thawing.

The behemoth of a man observed me further, fist still raised, but I didn't think he was even aware of it at that point. I hung in his grasp, wordlessly begging him for violence, for anything to make it all end.

His arm slowly lowered to his side as he mimicked my drooping posture. That's when I noticed the scruff riding his jaw, the suit jacket he wore inside out, the scent of liquor coming through his pores. The scent wasn't fresh, more like his body was still ridding itself of the harm he'd done to it over the course of a week. He took in the wedding band I hadn't managed to take off, and I took in his.

"*You*," he whispered, seeming to realize that I wasn't the other half to his wife's affair but another victim of it.

"You," I parroted back, voice hitching as I acknowledged him in the same way, acknowledged his pain. A flood of moisture rushed to my eyes, and I didn't know if I moved first, if I hugged him or if he hugged me, but I clung to him. Clung to this stranger, who, through our current shared experience, I had so much in common with. We'd be forever connected now, and I didn't even know his name.

◆ ◆ ◆

Unfortunately for me, sleep didn't cure headaches. I blinked awake, my cheek resting on something warm and solid, my hair veiling my face. Groaning and pushing myself upright, I noted the rock-hard expanse of a muscular chest under my hands. My gaze widened, shooting to the inquisitive eyes of the man beneath me, the man whose steady heartbeat fluttered against my flattened palm.

One of his strong hands grabbed me, saving me from falling onto the floor, while the other brushed my hair back. I disentangled myself from him, moving to the other side of the couch.

"H-how..." I massaged my forehead, trying to sort through the last thing I remembered. It came back to me in a dizzying rush, and the man—Noon, maybe?—watched me with concern.

My face heated as I recalled holding on to him like a dog with a bone, and not letting go even as he'd led us inside. A dam had broken, the slight numbness of the last few days wearing off due to our instant kinship—whether we wanted it or not. I'd been delirious with sadness and grief.

"What time is it?" I rasped, turning toward the window. It was dark out, and the snowstorm the weatherman predicted had arrived on my doorstep.

"It's officially tomorrow," he said, holding up his phone.

"*What*?" I squinted at the screen. It was midnight. "What time did you get here?" I couldn't say when I'd last checked the time. Each day blurred into the next. My lack of sleep and binge drinking hadn't helped.

"Ah, very early yesterday," he said, thinking hard. He seemed off-kilter too, and rightfully so.

"And I kept you trapped under me the whole time?" I asked, more than a little appalled.

"Not the *whole* time. I took a few bathroom breaks, sat on this end for a little while to get the blood flowing in my limbs again, but you found me in your sleep."

My whole body burned now, down to my toes.

"That shouldn't embarrass you," he said. He was right. I hadn't been myself and he knew it. If anyone understood that it would've been him.

I exhaled an extended breath. "You should have woken me up."

"Seemed like you needed sleep more than I needed blood circulation." His words were light, suggesting humor, but his amusement didn't reach his eyes. "Really, I didn't mind. How are you feeling?"

"Not good," I said, and he nodded. I tried to ask him how he was doing, tried to form the words, but they got stuck somewhere in my chest. Probably right where the broken pieces of my heart lay scattered.

"I've been better myself," he said. That familiar ache I witnessed on the porch returned, and I twisted around to see if the front door did, in fact, have a fist-size hole in it.

"My name's Noon," he followed up with, confirming the name I'd heard his wife call him at the museum. I stared mutely at him, so disoriented by pain that I couldn't see straight. "If you're going to drool on me, the least you can do is give me your name."

Another stab at humor, even though his bloodshot eyes indicated the world of hurt he was in.

"You don't need to worry about me," I said, picking up on a theme. My husband played a role in ruining his marriage. How he could manage to care about my well-being and assuaging my embarrassment went beyond me.

"Sorry. Nasty habit of mine." He slumped against the back of the couch like I'd given him the permission he needed to be weak for a moment.

"I'm Solace," I said, suddenly conscious of how haggard I appeared, and that I was in desperate need of a shower.

"You caught them, didn't you?" he asked, barely above a whisper.

"Yes," I confirmed, and he turned away.

"She'd been crying," he whispered, reminding me of her runny mascara. "She wouldn't tell me what was wrong until we got home. And then she wouldn't even tell me who he was. How they met. Wouldn't give me a name."

"His name is Patrick," I said, wondering how he knew to come here if she hadn't given him those details.

He huffed. "I know that now. No thanks to her. I got into her phone logs and took a chance on a number that popped up often. Too often. I called the number repeatedly but got no answer."

That must have been how he got Patrick's name. Through his voicemail message.

"Did you know there's an app that spits out a list of possible addresses when you punch a phone number into it?"

I shook my head. I hadn't known that.

"You were my sixth stop today. I've been making stops all week. I thought you were him," he said. "When you opened the door, I remembered you from the charity ball."

Patrick must have remained out of sight then, after their little clandestine tryst in the museum. Likely slipping out of a back door.

"Makes sense why you were so upset that day. I've been curious about whether you were okay or not." The weariness was absent from his voice when he spoke again. Anger and determination replaced it. "Where is he?"

It crossed my mind that maybe he'd stayed in hopes of confronting Patrick. Then I thought about the rawness of his embrace outside, thought about the vulnerability in it, the way it wordlessly conveyed that he needed a pillar too. I thought about the ill-timed humor meant to lighten the moment, and how he'd put his own rage on pause while I rested. Thought about it all and knew without a doubt his reason for still being here had little to do with Patrick. He'd stayed for me. For *us*. Something like gratitude took up space in my heart.

"He's gone," I answered, realizing he didn't know.

"We'll have the next three months together," Patrick had said to his wife.

Noon shot up like a spring, his breathing loud and jagged. "They're together," he said roughly, giving me his back.

"Yes." I hated that I had to be the one to tell him. Hated that he had to be told at all.

"Son of a bitch!" He tugged at his hair as he spun, gaze darting everywhere, as if searching for something to break. He must have remembered nothing here belonged to him, that he didn't have a right to destroy any of it, because he strode briskly for the front door, tearing it open before charging out and roaring at the snowy night sky.

Our house was located at the end of a cul-de-sac, with nothing but woodland to the left and rear of us. There were still a couple neighbors along the street to take into consideration.

I couldn't find it in me to care if Noon's bellows awoke them, though.

I sat with my head lowered, listening to him purge his agony, wishing I could do something for him. I was too busy screaming inside myself, though. Eventually the night fell silent again, and I went to check on him, finding him on his knees, chin lowered to his chest.

Slipping into the boots I kept by the door and tightening my robe, I trudged the distance to him, snowflakes dampening my hair. Coming up beside him, I squeezed his shoulder in silent support. He reached up, holding my hand there before aiming tear-filled eyes at me. "She told me the truth," he said shakily. "She told me the truth. She saw what it did to me, and she..."

"And she left anyway," I finished for him, knowing where his thoughts had gone, because mine were there waiting. "And he left anyway too." My fingers protested at the pressure he applied to them, but I willed my bones to absorb his pain, to hold up under it for just a while longer.

"Come back inside," I said. "I'll make us some tea."

♦ ♦ ♦

I turned the fire down under the tea kettle and excused myself to take a quick shower. Ten minutes later I was securing my damp hair in a bun and rummaging through my closet for a pair of sweats and a t-shirt Noon could change into. His pants were soaked from the knees down. It didn't escape me that he wore the same suit from the charity ball, only now it was rumpled, likely from him sleeping in it for days.

I paused at the top of the landing, watching him fix the photo of Gavin that I'd placed face down. He then picked up the photo of Patrick, staring at it with a look of recognition then anger.

"You've seen him before," I said, descending the stairs.

"At the museum, that night," he said, looking over at me before setting down the frame. "I'd caught him staring at my wife. I thought nothing of it. She's beautiful. Everyone stares at her. *I* still stare at her," he ended, as if he couldn't comprehend why she'd need Patrick when he still loved and appreciated her, when nothing for him had changed. I held out the sweats that were at least two sizes too small for him.

"These were the best I could do," I said, when he peered down at the bundle in my hands.

"Do they belong to *him*?"

"No. I wouldn't do that to you. They're mine, but they're both roomy on me, so hopefully you'll be able to get into them."

"Sorry," he said, scratching a thumb over his brow and then jamming his fists into his pocket. "Thanks, but it's not necessary. I'm gonna head out soon. Before the weather gets worse."

The kettle whistled, and I set the clothing on the arm of the sofa before venturing into the kitchen. Noon sat on a stool at the island while I pulled two mugs from the cabinet along with a few ingredients for the tea.

"So, how many front doors have you nearly knocked down in your hunt for Patrick?" I asked as I filled the mugs with the steaming water.

"Around thirty. I've barely gotten any sleep. And I've never reacted as aggressively as I have today. I was at the end of my rope by the time I got here. You were last on my list. Sorry."

Noon was a man of action, whereas I was one of deep contemplation and self-loathing. I slid him his tea and sat across from him. His size ate up the space, causing our knees to bump under the island. I had to crane my head up to meet his eyes, eyes weighed down by exhaustion, the skin beneath them stained purple.

"I got tested," he said without buildup. "There's a clinic not too far from my house. Maybe you should consider doing the same. You never know."

"I'll do that," I said. It was on my list of things to do, especially since Patrick hadn't been wearing a condom. He and I hadn't had sex in a while, but who knew how long they'd been sleeping together unprotected. And who knew if there were other people he'd slept with besides me. Besides *us*. Neither of them could be trusted. Since Noon had already gotten himself tested, I didn't bother informing him of the danger his wife had put him in.

"This is good," he said, like he hadn't expected it to be. "I can count on one hand how many times I've had tea, and I'm pretty sure it was always cold and had the word "iced" in front of it."

"It's chamomile. My grandfather's recipe." I pushed a tin of tea biscuits toward him, and we sipped and munched in silence.

"What's she like?" I asked, staring into my mug. I waited for him to tell me that it was none of my business, that I didn't have a right to know. He said neither.

"Stacey's smart and funny," he started, and I flicked my gaze up to find that his eyes had softened on me. I needed this. For whatever reason, I needed to know what she had that I lacked, and Noon didn't seem to judge me for it. "She's spontaneous and loud. The life of any party."

"I'm reserved," I said, as if it were a strike against me. "I'd take a night in reading by the fire over attending a party." Maybe that was it. Maybe I bored Patrick—at least maybe that was one of the reasons. If I were being honest with myself, there were signs of infidelity long before this affair was blown out of the water. Patrick leaving the room to take calls, working extra shifts at the hospital—or so he'd told me. Small signs, ones easy enough to ignore or that could be attributed to Gavin's death, to my role in it. I should've taken steps to unearth the truth. Instead, I'd kept my head in the sand.

"Secretly, so would I," he whispered. "I just wanted her to be happy, and for a long time she was, then she wasn't, and it made me feel like a failure. But I never stopped loving her. *Never,*" he said, voice thick with emotion. His gaze held a plea, one I recognized. He wanted answers too.

"He's a protector and a provider. A great friend." *He used to be all those things to me,* I thought. "But he can be emotionally unavailable. Patrick would rather sweep a problem under the rug than talk at great length about it. We're so opposite in that way. He says I'm too soft, weak-hearted. Maybe I am."

"Don't," Noon said sharply, drawing me up a notch. "You've shown more strength in the short time that I've known you than they ever did. It takes strength to face your problems head-on instead of cheating and then running from them like a coward."

That was exactly what they had done. Stacey and Patrick. They'd cheated and then ran from the consequences.

"Thank you," I said, biting into my quivering bottom lip. Noon tugged it free, his fingers warm and soft. My lip shook uncontrollably now, and I thought I might break open under his stare.

"There you are," he said, his smile wobbling. "Perfect."

It was either keep talking or start sobbing, so I kept talking. "Our son died a year ago." I stared through the patio sliding door to the in-ground pool that had since been cemented over. Noon followed my gaze.

"I was supposed to be paying attention, but I wasn't," I confessed in a small voice. "All I ever wanted was to be a father. I had to talk Patrick into it. We were still young, and he'd just started his residency at the hospital. We used a surrogate. We loved him. So much. And within the blink of an eye, he was gone. I'm so sorry," I said emphatically, "because maybe if I hadn't fractured my marriage with my carelessness, yours would have been spared."

Noon shook his head in objection, and I closed my eyes to it. He cupped my chin like he had at the charity ball, and I nearly sobbed from the contact. "Look at me," he said, and waited until I did. "Stacey wanted to start a family, but no matter how hard we tried, we couldn't conceive. We tried everything, but nothing worked. Turns out the problem was me. I'm someone who needs to be needed, who needs to take care of the people around me. But the one thing she needed from me, I couldn't give her, and so she stopped needing me. I tried to compensate by loving her more. It was never enough, and I knew it, although I never stopped trying. So, I'm sorry too."

I leaned into the hand now cradling my cheek. Did he know how badly I needed touch? Did he sense how deep Patrick's neglect went? Was it written all over me? And did he think I was too needy, like Patrick did? I'd told him he didn't need to make things okay for me, but I'd have been lying if I'd said that him trying didn't feel good.

"Why weren't we enough?" I asked.

"I was hoping you knew," he rasped. "I was hoping you knew."

I didn't know either, and so we sat there at a loss, trying to come up with a million reasons why together.

After a while, when our cups were bone dry, Noon spoke. "She told me she'd fallen in love with someone else, and that she was leaving me for him. She said she was sorry. Said she never meant to hurt me. We argued into the wee hours of the morning. I begged her to cancel her trip, to not leave until we figured this all out. She agreed under the condition that we would get some sleep and pick things back up afterward. It had been a long day, she'd said. She was tired, and I was nowhere close to done. I can be like that sometimes."

He'd probably driven through countless surrounding cities and states on the hunt for Patrick. I had no trouble imagining him fighting tooth and nail for his marriage, refusing to get a wink of sleep until they'd worked it out, until he'd given his all in trying.

"I don't know if it was love, stupidity, or arrogance that made me believe her. Maybe a little of all three. I took the guest bedroom, and when I woke up, she was gone. She left her rings on her nightstand." He spread his fingers, staring down at his own wedding band. "Any other day I would've said she removed them before falling asleep and then forgot to put them back on."

"And now?"

"Now I know that her leaving them behind was a declaration. Our marriage is over." He fisted his shaking hand. "I've never taken mine off."

"Neither have I."

He hid his hand under the table. It reminded me of when Gavin would hide things behind his back. Things he didn't want taken away from him. "I'm not ready yet," he said simply.

I understood what he didn't say. Understood the questions he didn't ask. Who were we if not theirs? Who would we be once the rings came off? He wasn't ready to find out. Not quite yet.

"It's okay," I said. "I'm not ready either."

Eventually needing a distraction from the hell we were in, I made more tea while Noon made us omelets. Breakfast food was his specialty, he'd said. Neither of us ate much, and any rare moments of levity we found were eclipsed by the silences we fell into. The reminders of what happened to us lived in the silence. I couldn't wait to curl up in bed again with a stiff drink, but I also couldn't bear to be alone.

"I should go," he eventually said, like leaving was the last thing he wanted to do, like he had nothing to go back to. "They'll close the roads soon, if they haven't already."

He stood, peering down the hall leading to the front door. I didn't allow myself to think as I grabbed his hand and said, "Stay. Please...stay."

CHAPTER 5

Now

MY MORNING SELF-CHECK-INS began with a run-through of my memories. Every day I awoke on the metaphorical edge of my seat, wondering if my world had righted itself while I'd slept. Today was no different, and as per usual, the results of that check-in were disappointing.

I untangled myself from the blanket, and, not for the first time, I considered if getting all my memories back would be such a good thing. If they returned, Stacey would still be gone.

The fire had burned out in the middle of the night, and I shivered against the chill in the house as I approached the floor-to-ceiling windows to watch the final dregs of darkness dissipate.

I didn't know when my fascination with dawn began, but if I had to pick a favorite time of day, that would've been it. That sweet spot between night passing and day emerging, right before nature and the world came to life. Even with the disappointment of waking to learn that what I wanted more than anything hadn't come back to me, my thoughts weren't as erratic at dawn. I was usually able to reason with myself, to be more patient and temporarily content with what I didn't know within the quiet privacy of my own mind.

It became harder to hold on to that contentment as the day progressed. My reasoning began to fracture, and exhaustion would start to kick in after a full day of once again not remembering everything. Of not being the person everyone else remembered and so desperately wanted me to be. By nightfall chaos tended to erupt, both internally and externally, and once dealt with, once worked through—like I had last night with Solace's help—I'd earn a fresh start, or more like a reprieve, at dawn.

I would've given anything to take a walk right then, but I didn't want Solace waking up to find me missing and worry. I also didn't want to get lost. Seemed my sense of direction only functioned when inside the city.

I wasn't sure if Solace was an early bird, but I decided to have breakfast ready for him when he woke up. It was the least I could do after the panic attack he talked me down from last night, and for allowing me to stay over. Part of me said I should've been wary of his kindness, but I didn't want to listen to that part of me because something about him felt right, and I wanted to cling to that, if only for a little while.

In a perfect world, we'd tour the town and I'd remember why this place felt so vital to me, then I'd return to my life in the city, leaving Haley Cove and Solace behind. Or maybe we'd end up being lifelong friends from here on out. That thought brought a smile to my face.

Thirty minutes later, the food was done and Solace still hadn't made an appearance. I lowered the oven setting to warm, then placed everything inside before setting two mugs on the counter—a subtle hint when he showed up that his grandfather's chamomile tea would be greatly appreciated.

With nothing left to do, I did a second walkthrough of the lower level, fully able to take in every detail now that I didn't have Solace unintentionally distracting me with his cloudless blue gaze. Those oceanic eyes of his made it hard to focus on anything else.

Before realizing it, I was at the top of the stairs, walking toward his open bedroom door and then beyond it. A voice in my head screamed that I was crossing a line. We didn't know each other well enough for me to be traipsing into his bedroom without invitation, but my feet didn't get the memo.

Solace lay sprawled out on his back in the center of the big bed, his bare chest rising and falling, his hair spilled across his pillow.

Even in sleep he was elegant. His limbs were delicately etched with muscle, not carved with the bulging kind found underneath my clothing.

The sheet covering him stopped below his navel, and the blanket hung partially on the floor, as if it had been kicked there by the long leg poking out from under the sheet. I thought of regal beauty when I looked at him, but although his physical appearance called for immediate attention, it wasn't what held it. Solace had the temperament of someone wise and thoughtful with an infinite amount of tolerance for others. He exuded goodness, and that made me feel safe with him.

That I'd had those thoughts scared me, that I couldn't stop moving closer to him terrified me even more. Everything in me began to burn when those beautiful eyes of his fluttered open to land on me without surprise, as if my being there was perfectly normal.

"Morning," he said groggily, stretching his arms above him.

"I made breakfast," I blurted, hurrying to give an excuse for being at the foot of his bed. "I didn't mean to wake you."

"You didn't." Remnants of sleep made his voice husky, and he pushed himself up against the headboard before sniffing the air. "The smell of bacon did. I hope you made extra."

"I can make more," I said, chuckling at his look of delight. "It's keeping warm in the oven. I just wanted to see if you were up." I pointed toward the hall. "I'll wait for you downstairs."

"Okay," he said, scrubbing a hand over his eyes. My gaze traveled down his chest to the faint hairs vanishing below the waistband of his boxer briefs, and every part of me stirred.

"Okay," I repeated in a gravelly tone, already walking away. My reaction to him confused me, and it had nothing to do with him being a man. It was that it felt against my will. Like my body had begun to work independently from my brain. I couldn't call it attraction, because the only attraction I felt—the only attraction I *should* have felt—was toward my wife. It was a sudden and intense awareness of him, though, and maybe a sign that I'd gone without the comfort of another for too long.

Back in the living room, the photo of Gavin caught my eye. I picked it up, bringing it close enough to make out the album title and artist name on the vinyl record he held.

Eric Clapton. *Unplugged.*

A prickling sensation started up in my head, and I placed the frame back on the mantel to pull up the album in the music app on my phone. I randomly shuffled from song to song, about to call it quits when the prickling stopped, but then the acoustic guitar kicked in on "Tears in Heaven," and the hairs all over my body rose.

I'd made it through my second run-through when that elusive string in my head begged to be pulled, but no matter how hard I tried to grab on to it, it remained out of reach. Time meant nothing as I fought to get to that place that held all the answers hostage.

The third replay of the song ended, and I remained transfixed by the flutter of familiarity. So much so that I hadn't heard Solace's approach until his hand landed on my shoulder. Startled from my trance and forgetting where I was, I spun around and grabbed his forearm with more force than necessary.

"Solace?" I said in confusion. I peered around, getting my bearings, then remembered I still held on to him. Jerking my hand back, I watched the indentation of my large fingers fade from his porcelain skin.

I took two steps in the opposite direction, giving him breathing room, shrinking in on myself to appear non-threatening. "Sorry," I said. "I wasn't…" I stopped before saying "in my right mind." If my rough handling of him hadn't sent him running, saying that surely would have.

"Don't be sorry," he replied, reminding me of his request from last night. "You don't scare me, Noon." A flush stained his cheeks, but he hadn't flinched away from my grasp. Hadn't seemed afraid of me.

"That doesn't make it okay," I said, horrified with myself.

"I startled you."

"That's no excuse," I snapped. Solace observed me in that patient way of his, as though understanding that I didn't need him to make this moment okay for me. He was respecting me, letting me feel whatever it was I needed to feel.

"I get stuck sometimes," I explained. "I feel something there, and I get stuck trying to latch on to it."

Solace's mouth tightened, then opened, then slammed shut again. He seemed torn, and I couldn't understand why. "I admire you," he said, eyes lowering for an instant. "You're a fighter."

"So are you."

"No, I'm not." Conviction lit his gaze. "I take things lying down, and I hate that about myself. You make me want to fight. You remind me that some things are worth fighting for. You always—" He cut himself off, shaking his head. What had he been about to say? He carried on before I could ask.

"How does someone who never fights know how to fight? How do they know if they're doing it correctly?" He now stood so close that I could make out the three tiny freckles along his nose. "How do I know if I'm doing the right thing?" He was struggling with something, had been since the moment I spotted him in my camera at the tavern, and now he was looking at me like I had all the answers. I felt the need to hold him, to fulfill my sudden urge to litter his forehead with kisses. And it had nothing to do with attraction or lust. I simply wanted to make him feel better; to do so felt instinctive, and I was so close to not caring about how inappropriate that would be.

"What does your heart tell you?"

"That I'm doing the right thing."

"Then always go with your heart," I said, "because yours seems pure, like only good can come from it."

"I hope you're right," he whispered before brushing my unruly hair from my face.

◆ ◆ ◆

"Are you sure you can do this?" I eyed the scissors in Solace's hands as he drew closer. He'd asked if he could cut my hair after our talk in the living room, and I'd responded with an emphatic no before striding for the kitchen. He'd worn me down over breakfast, though.

"I used to trim Gavin's hair all the time," he said, as if that would make me feel better.

"My hair's a little more challenging than his. You can't really go wrong cutting a head full of curls. What I've got going is a mishmash of textures. You've got to be an expert to get this right."

Solace shrugged. "What's the worst that can happen? It's hair. It'll grow back."

"Well, when you put it that way," I said, giving in and getting comfortable in the seat he'd dragged over from the breakfast table. I caved because of the sweet thrill shining in his eyes, but he didn't need to know that.

He wrapped a towel over my shoulders before sectioning my hair, stopping to touch the raised scar where the hair grew thinner.

"Where were you both headed?"

"Home. I think. I'd picked her up from the airport. She'd been gone for three months on a humanitarian trip. After all that time apart, I must have been beyond happy to see her," I said reflectively. "I often create stories in my head about what our reunion must have been like. They all start with her running into my arms and me kissing her in the middle of the airport baggage claim. Letting my imagination run wild helps, believe it or not."

Solace didn't answer as he continued to prep me for the haircut. I was glad for it. I needed a break from missing her.

"No swimming pool?" I asked, staring into the backyard. There was more than enough room for one.

"No swimming pool," he said without further explanation before he got started.

I was afraid to speak as he worked. I didn't want to steal an ounce of his focus away, but not talking meant I was stuck inhaling his scent of cedarwood and sage and then having to think about how that scent made me feel. Risking a botched haircut seemed safer.

"Why were you so upset when I bumped into you at the tavern?" I asked. He paused to ponder my question, maybe deciding if he'd even answer it.

"I go there a lot." He worked as he spoke. "Each time I go, I tell myself it'll be the last time, but then I find myself back there again. Waiting again," he murmured. "Being there brings back memories."

"Of the guy you lost?" I hedged, wondering how anyone could walk away from Solace. It couldn't have been willingly.

"Yeah. We were supposed to meet there a while ago, but he never showed."

"He stood you up?"

"You could say that," he answered noncommittally. "You sound offended on my behalf."

"I am. I'm gonna track him down after the haircut," I joked.

"It wasn't his fault," he whispered. "The universe had other plans for us."

"You loved him," I said gently.

"With all of me. He came into my life at a time when I had both feet off the ledge. He caught me as I was falling."

It felt wrong for me to experience the raw, palpable love in his tone. It felt like the love that filled every fiber of my body, the one I associated with Stacey. "Maybe you'll find each other again, work things out. Maybe it can be like it used to be." My body tensed, as if rejecting the idea, even while I wanted nothing more than for him to be happy, whatever that looked like, whatever it meant.

"I used to want that more than anything," he said, coming around to work on the front of my hair. His tongue peeked through the corner of his mouth as he concentrated on the task. Another thing to add to the list of what made him adorable.

"And now what do you want?"

"A second chance," he said, now looking at me directly. "It doesn't need to be the same, doesn't need to be exactly as it used to be. I'd settle for a second chance at loving him. At being loved by him. In fact, it wouldn't be settling at all."

My heart constricted as his words worked their way through me, as they made me consider another possibility. Could I move forward without regaining what I'd be leaving behind? I'd been searching for a second chance at my past, and now I wondered if a second chance at life, at love, would be even better. Solace made me consider it. I had a feeling he could make me consider anything.

"All done," he said with pride, brandishing a handheld mirror in front of me.

"Not bad." I accepted the mirror from him. The sides were short but not shorn, and he'd left the top long enough to comb back.

"Not bad?" he scoffed. "You look handsome."

"You think I'm handsome now?" I asked, forgetting to keep my tone light. I'd dissected his looks and attributes, feeling guilty about it every step of the way. I hadn't once considered if he'd been doing the same to me. The longer he took to answer, the more charged the moment became.

"You were handsome to begin with," he said, "but now the world can actually see it."

"The world, huh?" I glanced in the mirror again, angling my head this way and that way. "My size attracts too much attention as it is. I'm not sure I'm ready for the mayhem my good looks might bring."

He considered me. "You're right." He ruffled my hair until the longish top layer curtained my eyes. "We don't need the townspeople fainting on us."

"Hey," I said in mock outrage. "Don't be jealous because you'll no longer be the prettiest thing in town."

I shoved my hair back, and he ruffled it again. I tugged on the thin elastic band keeping the braid draped over his shoulder together. It popped, sending the braid unraveling. I laughed, fixing my hair again, only to have him screw it up once more before attempting to dash from the kitchen. I snagged him around the waist as he reached the living room.

"Two can play that game," I said, messing up his hair in return. He chuckled, twisting us and batting my hands away. The move caused me to trip on the living room steps. I ended up tumbling down and taking him with me. "Oof," I groaned, landing on my back with him sprawled over my chest.

Solace pushed his hair away, looking down at me in alarm. I winked at him, letting him know I was okay, and then we exploded into a fit of laughter. We kept laughing until it hurt, until we forgot that life was hard and unfair and that we probably should've been crying instead.

Laughing with Solace felt like the most real thing I'd experienced in a while. It felt like a second chance.

CHAPTER 6

Solace

Then

AFTER TIPTOEING TO the guest room to find Noon gone, and the clothes I'd given him to sleep in last night still folded on the chair in the corner, I headed for the living room. "You're up," I noted as I descended the stairs. We'd stayed up for hours talking—and sometimes not talking—after he'd agreed to stay the night. We'd only gone our separate ways a few hours ago, promising each other we'd get a little shuteye. Looked like neither of us held up our end of the deal. "Did you sleep at all?"

Noon spared me a glance before turning his attention back to the window. "No, but at least now I know what I've been missing by sleeping in all these years."

"Sunrise?"

"No," he replied contemplatively. "Dawn. The moment right before."

"You're leaving," I said, noticing that he'd put on his suit jacket and shoes.

"The roads are closed, so you're stuck with me a while longer. I'd planned on at least taking a walk, though. Get some thinking done, maybe let out another scream or two. But aside from the insane amount of snow that accumulated overnight, I realized I didn't want to get lost out here. I'm someone who needs a GPS to get to the same place I've been to a million times, and unlike the city, there are no street signs or cabs to hail when I get turned around in the woods."

We lived far enough away so it didn't feel like we were near the city but close enough to access it. Hard line to straddle because Patrick needed to be close to work, but we'd wanted Gavin to grow up similar to how we did, surrounded by woodland and with plenty of outdoor space to play freely. "I would've found you," I said.

"I'm gonna hold you to that tomorrow." He looked more exhausted than he had yesterday. Even his tone seemed tired. "I suppose I could walk along the shoulder of the road," he mused, still staring beyond the boundary of trees along the house.

"But it's not the same," I said.

"No, it's not."

We didn't have sidewalks like in the city, and there weren't any sights worth seeing in the vicinity. Gavin and I would roam the woods as well, choosing nature over neighborhood.

"Did I wake you?"

"No. I couldn't sleep either." I tightened the sash on my robe.

"You need sleep, Solace."

I almost reminded him of the extended nap I took on his chest yesterday, but I'd have to relive my mortification to do it. Besides, I was still so damn tired, so in the end he was right. "And you don't?" I asked. "I'll sleep when you do."

"That might be the motivation I need," he said softly. "How are you feeling today?"

"Not much better."

"Yeah, me either." He scratched at the scruff covering his jaw. It had grown during the hours we'd been apart.

"I was going to make some tea. Would you like some?"

"Chamomile?" he asked, perking up.

"It's the only kind I drink."

In the kitchen, I grabbed the kettle from the stovetop and set it under the running faucet.

"Omelet?" Noon asked.

"I'm not hungry." The thought of eating made me sick to my stomach. I couldn't recall the last time I'd had a full meal.

"Neither am I," he said, pulling the carton of eggs from the fridge anyway. I didn't have the strength to fight him, so I resigned myself to wasting another one of his delicious omelets.

Noon moved around the kitchen without hesitation or permission. I'd never met anyone so at ease with making themselves comfortable. It made me more comfortable in turn.

"Thank you," I said.

"For what?"

"For staying. Being here by myself... It was hard." Cutting the water off, I pressed my palms to the counter, feeling light-headed and shaky. I was used to this by now. Used to feeling as close to okay as possible one second, weeping uncontrollably the next, then feeling numb to it all.

I also bounced between anger and jealousy. Then there were the moments when I wanted Patrick back. Moments when I hated him but couldn't help but still be in love with him. Most times the mere thought of him touching me again made my skin crawl, but then other times the thought of him never touching me again snuffed the air from my lungs.

Then I'd remember none of that mattered, because he didn't want me anyway. Right now, it was grief's turn to have a spin.

Noon's footsteps were tentative as he approached, but his hands were sure as they urged me around and into his arms. He stroked a hand up and down my back as I struggled with the rising panic.

"Breathe," he coaxed, the scent of him filling my lungs. He'd showered last night, but beneath the cedarwood and sage fragrance of the body wash I'd given him, lingered a scent that was all him. A scent that mingled with the others to form a comforting balm. I unconsciously pressed my nose deeper against him, feeling better soon after.

"Has anyone ever told you that you're terrible at respecting personal space?" I murmured. Regardless of my words, I didn't let him go. I didn't move away.

"Yes, but they're all liars," he said, earning a chuckle from me. "It's hard to gauge space when you're usually too large for any space you're in. Everything feels close, but I like it that way. My best friend pretends to hate it, but behind my back he calls me a big cuddly bear." He made to back away, and my fingers tightened on his jacket. He relaxed, squeezing me tighter.

"Thank you for letting me stay," he whispered into my hair. "I wasn't ready to leave."

"You're welcome." I looked up at him, spotting the dry patches at the corners of his eyes. My forehead creased. "You've been crying."

"Crying is good for the soul. Don't let anyone tell you any different." He tracked the tear stains along on my own cheeks. "You've been crying too."

I'd been about to apologize for it, but then I gazed at his eyes again, at the strength behind them even as the proof of his emotions rimmed them red. "Yeah, I have."

"Good," he said, as if I'd made him proud. Noon made me feel seen, understood by someone, even though we were little more than strangers. He was confident in his vulnerability, generous with it, even after having been crushed in the worst possible way by the person he loved most. And at every turn since showing up on my doorstep, he'd put my needs ahead of his own.

"Better?" he asked, and I nodded. Noon let go of me to get started on breakfast, and I started on the tea.

We took our food and tea to the dining room this time because I couldn't bear the view of the backyard that the kitchen provided. Noon pointed to the large black and white photo of me, Patrick, and Gav hanging on the wall.

"You look so young," he said. "How long have you two known each other?"

I peered at the photo before returning to my steaming mug. "We started dating in high school. Patrick and my brother were best friends. They played on the football team together. I was known as the jock's geeky, introverted brother. My head was always stuck in a book. Patrick didn't notice me until my junior year when I let my hair grow out. He and Gav were seniors by then." I forced a bite of eggs down after Noon gestured to my plate. "Your turn," I said, motioning to his untouched food. If I had to eat, then so did he. He obliged, taking a deep breath first, preparing his body for something it wasn't in the mood for.

"Did you grow your hair for him? To get his attention?"

"God no. Dating an athlete was the furthest thing from my mind. I'd been approached by a modeling agent while I was studying at the park one day. She gave me her card. Insisted I could make good money doing it. Figured I could use the money for college, so I decided to give it a shot. She said growing my hair would add to my 'mystique.' I believe her exact words were 'Your kind of beauty only comes around once in a lifetime.'" I dipped my head under the guise of wanting another forkful of eggs to hide my cringe at having repeated that.

"Are you blushing?"

I peered at him, expecting to see amusement at my expense. Instead I found something close to wonder within his eyes, lines of fatigue dragging down the corners of them.

"Are you making fun of me?" I asked to be sure. Patrick never missed an opportunity to poke fun at how easily I became embarrassed or bashful. It'd made me self-conscious over the years.

"No," he said, brows lowering at my assumption, "far from it. It fascinates me that you've managed to hold on to that innocent part of you that so many leave behind once they get a taste of how cruel the world can be. Cynicism and indifference taking its place. It's refreshing, and admirable. Besides that, I'd never make fun of you for being who you are, Solace."

I'd never looked at it that way. I'd spent so much time beating myself up for it, thinking it made me childish. If Noon were to be believed, it actually made me brave. It meant that there was something good left in me, something Patrick hadn't succeeded in carving away. I fought to hold his stare, my insides now feeling as warm as my exterior. I broke the connection first.

"It was honest work, and it paid for my education," I said once I was able to.

"What did you go to school for?"

"Teaching."

"Now *that* adds up," he said. "You have the temperament for teaching."

"You don't think I'd make a convincing model?"

Noon considered me, slinging an arm over the back of the neighboring chair. It was hard not to hide behind a sip from my mug as the weight of his attention bore down on me.

"You have the looks, and you can definitely nail the pensive gaze. I don't know," he ended with a shrug. "I can't see you fussing over the perfect look and the best angles."

"Thankfully, other people were paid to handle that side of it." A wave of nausea rippled through me. I wasn't sure if it was my system rejecting the nutrition it was no longer used to getting, or my emotions moving on to another stage. I pushed the plate aside, more than half of the breakfast uneaten. Noon reached over to take my hand, squeezing, letting me know it was okay.

"If you're not careful, I'm going to get used to you touching me." It was out before I'd thought it through. "I didn't mean it the way it sounded. I just meant you're making it too easy for me to lean on you."

"I know how you meant it," he assured me. "And it's okay to lean on me. I sure as hell have been leaning on you since I arrived." Again, so open and honest. "It says a lot about my current state of mind to lean on anyone. I keep reminding myself not to."

"You don't have to remind yourself not to lean on me," I said. "It doesn't feel like I've done anything to help you, though. I can't even help myself."

"Not being alone helps more than you know."

"I'm terrible company."

"You're not," he disagreed, "but I don't mean *alone* in that sense. There could be an army of people here and I'd still feel alone without you. Having someone who completely understands what I'm feeling means everything. Having someone to look after means even more." Noon needed to feel useful, and I needed to feel cared for.

"How long have you and your wife been together?"

"A little over a decade. I'd just, once and for all, ended a two-year break-up-to-make-up cycle with my boyfriend at the time. The plan was to stay single, nothing but casual hook-ups. I spent a few months living according to plan, then I ended up in Stacey's emergency room with a bad case of food poisoning. The rest was history. She was still a nurse at the time."

"How many years have you two been married?"

"Six."

"You told me what she's like, but what attracted you to her? What made you decide she was the one?" I both hated her and wanted to know everything about her. Both disgusted and obsessed with her. Deep down, I understood it wasn't about her, that my obsession was more about what *I* didn't have to offer than what she did.

Noon inched my plate back in front of me, giving me a look that said he'd keep talking if I kept eating. "We had similar backgrounds. Single-parent households, odds stacked against us. We were ambitious, we challenged each other, we both wanted to make something of ourselves and get the hell out of Seattle. She got accepted to Cornell Medical School, so we packed up and headed for New York."

"Did you know?" I asked. "Did you suspect anything at all?"

Noon relaxed in his chair, staring at his plate, like maybe the answer lay between the food he'd pushed around on it. "I've been asking myself that question every day," he whispered, sighing. "I don't know. I'm sure I could look back and find a whole host of signs. Our sex life hadn't been what it used to be as of late. We'd lost the intimacy, the joy of lovemaking, from all the pressure we'd put on ourselves to conceive." His lips pressed into a hard line. "We were friends before we were ever lovers, though, and I guess I believed my friend would never hurt me in that way, no matter what we were going through. I think the answer is that I never saw this coming. I didn't think she was capable of it. Some may call that naive."

"They'd be wrong," I said. "Seeing only the best in the person you love is not naive. It's fearless. You loved her unselfishly, without ever stopping to consider if you'd be hurt in the process. You kept loving her, loved her more, even, when things grew challenging. And something tells me you don't plan on letting your pain change you. *That's* courageous." We'd risked our hearts on people who ended up not being worthy of it, and where I would have remained curled up in my corner to never trust again, Noon was here showing me the benefits of not allowing the pain to close me off. He led with an open heart and mind, even while knowing what doing that had cost him. I found that courageous. It was my turn to touch him. My turn to squeeze his hand. His answering smile conveyed gratitude.

"Dig in," he said, nudging his chin toward my food.

"So bossy," I muttered, stealing Gavin's favorite phrase.

"Is that something your son used to say to you?" he asked, surprising me.

"Yeah. How did you know?"

"Your voice changed. Like you were mimicking him. Most parents do that when explaining something their kid said." His own tone turned mournful, and I remembered he hadn't been lucky enough to have children. Considering the constant, all-consuming pain I felt at having lost my child, I wondered if maybe Noon was, in fact, the lucky one.

"You can talk about him," he said. "If you want."

"It usually followed him being told to eat all his vegetables or to brush his teeth before bed. In actuality, I was the more lenient parent. Or maybe the more..." I reached for the right word.

"The more emotionally available parent?" he supplied, no doubt remembering my description of Patrick.

"Yeah, that sounds more accurate."

"I was going to suggest other options when she got back from her trip," he confessed, jaw working. "The baby didn't need to be biologically mine. I'd have loved any child."

"And any child would have been fortunate to have you as their parent." I believed that with every fiber of my being.

We spent the next couple hours trading war stories and holding hands when needed. Noon had kept me distracted and engaged in conversation, keeping me occupied from my pain—even during the topics that saw me diving headfirst into it. I hoped I'd returned even an ounce of the comfort he'd given me. He'd taken care of me, and when he tilted his head toward my plate, I looked down to find it empty. I'd unknowingly devoured all my food.

That night, in hopes of reducing how often my mind drifted to Patrick and everything that happened, I moved into the other guest room. Leaving our bed didn't help. Images of Patrick having sex with Noon's wife still slaughtered me. The sound of his desperation when he told her he loved her, kept me from sleeping.

Eventually, the bedroom door creaked open and closed and then the bed depressed as Noon curled behind my trembling form. I turned to face him in the dark, to meet him there, to commiserate with him there too, because his body shook far worse than mine. He hauled me into his arms, and I went willingly, sighing in unison with him. He placed a kiss on my forehead, and it didn't feel driven by lust, only the desire to make me feel better.

His body temperature ran hot, likely due to his size, and my body thawed, my limbs going slack. Within minutes his soft snores filled the room, and I was on my way to join him in deep slumber, already knowing I never wanted to sleep without him again.

CHAPTER 7

Noon

Now

SOLACE AND I agreed it would be best to explore the town before the rest of his property. That way we'd be off the major roadways before the second round of heavy snowfall touched down that evening. There was also the concern of businesses closing early in preparation of the inclement weather.

We'd stopped at the museum, had a late lunch at one of the more popular places in town, then watched a local band play a short set at the cultural center. None of it sparked new memories—or old memories, rather. There were no tugs, no flickers, not even a soft buzzing in my brain. None of it felt familiar to me. Defeated and angry, I'd called it quits before venturing to our next and final location.

Solace convinced me to spend another night at his place, and so we stopped at the bed and breakfast for some of my things. He seemed worried about me, and I got the impression he didn't want to leave me alone to wallow in my self-pity all evening. I felt terrible for dragging him into my mess, especially when he too became solemn on the drive back to his place, as if my mood had rubbed off on him. He'd spent the whole ride staring blankly out the window, his heavy sighs filling the cabin of the truck.

"Keep driving," he said when I veered toward the front of the house.

"I figured you weren't up for the tour anymore. Figured you needed a break from me," I said, even as I continued down the snowy path.

"Why would you think that?"

"You're introspective. I guessed that within minutes of knowing you. But your silence now feels different. I can't help but think I've ruined your mood. Your day."

"You didn't ruin my day," he said, then huffed. "If anything, I thought I'd ruined yours."

"How so?"

"Nothing worked. You didn't remember."

"That's not your fault," I assured him, but he didn't seem convinced as he crossed his arms and went back to gazing out his window.

I didn't know what else to say, so I kept quiet about it and turned in the direction he indicated.

"You have someone who comes out and plows the snow for you?" I asked, noticing the snowbanks off to the side, rock salt crunching under my tires.

"My friend Pauly. He owns a bistro in town. He offered to plow while we were out."

"That was nice of him," I said, even as I wondered why someone who had his own business to run would take the time to plow and salt a property of this size.

"Yeah, Pauly's great like that." His tone held affection, and his disposition became lighter. My hands tightened on the wheel. I wanted to be the one to make him feel better.

We passed a rundown loafing shed and a barn. The wire fencing, which I assumed had kept the cattle in once upon a time, sagged in spots. Otherwise, the old farm was beautiful and spacious. I imagined how it would look when winter cleared out and the tree limbs filled in and the grass was green again. The sudden need to capture that future on camera became a living thing inside of me.

My mind began firing on all cylinders the farther we drove, and that overwhelming sensation of knowing started crawling up my spine. I couldn't verbalize what it was that I knew, though. I sat straighter in my seat, my gaze darting all around me.

We pulled up to an old white farmhouse that obviously hadn't been in use for a while. The window shutters would have benefited from a fresh paint job, and the wooden porch steps looked unreliable. Aside from a few other minor repairs needed on the exterior, the bones of the home were lovely.

"This was my grandfather's house." Solace offered up his first smile in hours. "My brother and I used to spend our summer vacations here. He stopped coming once he started high school. He had football camp and groupies at that point," he said wryly. "I stopped once I started modeling to save for college."

"I'm still trying to wrap my head around that," I said, throwing the truck in park.

"I was surprisingly good at it."

"Staring thoughtfully into the distance? I don't doubt it," I said, and he laughed, the sound throaty and sinful. Shame stretched across my gut as soon as that last description entered my thoughts.

"Why did you build your house at the other end of the property? Why not remodel this one?" I asked as we exited the truck.

"It hadn't been a working farm for years. I didn't see the point in being way out here. The plan was to add the stables to this plot of land. That didn't end up happening."

"Too much for one person, right?"

"You remembered," he said with a grin.

"I have plenty of room to store new memories now," I muttered.

"Are you making any? New memories," he clarified as he fished a set of keys from his pocket and unlocked the front door. He stepped inside before I could admit that I hadn't been.

Regardless of what I'd said that night we met at the tavern, I was afraid to make new memories. I feared doing so would cost me what I'd lost forever. That I'd move forward and never look back. But when he spoke of second chances earlier, he'd made it sound so tempting.

Instead of answering Solace's question, I decided to take it for what it seemed to be. A reminder.

"I'd considered selling off this half of the property. Creating an entry point in the back for the would-be new owners, and fencing off the front where I live. I couldn't bring myself to do it, though. Plus, one day Gav will retire from the military, and maybe he'll want to build a life here."

"Makes sense," I said absently, trying to work out why my chest tightened the moment I'd crossed into the dust-covered foyer. Solace disappeared into rooms and down halls, flipping on lights as he went, while I fought to remember how to breathe. I turned toward the living room, my hands twitching at my sides.

"You okay?" Solace asked. I hadn't heard him return, but I glanced back to find him watching me, his gaze probing for something.

"Yeah, why wouldn't I be?" I faced him, hiding my shaky hands behind my back, attempting to appear normal, when in actuality my heart had begun the trek up my throat.

"Just checking. Thought maybe you remembered something."

"No," I said, even while mentally clawing through every corner of my brain for that dangling string. "The upkeep on this many acres must be expensive."

Solace didn't reply right away, and for a moment I thought he might call me on the pretense I was putting up. He looked like he wanted to. "Not as expensive as you would think," he finally said. "The mortgage on the land is paid off, taxes are relatively cheap. Although the lawn mowing bill never fails to take my breath away. Come on." He aimed for the stairs. "Let's start at the top." He ascended halfway, stopping when I remained rooted to my spot. "Coming?"

"Ah, yeah," I said, snapping free of my shackles and catching up to him.

By the time we were done, the tightness in my chest had spread through my entire body, until it felt like my lungs were being strangled by an invisible fist.

"Noon?" Solace asked, his voice sounding distant even though I could feel him by my side.

"One second," I hissed, focusing on that tug I hadn't experienced all day. I shuffled into the living room. "It's...it's right there." Bells rang in my ears, and sweat beaded along my brow as I yanked and yanked on that string. Flashes of the sun and moon and skin slicked with the aftermath of sex assaulted me. Quick flicks, faster than the speed of my camera shutter. There one millisecond and gone the next.

"Please, please, please," I begged my broken mind and God. "Please!" I lunged for the memory, but it was too late. It had slipped away.

"Fuck!" I yelled, ripping off my jacket and scarf, bumping into the furniture and nearly tripping over the hem of the sheet covering them. "Fuck." I counted and breathed, counted and breathed, and fucking counted and breathed again. By the time I'd calmed myself down, my t-shirt was soaked through with sweat, my face drenched in it too.

Solace. I twisted around, finally remembering he was there. He observed me from the other side of the room, as if giving my crazy the space it needed to break free. His face was a blur.

"You're beautiful when you cry," he whispered, voice taut. So that wasn't sweat pouring down my face. "There's no shame," he went on. "No pretense of strength. You just...let go."

"Y-you say that like you've seen me cry before," I said before drying my tears with the backs of my hands. "I'm sor—" I couldn't say it. I was sick of being sorry. So damn tired of it. "I should head back to the inn." I nodded, sniffling and peering around for my jacket. I shook my hands out at my sides, attempting to rid myself of the raging energy still surging inside of me. I needed to dump it. I didn't do well with keeping it in.

"You need to break something," Solace said, but I ignored him, grabbing my coat and then scanning the floor for my scarf. He began ripping the sheets away, exposing porcelain lamps on end tables, a glass-topped coffee table, vases along a wooden console.

"Wha-what are you doing?" I asked.

"Break it," he said, his shoulders set with determination.

"What are you talking about? I can't—"

"They're things, and things can be replaced. You need to get whatever it is inside you out. Break it," he ordered, his tone gaining strength as mine grew weaker. In demonstration, he slung an ornate vase at the wall. The crash of glass breaking rang out as he heaved. "Break it all. Do whatever you need to. And don't you dare feel sorry about it afterward."

My gaze flickered around the room maniacally until I spotted a poker by the fireplace. I grabbed it, letting out a roar as Solace backed out of the room. I shattered everything, tore the innards from the cozy armchairs, and put a few holes in the walls. Not even the darkness outside could compete with the darkness within me.

My muscles were liquefied by the end of my rampage of destruction, and I would've sunk to the floor if it weren't for the shards of broken things scattered everywhere.

The poker fell from my numb hand, and I eyed Solace, who'd remained an unshakable presence in all this.

"Are you done?" he asked. "Did you get it all out?" He seemed fully prepared to let me tear down the whole house if I had to.

I took in the mess I'd made, his childhood memories I'd ruined, and I wanted to crumble. Wanted to find a corner where I could draw my knees to my chest and wither away in peace. I rubbed at my temples, swaying on my feet as Solace swiftly approached to steady me.

"Will you do something for me?" he asked quietly, pulling my hands away from my face.

"Yes," I said, voice shredded. I would do anything for him, anything to right the wrong I'd just done.

"I want you to try something." He reached for my clammy cheeks, and I bent forward to make it easier for him. Similar to a cat starved for affection, I leaned into the touch. "For the rest of your stay in Haley Cove, I'd like you to stop trying to remember and just *be*. If you need someone to tell you that it's okay to let go, I'll be that someone. Let it go, Noon. If only for a little while."

"But it feels important," I said. "Remembering feels so important."

"*This* can be important too. This moment, right now, me holding you like this, you taking comfort in it, us not being alone. This can be important too, and all the moments that come after it. Don't miss out on making new memories by spending every waking hour trying to recapture old ones. Live, Noon. Live and let the universe take care of the rest."

Solace seemed as heartbroken by the idea as I did, but his unflinching stare said everything would be okay, the ocean within that stare ushering me safely to shore.

"Why do you care?" I breathed. "You hardly know me. You *don't* know me."

"What if I said it feels like I do?" he asked, head lowering.

I forced his gaze up with a gentle pull on his braid. "I'd say it feels like I know you too."

He took my hand, leading me out of the rubble. "Let's go home," he said, and my brain snagged on the word *home*, because that was how Solace felt. Like home. "You can take a hot shower while I cook us dinner."

"But you don't know how to cook," I said with certainty.

Solace spun on me, his expression a mix of confusion tinged with surprise. "How do you know that?"

"I-I don't." I had no clue why I'd said it, and now I worried that I may have insulted him.

His gaze dug deep into me, then dropped as if coming up empty. That was how I felt. Empty.

"Well, you're right. I'll order us pizza. Come on." Solace drove us back, cranking up the heat when I began to shake from the loss of adrenaline.

Back at the house, I showered, standing under the hot spray for about an hour before dragging myself downstairs in search of Solace, both the man and the feeling.

I froze as I entered the kitchen. He stood with his back to me, hands pressed into the marble island, head hung between his shoulders. He seemed exhausted too, and I was hard-pressed to think of reasons other than myself for why that would be. I backed away, making sure to create noise before re-entering. My heart pitched toward the floor at the smile plastered across his face. It was a show. Intended for my benefit.

"The pizza's cold," he said. "But I can reheat it."

"It's okay. I don't really have an appetite anyway. What I could really use is some sleep."

"Alright. I already got a fire going for you in the living room. I assumed you'd want to sleep on the couch again." He made his way to the living room with me in tow.

I looked at the front door as he settled onto one end of the couch.

"I can hang out here until you fall asleep."

"I really should go."

He followed my gaze to the door, then tilted his head at me. "Is that what you want?"

"No, but I should want it. Not wanting to leave here doesn't make sense," I said, every syllable loaded with confusion and despair.

"Does being here feel right?"

"Yes."

"Then hold on to that. Hold on to what feels right." He offered me his hand, and I took it, holding on to him, because that felt right too.

Solace tugged me down, patting the pillow he'd placed on his lap until I rested my head on top of it. I settled in, each blink heavier than the last.

He hummed while playing with the damp strands of my hair, and I tried to hold on for him. Tried to stay awake for one minute longer, because his touch and his voice somehow made everything better right then.

The humming stopped, and so did his fingers. My eyes opened sluggishly. I couldn't see him from this angle, so I concentrated on the fire while hoping he'd pick up where he left off. His nails lightly dragged along my scalp, and I exhaled in relief.

"Gavin hated being dropped off at daycare," he whispered, like maybe the crackling fire had ears and would spread his secrets if he wasn't careful. "Taking him was my job. He didn't understand why I had to work, why I wanted to be with other kids more than I wanted to be with him."

"You were a teacher?" I guessed.

"Yes. I didn't have to work, but I loved my job and believed I could do what I loved and be a good father. Gavin couldn't wait to be old enough to go to school with me. We started a countdown calendar after his fourth birthday. He'd get to go to school with me when he turned five." Solace's voice took on a faraway quality. He was no longer in the room with me. His memories had taken him somewhere else, and I bunched the knees of his sweats between my fists in dreaded anticipation.

"We were a day away from that long-awaited first day of school. 'We made it, Dad!' he'd said. Lunch was packed and in the fridge, and with my help, he'd ironed his clothes like a big boy. I don't even think he got a wink of sleep that night." He gripped my hair as if bracing himself. "And then the morning came, and so did the first of many seizures." Solace swallowed, and my stomach hollowed out.

"I ended up quitting my job to homeschool him, which was a nice consolation for him, but over time it secretly made me resentful. Gavin's father is a doctor, and he tried his best to fix Gavin. Called in the best pediatric specialists, the top neurologists, but nothing worked. It took a toll on our marriage, although the complete fracturing of it would come much later."

I rolled over to face him then, brushing back his loose strands of hair blocking his anguish from me. I needed to see him clearly, and I needed him to see me. Needed him to know I was right there with him.

"He loved to swim, always had, but now we needed to be careful. Every second he spent around bodies of water had to be supervised at all times. *Every* second. I knew this. I understood it. One day I wasn't careful. He was splashing around in the pool, having the time of his life when I received an important call. A call I'd been waiting for all week, one that would've allowed me, in some capacity, to go back to doing what I loved." He took a second to blink up at the ceiling, and I wanted to tell him not to fight it. I wanted to tell him that it was okay to cry. I settled for being a listening ear instead.

"Gavin's happiness couldn't be contained, and his shouts of glee escalated until it became impossible to hear the person on the other end of the phone. I stepped inside for what felt like only seconds to wrap up the call. A lot can happen in a few seconds," he cautioned, his voice dipping lower. "I wanted more, when I already had so much. Because of my ungratefulness, I ended up losing the person I loved most. I hadn't noticed when the splashing stopped. I wasn't careful."

His fingers were so soft and calming as they combed through my hair again, and I wondered how he could focus on me in any way as he recounted what had to be the most painful, and life-altering experience of his life. I hadn't gotten to meet my unborn child. The accident had robbed me of that. But the pain of losing someone who I hadn't gotten to meet, but who was still a part of me, left me riddled with pain every time I thought about it. I couldn't even begin to comprehend the magnitude of Solace's pain.

"It wasn't—"

He pressed a single digit to my lips, silencing me. "Don't," he said. "I didn't tell you so you could make me feel better. I'm okay. I've already made peace with it."

"So why did you tell me?" I wiped the wet corners of his eyes with my thumb.

"There are things I didn't think I could survive, didn't think I could live through, but I did—" He shook his head, starting over again. "I can't watch you fight to regain your life and not try to help. I'd like to believe that every time I share something with you, it's helping, or will help, in some way. That's my way of fighting in return. Now, sleep," he said, the calming effects of his hands in my hair resuming.

For the first time, I didn't try to understand what he meant, didn't search my mind for the deeper meaning, for the familiarity of it. I surrendered to living in the moment, to believing that my hardships had inspired him in some way, even if I didn't understand how.

I brought one of his hands to my chest, keeping it there as I drifted to sleep.

That night I dreamt of vinyl records and dancing in the snow. I dreamt of "Tears in Heaven." And in between those dreams, Solace's warm breath tickled against my ear as I imagined he whispered, "You once took care of me, now it's my turn to take care of you."

CHAPTER 8

Solace

Then

I'D JUST ZIPPED up my coat when Noon crossed the tree line onto the front yard.

"I was about to come looking for you," I said as he stomped through the front door. He'd been here over a week now, and without fail, he went for a stroll through the woods every day at dawn. I'd had to find him twice after more than an hour passed and he hadn't returned.

"These came in handy." He held up the strips of torn sheets I'd given him yesterday with the suggestion to tie them around tree trunks and branches as he went. "Thanks."

"Glad I could help," I said with a grin as I rehung our coats. The storm ended days ago, and almost all traces of it had melted under the now abnormally warmer temperatures. Noon hadn't gone home, and neither of us had pointed it out.

He tried to smile for my benefit, always for my benefit, but I knew him by now. Enough to know when his smiles were real or faked. They were always insincere after his walks. His bad moods returned with him.

I wished he didn't try so hard to appear better for me, but that was how he operated, I was beginning to learn. It wasn't that he didn't let me witness his pain, but he'd express it and then shake it off just as fast, as though he thought that only one of us could break down at a time, and that pleasure often fell upon me.

I couldn't fight it, couldn't insist I'd be okay for a while if he wanted a break from being strong. I was too damaged to pretend otherwise, even for a brief moment. But I tried to help him in any way I could.

"You need to break something," I said. "Staring at nothing doesn't work for you, not like it does for me. You need an outlet for your emotions."

"I'll be fine. The walks help."

"Is that why you were snarling to yourself and kicking up dead grass on the way to the porch?"

He dropped onto the couch in the same suit he'd arrived in. He needed more things, but he'd have to leave to get them, and I was scared that if he left he wouldn't come back.

"I'm not going to break anything, Solace."

"Okay." I shrugged. "Then we'll settle for burning it."

Noon raised a brow as I headed for the staircase, my steps purposeful. I returned with a handful of Patrick's things, striding for the kitchen and then through the patio door. I dumped the expensive suits into the large fire pit, making several more trips through the house until every article of clothing he owned filled it.

"How can I help?" Noon eventually said. I hid my smirk and told him to start with the awards and framed degrees in Patrick's office. He snapped the trophies in half before tossing them in.

"I guess you're breaking something after all," I said, passing him the guitar signed by every member of Patrick's favorite band. It was worth a lot. Noon cracked it over his knee before adding it to the raging flames. As items burned, creating more space, we added more, until the only thing that remained of my lying, cheating husband were the memories lingering in the house. I thought about razing that to the ground too, but Noon talked me out of it.

"Thank you," he said later on as we sat by the fire pit sharing a drink. He opted for beer, and I returned to my usual: red wine. "I needed that."

"Was the exhilaration only temporary for you too?"

"Yeah," he admitted. "But just because our problems were waiting to greet us once the high wore off, doesn't mean that it wasn't needed. I no longer feel like I'm about to explode."

The destruction of Patrick's things had only been a fleeting distraction. Now that the rush was gone, we were back to the truth, back to figuring out how to pick up the pieces of our shattered lives.

"What's that?" Noon asked, looking over at the photobooth picture I held of my brother and Gavin. I handed it to him.

"It fell from the pocket of one of Patrick's suits."

"Were they close?"

"Thick as thieves, even though their relationship was mostly long distance. My brother took his role as uncle seriously. My son got his love of music from him. Specifically his love of Eric Clapton. Greatest guitarist to ever live, Gav would say. He gifted Gavin his much-loved and worshiped signed copy of the *Unplugged* vinyl album one Christmas. I'd never seen my kid so happy."

"That's the album he's holding in the photo on the mantel," Noon said.

"Yeah. Weirdly, his favorite song was 'Tears in Heaven.' Patrick thought it was morbid that he loved that song so much. I thought it was cute when he'd promise to never forget my name, not even in heaven." I rubbed at the ache in my chest. "Hell, maybe I was the morbid one."

Noon handed back the creased photo, and I grazed a finger over Gavin's goofy smile. "I loved that they had something that was just theirs."

"Did you and Gavin have something that belonged to just the two of you?"

"Photography."

"Oh yeah?"

"Yeah. I knew my way around a camera from being in front of one for so many years, and it was the only other thing Gavin had taken an interest in other than music. We'd go off into the woods and take nature shots. We took a class together the summer he..." I swallowed, then decided I didn't need to say the words for Noon to hear them. He'd become good at picking up on my thoughts. "It was mostly something for us to do since he couldn't attend day camp like other kids. I didn't want him out of my sight. Ironic, considering that's how I lost him. Anyway, I didn't think I'd gain much from the class, but it sharpened the skills I'd picked up from doing photo shoots."

"My friend Leland is an artist. Because of him, I have an appreciation for it. Whether it's paint on canvas, photos of beautiful landscapes... I love it all."

"Wait here," I said before darting into the house and returning with my camera. I let him flip through some of the digital images, feeling bolstered by his praise.

"Can I take one of you?" he asked.

"Ah, sure," I said, self-consciously sifting my hands through my hair. I gave him a quick tutorial before relaxing in my chair and facing the lens.

He snapped a shot, then handed the camera back to me, smiling triumphantly.

"Where's my head? My nose and chin?" I asked. He'd completely botched the shot.

"I left them out on purpose," he replied smugly, taking a swig of his beer.

"You expect me to believe you meant to only capture my eyes?" My tone was more than a little skeptical.

"Yes, because it's the truth," he whispered. His jeweled gaze glowed in the firelight, intensifying the longer my stunned silence held. He removed the camera from my hands and began snapping away again.

"See?" He inched his chair closer to show me the photos. "Now we have your chin and nose."

"Better," I agreed. "Do it again. This time move a few paces away, lower to your haunches, and angle the lens upward. And here," taking the camera I messed with the settings, "let's add a UV filter to neutralize the colors, especially the setting sun behind me." I took a test shot, pursing my lips as I examined it.

"What's wrong?" He leaned over to see the camera screen. "It looks perfect."

"I'm trying to decide if it'd be better to switch from a wide-angle lens to a telephoto one," I mused, taking another photo of the woodland beyond.

"What's the difference?"

"A wide-angle is better to capture scenery. The vastness of the orange sky and how far the tree tops stretch into the distance," I explained, still flicking away. "A telephoto lens, on the other hand, would allow you to get a narrower view. It puts the subject at the forefront of the shot, so to speak."

"Then definitely a telepathic scope," he said, and I cursed my skin for heating when he gathered my hair to drape it over one shoulder, making it clear who the subject would be.

"It's a telephoto lens," I corrected, attempting to take the attention off me. I reached into the camera case to swap out the lenses.

"We're losing sunlight fast." I passed the camera off to him. "Make these shots count."

Between the wine, the fire, and Noon's sudden intensity, I'd grown too warm for my coat. I shrugged it off, careful to not screw up the way he'd positioned my hair.

Noon fully immersed himself in the task, taking his job as a pseudo-photographer seriously, and what was supposed to be a few photos before sunset turned into a full-blown photo shoot under the moonlight. He gave orders with confidence.

Moodier.

Less pensive.

Smile for the camera.

Pretend you're walking away.

Now look back at me.

He'd even gotten down on the slushy lawn, willing to do anything for the shot.

"I need more, Solace," he coaxed. "If you plan on making it in this industry, you're going to have to give me more."

"So demanding," I tsked, chuckling when he lowered the camera to reveal his own amusement.

Noon stood, watching me from across the fire as he dusted his pants off as best he could. "This was fun," he said. It was. For those couple of hours, I'd forgotten about everything that had hurt me, and I suspected that was the point. A piece of my heart not riddled with pain warmed for the man I observed through the fire pit's flames, and if his grin was anything to go by, something in him warmed for me too.

It scared and confused me, but I told myself being scared and confused was way better than being scared and alone. Noon made it okay to be terrified as long as we were terrified together.

"Let's see how you did." I circled the fire for the camera, ignoring the electrical current that ran up my arm when our hands briefly touched. "This isn't bad," I said, my voice huskier than usual.

"It's terrible," he countered, looking over my shoulder. His size eclipsed everything, even blocking out the darkened sky. The cold air didn't stand a chance at getting past him to me.

"There's some good stuff here," I said, wincing when I got to one missing half my body. "You did good for your first time," I amended.

Noon stepped closer to me, taking the camera back. Excitement flashed in his eyes as he scrolled through the remaining photos. They were the best, proving he'd gotten better with time. I loved seeing him happy. There was a childlike quality to him. As intimidating as he seemed on the outside, he was soft and mushy on the inside.

"Care Bear," I said in wonder.

"Huh?" He took a break from scrolling to look at me, his expression bewildered.

"Gavin would have called you a Care Bear. It's an old cartoon and stuffed toy. Way before his time. He was an old soul like that. The bears were created to help people express their emotions. They have this unique way of making people feel seen and safe." I shook my head, feeling silly. "Forget it. Ignore me," I insisted. Noon likely didn't remember, if he ever knew, who the Care Bears were. "I used to watch it as a kid. Gavin loved them."

Noon began singing the theme song then, and my chest burned from where my heart had begun to melt. I joined in, and when we were done, he shouted his request for an encore. We sang it three times before emotion robbed me of my voice. I pressed a fist to my mouth. It did nothing to hold the tears in.

"You're beautiful when you cry," he said, not making a big deal about it. "Which Care Bear name do you think Gavin would've given me?"

I blinked the remainder of my tears away as I thought long and hard. "This is tough because you could literally be all of them—well, maybe not Grumpy Bear."

"Let's revisit that after I get my appetite back and you've seen me hungry," he replied. I bit my bottom lip to stifle my smile, and he frowned, pulling it free. "You're just as beautiful when you smile too."

"Okay, let's see," I said, getting back to his Care Bear name. The way his eyes danced said that my stupid blush was thank you enough for his compliment. "The bear's gender doesn't matter here. This is strictly a personality trait thing."

"Of course," he said with mock gravity.

I went through all the Care Bear names and traits in my head before saying, "Maybe Tender Heart Bear. Or Always There Bear?" I asked with less confidence. We really could have gone with either.

"Or Bedtime Bear," he interjected, wiggling his brows. We'd never spoken about our new sleeping arrangement, but we hadn't spent a night outside of each other's arms since that first time he found me in the guest bedroom shivering in the dark.

"My dreams have definitely been sweeter since sleeping with you," I admitted, surprising him and myself. "And even when they're not, it's okay, because it feels like you're there with me."

"Samsies," he said, earning him an eye roll. He hummed thoughtfully. "I never had a nickname before. I'll take Care Bear. And then if the situation calls for it, you can address me by a specific bear's name at that moment." He nodded as if it was all settled.

"I'm pretty sure that's not how nicknames work." I crossed my arms, the cold beginning to set in again. "You can't assign yourself one."

"Says who?" he challenged, getting my coat off my chair and holding it out so I could slide into it. He still wore his suit jacket, but the cold never seemed to affect him like it did me. I'd been washing the whole suit for him every night, and the expensive, dry-clean only fabric now looked mangled.

"Says..." I couldn't think of who'd said it. Noon placed a

hand to his ear in the gesture of waiting for my answer. "Says everyone," I finished.

"Anyone named Everyone should never be trusted."

"You know what I meant."

He tapped me on the nose and again declared that Care Bear was now his official nickname. I gave in, because secretly I loved it and couldn't wait to drive him crazy by abusing it.

I sat while Noon added more wood to the fire pit. Patrick's things had long burned to ashes. "That suit has been through a lot," I noted after he collapsed onto his chair, the plastic and metal groaning in protest.

Noon sighed as the heavy weight of reality retook its place on top of us. "I don't want to go back there."

I knew he meant home. I'd known that was part of the reason for his still being here long after the storm had passed. It said a lot about our rapidly growing dependency on each other that he could even be here, in the home Patrick lived in. It said a lot about the man he was that he'd brave his discomfort if it meant not leaving me here alone. I was beginning to appreciate it more than I should have, for reasons that I shouldn't.

"So don't. We can pick up a few things for you in town tomorrow."

"I need to go back," he whispered.

"Is it work?"

He worked for himself, but that didn't mean he could afford to take time off.

"No. I think I've earned a hiatus, all things considered."

Perhaps he needed the privacy he couldn't get while here to fight for his wife. Maybe he wanted her back. Did I want him to fight for her? Did I want Patrick in a position to be forced to settle for me? No, I didn't want either of those things. Most of all not the former.

"Would you stay with her if you could?" I asked, once the suspense became too much. "Do you still want her?"

Noon considered the question for a long while. "I could have forgiven her for it all the night it happened—or the night she told me about the affair, I should say. We've been together for a long time, and marriage has its ups and downs. People make mistakes. I could have forgiven her mistake, even one this big." He peered into the dark, the breeze disturbing his hair. The ends—a lighter shade of brown than the roots—were beginning to curl in places, signaling his need for a trim.

"But I begged her to stay," he said, voice thick with emotion. "I begged her, and she told me she would, but when I woke up she was—" His mouth snapped shut, unable to say the words.

"She was gone," I said.

He nodded, gazing over at me. "Is it crazy of me to say that her not staying felt like the biggest betrayal of all?"

"No," I said, "because Patrick not coming home that night feels similar." It said they weren't sorry. It said they didn't feel bad about the pain they'd caused. It said they wanted each other more than they wanted us to be okay. More than they wanted to help us understand. That part of their betrayal had cut us both soul deep.

"She doesn't want me anymore." Even with the fire helping to light up his eyes, the life inside them dimmed. "So me saying that I wouldn't stay with her even if I could feels kind of pointless."

"It's not pointless," I argued. "I think your answer, *our* answer, to that question indicates if we're ready to move on or not."

"Would you stay with Patrick if you could?"

I sucked down a deep breath before responding; Noon tangling his hand with mine gave me the courage to. "If you had asked me that right after it happened, after I'd had a chance to admit to myself that I'd be lost without him, I would have said yes."

"And now?" Noon asked.

"Now I feel like I'm finding myself. Now I don't feel so lost."

Everything began to change the day Noon showed up, and it continued to do so. His tentative smile said he understood the significance of what I'd said and how it related to the timeline of his arrival here.

"He was my first everything. My first kiss, my first lover. My only kiss, my only lover... I'm used to him. Used to the way he makes me pay for Gavin's death. Used to the way he reminds me that I deserve it."

"I have a feeling that if I said what happened to your son wasn't your fault, you wouldn't believe me."

I released his hand to touch his forehead, the lines furrowing it smoothing away. "It isn't my hope to one day wake up and believe that it wasn't my fault."

"What do you hope for, then, Solace?"

"To one day make peace with the fact that it is."

Noon reclasped our hands together. He didn't try to change my mind or convince me that my outlook was wrong. He just sat in my grief with me.

"Being without him never gets easier," I said. "The wound never scabs over. The pain remains acute."

"I'm guessing the pain will always be close to the surface," he whispered, and I wondered if the ache in his voice was on behalf of my loss or in remembrance of his. Of the children he wanted but couldn't have. Knowing Noon, it was a mix of both. "I'm sure not being able to openly grieve in your own home didn't help, and not having the support you needed from your husband. He should have been leaning into you, not away from you."

"Being constantly watched through a lens of blame and scorn didn't help one bit," I admitted. It felt like that was what

Patrick needed, and because of what I'd done, what he needed had mattered most. I just wished what he needed had been me.

Noon got down on his knees in front of me after I'd closed my eyes and turned away to wrestle with my emotions. I took a shuddering breath, then gazed up at him. Even on his knees he towered over my seated form. "Has anyone ever told you that you're beautiful when you cry?" he asked with humor and awe, trying to be a light in my dark moment.

"Can't say I've heard that before," I said, playing along.

"Never stop doing it," he said. "If that's what you need, then never stop doing it." Noon withdrew his phone from his pocket, and after a few taps on the screen "Tears in Heaven" began playing. He maxed out the volume before setting the device on his unoccupied chair, then stood from his kneeled position, making a show of holding his hand out for me to take. "Shall we dance?"

My whole body trembled with emotion now. For once I didn't fight it or care, because Noon said it was okay not to, and I trusted him to be right. I let him pull me into his chest and wrap me up tight in his arms as we swayed to the most beautiful sad song ever written. And when I broke down further, when my sobs drowned out the song that he'd set to repeat, he didn't attempt to make me feel better with pointless platitudes. He didn't lavish me with words meant to make my well of infinite tears dry up. All he said was, "Grieve for as long as you need, Solace. I've got you."

True Heart Bear. That was who Noon exemplified in that moment. Kind, affectionate, and attentive. The most caring creature that ever was.

CHAPTER 9

Noon

Now

I'D CUDDLED BEFORE, but with Solace it was unlike anything I could recall ever doing in the past. When I woke up on the couch wrapped in his embrace for the third morning in a row, I added it to the things-the-new-me-enjoyed-immensely list—even if I shouldn't have.

Not wanting to wake him, I lay still, the events from a few nights ago replaying in my mind. The unfamiliar tourist traps of Haley Cove, the memories I'd tried and failed to grab hold of at Solace's grandfather's house, the subsequent rage and then the surrender to it. More importantly, Solace's steadfast support through it all.

The ordeal had left me near catatonic for days, so exhausted I could barely move from this spot to take care of my body's needs. Solace had kept an eye on me during that time, allowing me to rest but occasionally forcing me to eat too.

I'd gone from falling asleep with my head on his lap—and his fingers in my hair—that one night, to waking up to being spooned by him. I'd gladly sacrificed precious minutes of dawn to enjoy him holding me a bit longer, though.

The couch was surprisingly large enough to accommodate me, but it was a tight fit with the both of us. Considering the direction we faced, one wrong move and he'd end up crashing to the floor.

I felt more refreshed this morning, ready to take on the day, or at least attempt to. Eventually, the urge to both relieve my bladder and watch the sun rise became too unbearable to ignore. I carefully extracted myself from him, holding my breath and performing a few gymnastic moves to climb over the couch without waking him.

He rolled to his stomach, murmuring something unintelligible before falling silent again.

After a quick morning routine in the upstairs guest bathroom, I slipped into something warm before sneaking out the front door.

The smart option would've been to stick to the paved road, but the forest beyond the fence line beckoned me, so I set off that way, hoping I wouldn't get lost and die from hypothermia.

I walked longer than I'd planned, well beyond the time it took for the sun to rise above the horizon, and well beyond the point of being able to feel my fingers within my coat pockets.

Stepping into a sun-filled clearing with a landscape of untouched snow, I decided to take a chance that my fingers would survive another thirty minutes or so. Pulling my hat down over my ears, and zipping my coat all the way up to my chin, I stretched out on my back, closing my eyes on an exhale as the sun's rays warmed my cheeks. Shutting out the cold and the time, I relaxed there, practicing my promise to live in the moment.

"Hey, you're blocking my sunlight," I grumbled a short while later, cracking one eye open to see Solace peering down at me. The breathtaking smile he brandished took aim at my heart. All I could think about was how he'd been a soothing presence by my side since the day we met, and how he'd cared for me over the last few days. "How'd you find me?"

"I followed the crater-sized footprints you left behind. You were gone so long I thought you might need rescuing from your bad sense of direction."

"You make one wrong turn and they never let you live it down," I said dryly, getting to my feet and dusting the snow off me as best I could.

"The navigation was screaming at you to turn left," he said in reference to my driving mishaps during our tour around town. "Would you have thought to follow your own foot trail back to the house?" His pleased expression said he already knew the answer.

"Eventually," I said, taking the gloves he held out for me. "Thanks." It took a lot for my body to notice the cold, another indication of how long I'd been exposed to the elements.

He stuck his own gloved hands in his pockets, letting his gaze roam free. "I love this clearing," he said. "Wildflowers bloom throughout it in the spring. I hang out here sometimes, when it's warm. I can spend hours reading or just thinking."

"Sounds peaceful." I gazed around too, imagining the bare branches teeming with foliage and colorful flowers surrounded by the sunlight coming through the opening in the trees.

"It is," Solace said in a dreamy tone, shutting his eyes and tipping his face toward the sky. I cataloged every detail of his features, while he busied himself with a memory I wasn't privy to. His rosy, winter-kissed cheeks, his pale hair now braided down his back, the long lashes resting against the skin beneath his closed eyes. His tempting mouth, the fact that a few days ago that thought would have filled me with guilt, but in the moment—the one I was choosing to dwell in until it passed—there was no shame or guilt at all.

I hadn't realized he'd caught me staring at his lush lips until they moved, snapping me from my momentary preoccupation with them.

"What are you thinking about right now?" he asked, his entrancing eyes full of curiosity. He straddled a fine line between wholesome and seductive, without even trying for the latter.

"This." I gestured to the clearing, searching for more words to describe what surrounded us. "This stillness. It's contagious." Because for the first time in a while, I felt still. Mentally and emotionally.

"What else?" He came closer to brush snow off my shoulders, those near-invisible freckles that I adored coming into view. I didn't question why I adored them either. I just did. In that moment, I did.

"I'm also thinking about the other night. Thinking about you." My breath curled between us. "Thank you."

"For what?" He tilted his head at me.

"For sharing Gavin with me. That couldn't have been easy. For sitting with me these past few days. For being patient when you really don't have to be. And for helping me realize that I could still make a life. I'd like to try."

"Sharing with you is the easiest thing I'll ever do, Noon. Come, let's go inside. I want to show you something, and your lips are turning blue." He secured his gloved hand around mine and led the way back, cracking jokes about my shoe size as we went, claiming that my footprints almost swallowed him whole.

"Exaggerator has just been added to the list of things I've learned about you," I said once we were inside and peeling out of our winter gear.

"You've been compiling a list?" he asked with amused curiosity.

"I'm not telling you what's on it," I warned, already sensing where things were headed. I beelined for the fireplace, presenting my ice-cold palms to the flames.

"You can't tell someone you're building a list of their qualities and not tell them what you have so far," he complained, falling onto one of the armchairs and kicking his feet up on the coffee table.

"You're getting pretty comfortable for a guy who said he had something to show me. Is it in your pocket?"

"I'll show you if you tell me a few things on your list."

"That wasn't the deal," I said, laughing over my shoulder.

"Okay, just two things. That's it."

"You're lucky you're so adorable." I took a seat on the couch now that I'd defrosted.

"You think I'm adorable?" His tone held a seriousness that it hadn't a second ago. He lowered his feet to the floor, and the sudden intensity in his gaze had my body waking up in ways it hadn't before.

"Yes," I admitted. "Right this second, I find you adorable."

"What about this second?"

"In this second too," I confirmed.

"And now?" he asked, some of his playfulness returning.

"Now and forever. Does that make you happy?"

"Maybe." He shrugged, relaxing in his seat again. "I mean, I think I've aged out of the "adorable" bracket. Pretty sure the max age limit is eight. But it's better than "ghastly," I suppose."

My laugh was booming this time. Partly because I liked this witty side to him, and because I felt lighter than I had in ages. I wanted to do nothing more than sit there dangling my list over his head and feeding him bits and pieces of it all day.

"You owe me one more adjective."

"I never agreed to give you any," I countered.

"I was nice enough to count "adorable" as one, the least you can do is give me one more."

"Fine," I said, feigning exasperation. "If it'll get you to show me what was so important that you had to drag me from my bed of snow in the woods, I'll tell you." I thought back on all I'd gleaned about him during our short time together, on all the qualities he'd shown through both actions and words. I thought about giving him "helpful," "compassionate," "sad," or even "lonely," but one particular descriptor stood out most, so I went with it.

"Missing," I said, and Solace's anticipatory smile faded. "Like some part of you was missing, to be more exact. I remember feeling that strongly when we first met."

"And now?" he whispered. "Do you still sense that a part of me is missing?"

I looked to the mantel, toward little Gavin's photo, and wanted to say yes, but that felt too obvious. While I knew he missed Gavin, that wasn't the type of "missing" I'd picked up on. Then I remembered the man he'd lost, the one who was still somewhere out there in the world.

My stomach tightened, but it wasn't because I was sad for his loss—like I should have been—it was from fear of that person returning. I was starting to see Solace as mine, even if that confused me considering that our relationship wasn't a romantic one. I wanted to cling to the feeling I got when I was with him. I didn't want anyone showing up and taking that away.

"No," I said, lying to him for the first time. "I don't get that impression anymore. Not in the way I initially had. I think it was the loss of your son that I was picking up on."

"It was," he said, and somehow I knew he'd just lied to me in return.

Solace excused himself to make us tea, refusing my offer to help. I waited in the living room, giving him the space he seemed to need.

He returned, setting our mugs down before padding off to haul in a file box from the coat closet.

"What's all that?" I asked as he sat next to me and removed the box's lid.

"I was thinking about the photos you offered to take of me, and it got me thinking about my prior print work." He handed me a stack of magazines. I flipped to the dog-eared pages of him. "I forgot I had these in the attic. Thought it might be helpful to go through some of them before we start. This is my old portfolio." He passed me a binder next.

"You haven't aged one bit," I said, examining photo after photo, like there was hidden treasure to be found in them. There were shots of him with the winter landscape as his backdrop. Then a series of black and white photos where the only speck of color was the vibrant blue of his irises. My favorite was a photo of him in an oversized pinstripe suit. The legs dragged on the floor behind him as he peered away from the camera's lens, his expression pensive. The jacket's sleeves reached his knees, hiding his hands, and his hair had been artfully tousled. With his masculine but lean body hidden beneath pounds of fabric, I was left with only the androgynous beauty of his face. There was no way to guess at his gender, which seemed to be the point.

"Maybe we can recreate some of these," Solace said, alerting me to the fact that I'd been appreciating that particular shot for far too long.

"Yeah. Sure." I slammed the binder shut, then reached for my tea, hoping it hadn't gone cold. Maybe cold was what I needed right then. Something to cool off the heat in my blood, the blood traveling south through my veins.

"Great," he said. "How about we fire up the pit out back and make s'mores like we're in our teens instead of our thirties?"

I loved s'mores. "Sounds like heaven."

"Hear that, Gavin?" he asked, gazing heavenward.

"I bet he heard it loud and clear," I whispered.

"Do you always say the right things?"

"Have you not met me?"

"Pretty sure I have."

"Most times I blurt out the opposite of the right thing."

"Ah, that wonky filter right?" he shot back with a lopsided smirk.

"Correct. But saying the right thing helps when I'm talking to the right person." We were building a rhythm with our back-and-forth exchange, which felt a lot like flirting.

"Did you just make that up?" He raised a skeptical brow.

"I did. Was it cringy?"

"Extremely so," he answered. "Speaking of talking," he continued without missing a beat. "How about we do nothing but that for the rest of the day?"

"How about the rest of the week?" We'd both turned to face each other on the couch, our knees now touching. The rapid-fire banter made me breathless in a good way. I never wanted it to end, even as something like terror began to creep in.

"You should give up your room at the inn."

"I should stay here."

"You should," he agreed.

My heart hammered against my chest, my fingers seeking out his hair. The braid had come loose some time ago. "And we should do nothing but talk, sip beer—or wine—and make s'mores all day—"

"What happened to all week?" he asked, the lump at his throat moving up and down with his hard swallow.

"I like Easy Breezy Solace," I breathed.

"Just trying to keep my adjectives well-rounded."

We panted into the small space between us, long enough for my terror to gain ground.

"What are we doing?" I asked, releasing his hair. My fingers itched to recapture the silky strands, and other parts of me suddenly begged for more.

"Whatever the moment calls for." He caught and held my hand before it fell to my lap. "No comeback?" he asked when I remained quiet. Things could only escalate from here, and while I didn't want this moment or the next one to end, I wasn't ready for what his timid but heated gaze suggested. I didn't care if my body disagreed.

"I win," he whispered after I'd taken too long to continue our game of verbal ping-pong.

I cleared my throat and jumped to my feet, walking over to the fireplace. The loss of his skin on mine felt agonizing. I stared down at the hand that had been holding his, to make sure it was still attached to my body, because it felt like I was the one missing some part of me now, like I'd left it on the couch with him.

"We can get the rest of my things tomorrow," I said with a steadier voice. "I should probably check in with Leland as well. I wouldn't put it past him to form a search party to come looking for me."

"What if he asks when you're coming back? What will you say?"

"Never," I answered too eagerly, then amended, "I'll tell him I've still got some things to sort out before I head back."

"I like never better," he said. Despite his words, his tone was now absent of lust and innuendo, making his statement sound friendly instead of suggestive. The shift saddened me, and for the first time, I found myself mourning something other than my wife. I faced him, putting my back to the flames.

"I want you here," he said. "I want to get to know you more. And you don't need to hold back, Noon."

While that last part could have been misconstrued, his soft, reassuring smile said he'd simply wanted me to know I could speak my mind, that I could be honest about wanting to stick around a while longer. But the long column of his neck begged for the forceful grip of my hand, and his hair pleaded for my fist to take hold of it. I wanted to touch him. Wanted to do things to him that I hadn't thought about doing to anyone else. Not even my dead wife. Living in the moment and choosing the right moment were not the same things, though. And this wasn't the right moment. Might never be.

"Okay," I said with effort.

"Now, how about we get things going with the s'mores, beers, wine, and talking? We've got a long week of doing nothing ahead of us."

"Sounds perfect," I said. "And being here with you isn't nothing."

We spent the rest of the afternoon talking, as planned. I learned about Solace's childhood, about his summers spent in Haley Cove, and his years working as a teacher.

I mostly listened because I didn't have much to share. Or could it have been that I believed what Stacey and I had was too sacred to share? An even scarier thought was that maybe being here, being in this moment, was the sacred thing, and that I didn't want the memory of someone else to intrude upon it. A sickening feeling came with that potential truth, but in spite of it, I decided to use our talk as part of my starting point for building new memories.

I showed him my scars from the accident, and walked him through my physical recovery and my depression soon after. I redirected the conversation whenever a topic called for me to mention my wife. I realized that talking and thinking about her triggered my episodes of panic, and while I knew I needed to delve into that more, this wasn't the time.

We spent the next week going over staging for the photo shoot, ordering the proper lighting, and handing out adjectives. I'd learned that I was charming, honest, and blunt when at ease. I liked seeing myself through Solace's eyes. It made me feel like I still had so much to give, even if a good portion of what I'd had was missing.

We lived in the moment, every moment, and Solace wasn't afraid to do or say what was needed to reel me back in whenever I strayed too far from the here and now.

We watched TV, took daily walks to the clearing together, and spent every night on the couch, sleeping while nestled close together. We didn't overthink it, didn't overcomplicate it with questions and explanations as to why we needed it. We simply went with what felt good, with what felt right without crossing *that* line.

By the end of week two I was a firm believer that life was better when living it second by second, even if it was becoming harder to find and feel Stacey as the days went by. I had to believe she would've wanted this for me. Would've wanted me to move on.

CHAPTER 10

Solace

Then

NOON SCREECHED TO a stop at the top of the driveway. He slammed the truck door shut, then hurried toward me with his duffel bag. After weeks of rotating between his suit and a few of my baggier items, he'd finally gone home to pick up some things.

A part of me worried he wouldn't return, so I'd kept myself busy to avoid dwelling on that possibility. And also to avoid admitting to myself that wanting him to come back was no longer about me not wanting to be alone.

I'd used the time to run errands, and to open the email containing my test results. Like Noon, I was fine, and with that behind me, I had one less thing to worry about. It also meant I had one less thing holding me back from the bad idea I'd been increasingly contemplating the more time I spent with Noon.

"How many traffic laws did you break to get back here before sunset?" I asked from the porch.

"Too many to count," he said, dropping one of his now infamous forehead kisses on me. He'd said they made everything better. I had to agree because whenever his lips touched my skin, my problems faded into the background. My heart and mind soaked up his affection, affection that seemed to have ramped up in its frequency ever since we danced to Gavin's favorite song by the fire pit weeks ago. Other parts of me began to crave his attention as well.

Noon no longer felt the need to hold back, it seemed. If it were anyone else it would have come off as inappropriate, or a means to a sexual end. He wasn't the type to be guided by ulterior motives, though, and he didn't have a bad-intentioned bone in his body. Noon was honest, blunt even, and I'd have wagered that everyone in his life had experience with his overwhelming need to provide care and show love. I was short of both, so he'd never get any complaints from me about it.

Still, good intentions and all, I didn't miss the way he looked at me when he thought I wouldn't notice. Longing stares captured through the reflection of a window or glass door when my back was turned.

His doting, by nature, made it tough to discern what was real and what was a figment of my imagination, though, and I wasn't forward enough to ask. Wouldn't dare. Shouldn't even be considering it. We were both going through a lot, after all, and while it felt like I'd known him forever, in reality it had only been a short, trauma-filled time.

"I'll take a quick shower and then we can go," he said, entering the house and holding up the camera that dangled around his neck. That camera was now a permanent fixture at his side, and every evening he'd drag me to some park, or cliffside, or bridge to take photos of the sunset. He'd tried to drag me out at dawn, even promising me one of his delicious omelets—which I now scarfed down without having to be bribed to—but I'd returned to my normal sleeping patterns, and so getting up that early was out of the question.

I'd wake up to find his spot cold, and as a consolation for him being gone, he'd leave behind a Polaroid selfie of him holding me while I slept on his chest. He dated and time-stamped them all, down to the seconds. His way of letting me know he'd stayed with me, held me as long as he could before leaving to chase the sunrise. I saved every one of them.

"Why didn't you save time by showering at home?" I asked, removing my coat since we weren't leaving that second.

"I couldn't. I got in and out of there as fast as I could."

I nodded, making a mental note to be the one who held him tonight, the one giving instead of taking. He made it so damn easy to be selfish because he had an endless supply of everything good to give, but thanks to him, now so did I.

"And can I *please* burn that suit when we get back?"

"It's yours to do whatever you want with," he said, chuckling as he jogged up the stairs.

Ten minutes later, we were racing for the icy cold beach, barely making it onto the boardwalk before the moon would have its turn with us. Noon got the shots he wanted, though, and that giddy smile he directed at me was worth the frigid air shredding through my parka and thermals.

"Damn you and your high body temperature," I said, teeth chattering. He hadn't even zipped up his coat. He swooped in until only inches separated us, bringing his cozy warmth with him.

"Don't be jealous," Noon said around a laugh. "Summers are brutal on me."

"I'd still t-trade with you r-right now," I stammered.

"I'll tell you what," he started, wrapping an arm around my shoulders and leading me to the parking area. "I'll get the fire pit going when we get back, and we can sip beer—and wine— and make s'mores. I'll even let you ruin a perfectly great meal by adding those God-awful chocolate-covered peppermint patties to it." He shuddered at the thought.

"First of all," I said, highly amused, the cold now forgotten. "S'mores are not a meal, and your obsession with them needs to be examined by a shrink. Second of all, peppermint is the greatest thing ever invented."

"You put peppermint in your grandfather's chamomile tea, screwing up his tradition and recipe." He'd accidentally picked up the mug meant for me the other day, gagging when the taste of mint hit his tongue.

We shut ourselves inside the truck, and I grinned as I dug into my pocket to reveal a peppermint candy. Noon cranked the heat up, shaking his head at me in mock horror before driving off.

"There's mint in the toothpaste and mouthwash we use every day."

"And the floss," he interjected. "Don't forget the floss. Oh, and the air freshener plug-in thingy in the bathrooms."

"Point is, you never complain about—"

"That's different. I'm not ingesting those things. Peppermint should never reach the digestive system."

"You're such a strange giant."

"I think strange comes with giant territory."

"We should tattoo 'strange' on your arm."

"I vote for my big burly chest."

"Why not your big forehead?"

"But then where would the kisses go?" he gasped.

"I would say we could use our lips, but then you'd be forced to taste peppermint."

"I guess I could make an exception," he said in a put-out tone.

"I'd love it if you did," I whispered, not recognizing my husky tone and shocking myself further with my brashness. I'd turned our playful banter into something that shouldn't even be contemplated. Noon stopped at a red light and faced me, as if needing to read my expression for the truth. Even though I knew flushed cheeks greeted him, I still winked and responded with an ease I didn't feel, "I win."

"You play dirty," he said, swallowing hard. The light turned green and he took off again, but the thickness in the air hadn't thinned, not until several miles later when he started our banter up again.

We'd go back and forth about the silliest things sometimes. It was fun to see how one topic rolled into a new one, fun to watch the other try to keep up without missing a beat, fun to win every time. It was our game, it kept our minds busy, kept the heavy things still haunting us locked away for a while.

I'd never been a playful person, but everything about me was different with Noon. Everything about me was better. And the things that were the same were better too, because I was beginning to accept them instead of trying to change them. I was fine the way I was.

Noon suggested a movie night after we were done talking and drinking over s'mores by the fire pit. I'd thought he'd want to watch one of the action adventures he loved so much, but when I grabbed the remote from atop the media console and joined him on the couch, he whispered a new request.

"Do you have any videos of Gavin?"

"Tons," I admitted with hesitancy. I'd done a lot of emotional unloading over the last two weeks—more if we were counting from the moment he showed up in my life—and Noon had held me together through it all.

Whenever I'd insist that he must be tired of hearing me talk about Gavin, he'd tell me that I needed to talk about him more. I'd make dinner, or try to, before surrendering to the fact that I couldn't even toast bread. We'd end up ordering pizza and eating on the living room floor as we went through Gavin's baby books.

"How is it that I miss him, when I didn't even know him?" he'd asked me one of those nights. I'd broken down into the

crook of his neck as he hugged me so tight that my ribs ached for a few days afterward.

"For as long as I live, there's nothing that anyone could ever say to me that will mean more to me than that," I'd said once I'd come up for air. He'd just smiled at me before kissing my forehead.

"Are you sure?" I asked, leaving the memory of that night behind. "We can watch whatever you want."

"I want to watch Gavin," he assured me, brushing his knuckles over my warm cheek. "If you're up for it."

Noon made it impossible to keep the scales even between us. I had to constantly remind myself that allowing him to care for me was my way of giving back to him.

I grabbed my laptop and cuddled up next to him on the couch, going through the options in the Gavin folder before deciding to start from the beginning. I'd never watched any of these videos since taking them. Had been too busy before he'd passed, and too afraid to after.

Our movie night started out well enough, and I knew I'd made great strides with my grief when I found myself laughing instead of crying. Things took a turn when video after video played and I began to pick up on a central theme I hadn't noticed before.

"You're doing it all wrong," Patrick could be heard shouting in the background as I attempted to light Gavin's birthday cake. He'd turned two.

"Where would you be without me?" he said in another clip as I recorded Gavin strapped into his booster seat. He'd officially graduated from the car seat. I hadn't gotten the buckling of it correct. Patrick had stepped in to fix it.

"Can you do anything right?" he asked over Christmas breakfast. I'd burned the toast. *"Who can't toast bread?"*

Through it all, Gavin remained cheerful. His life hadn't been wrecked by my supposed mistakes, but for whatever reason, Patrick's had. I could see it in the thinning of his lips, and hear it in his long-suffering sighs. To anyone else watching, it wouldn't have been a big deal, wouldn't have been something they noticed. *I* hadn't even noticed at the time. I likely thought it was just Patrick being Patrick. Grumpy and impatient.

But now, looking back at the state of my self-confidence prior to Noon showing me what it meant to be treated with dignity and respect, and looking back on Patrick's affair, and the way he'd treated me after Gavin's death... It became crystal clear. He'd been gradually beating me down from the start, and I'd let him.

"Even this he's ruined for me," I said into the now quiet living room after pausing the video I could no longer enjoy.

"Solace," Noon started, but I was already heading for the stairs.

After a hot shower and a decent amount of self-loathing, I stood in front of the mirror in the bathroom Patrick and I shared, wiping away the condensation so I could see myself better. So I could see myself better than Patrick did. It wasn't easy, because on the heels of every mental self-affirmation came his put-downs from the home videos. By the time Noon knocked before entering and stepping in behind me, I couldn't even think of a good reason for still being here, for existing.

He removed the brush from my hand and began the process of detangling my wet hair while he watched me through the mirror. Droplets of water trickled down my spine, vanishing below the towel wrapped around my waist.

"For the life of me, I can't understand how he could possibly take you for granted," he whispered in astonishment. "Being around you is comparable to the experience of watching a flower bloom. You're guileless, generous with your emotions, soft-hearted in a world full of vipers."

"All the things he hated about me," I said in a flat tone, so numb I couldn't even blink.

"Because they were all the things he didn't deserve, and he knew it. He had to find reasons to justify hurting you to make himself feel better about it, Solace. Even your name speaks to the heart of who you are. The world needs more of you and less of him." Once the brush glided through my hair without snagging, he set it aside to braid the strands the way I'd taught him to.

"What do you see when you look at yourself?" he asked, observing me as he worked.

"I...I don't know," I admitted. I was too tired to fight the bad voices anymore.

"Okay. What do you see when *I* look at you?" It was as if he knew focusing on him would be a task much easier for me to complete right then. His green eyes were wide open to me, as always, but this time I paid attention to what they said about me instead of what they said about him.

"I see respect," I said. "For me."

"Go on," he encouraged.

"Admiration. Appreciation..."

"And?" he prompted, beaming at me, and without realizing it, my shoulders drew back.

"Strength. You see me as strong. I see fascination there too. I see...wonder."

"And the list of adjectives keeps growing every day," he said. "What else do you see reflected in my eyes, Solace?"

"I see my smile," I said, reaching up to touch my upturned lips. "I see myself."

"Whenever you forget, whenever he makes you forget your worth, what you have to offer, you look at me. Your reassurance will always be here." He pointed to his eyes. "And here." He laid a hand over his heart.

"What about when this ends? We can't stay in this bubble forever, Care Bear." I'd had to remind myself several times that what we shared under this tainted roof was for this specific space of time only, that our trauma bond would end once our spouses returned and reality kicked in. Those reminders typically came when I found myself admiring not only the attributes of his heart and soul, but his physical ones as well. The way his strong arms and body cocooned me at night, protecting me from my worst thoughts. And the way that powerful body ate up any distance that separated us when he could tell that I needed a hug. The idea of us going our separate ways saddened me on a daily basis.

He finished up with my braid before turning me around by my shoulders. "I was under the impression that no matter what happened next, we'd always be friends."

"I'd like that," I said, even though my stomach roiled as if my words were rancid. I didn't want to be friends. I didn't want to sit by and watch him move on, watch him eventually find love with someone else while I played the supportive friend role. *I* didn't want to move on and find anything with anyone but him. I saw the same thing written across his face, and decided to take a chance. To take a gamble that our thoughts were aligned. "I'd like more," I whispered brazenly, even if I didn't know what that meant beyond that point in time, or what it meant in the long run. At the very least, I knew I needed more right then.

"Thank God," he said, lowering his lips to my forehead, sealing them there as our bodies tensed, as we braced ourselves for more.

"I'd like to kiss you," he said, tracing my cupid's bow. My cock swelled beneath my towel, pushing against the fabric and loosening the knot holding it together at my hip. Noon shuffled closer, letting me feel his response to me as his hardness poked at my stomach through his jeans.

"What about the mint?" I asked to buy time. I wanted this, so much, but the sensations flooding my body were too extreme to experience all at once. I didn't know what to do with my feet or my hands, and my lungs had no idea how to manage my shortness of breath.

"I have a feeling mint tastes different on you," he said, making me smile through my nerves.

"Thank you," I said. We were approaching the end of an era for us, bravely crossing over into the next. I needed him to know how much I appreciated what he'd done for me thus far. "Thank you for being the best thing that's happened to me in a while. Thank you for taking good care of me."

Noon placed his palms on my cheeks, angling my head up as he hunched, making a slow descent for my parted lips before whispering, "Thank you for letting me."

CHAPTER 11

WE TOOK A break from our self-imposed isolation to drive into town. I needed to upgrade my MacBook in order to install the photo editing software needed for the shoot, and I also wanted to purchase a state-of-the-art camera.

"You think you got enough stuff?" Solace asked sarcastically from the passenger seat, turning to finger through the shopping bags piled on the back seat and floorboards. He plucked up a small LED panel that would attach to the camera itself.

"It's not just for the shoot." As I spoke, I kept an eye out for the restaurant we were on our way to for dinner. "I'm switching careers. I should be passionate about my current job," I said, even though I hadn't worked since the accident. "I did love it. Right now, though, photography is what breathes some semblance of life into me, so I've decided to focus on what I love to do right now."

"I think that's a great idea." Solace's approval boosted my confidence.

"I've got a lot to learn. I can take a photo, but I need to be able to edit them."

"Well, you've got a couple weeks to practice. I'll help you."

"I'd like that." Our gazes lingered on one another.

Solace tipped his head toward the streetlight, smiling as the car behind us tapped on his horn. "You've got the green light."

Clearing my throat, I eased my foot onto the gas, and a couple blocks later pulled into the parking lot of Pauly's Bar and Bistro.

"So, I finally get to meet Pauly-the-snowplower," I said dryly, to which Solace chuckled. We'd gotten more snow, and so I'd ordered a plow device to attach to my truck, intent on being the one to help Solace. I woke up today and there was nothing left to plow off the property road. Pauly had beat me to it in the middle of the night.

"He's a night owl." Solace climbed out of the truck. "I'll let him know his services are no longer needed, for now."

For forever, I wanted to say. A bold statement I had no right to make.

"And you say he does this out of the kindness of his heart?" I synced my pace with his as we meandered toward the entrance.

"Of the few friends I made in Haley Cove as a kid, he's the only one still here. He took over the bistro when his dad passed away. Before that he ran a sort of handyman business closer to town. Property plowing was one of the services offered. I'm not the only one he helps out when he can."

Unlike the tavern, which kept its historical charm, Pauly's Bar and Bistro had a more eclectic aesthetic. The four-seater tables had mismatched chairs, and the upholstered seats atop the barstools had dissimilar patterns.

I hung my coat on the rack near the door, then took Solace's and did the same.

"Where do you want to sit?" Solace asked.

The music was lively, and there was a decent-sized crowd gathered at the dartboards in the back. The place hadn't reached full occupancy yet, and so we had options in terms of seating.

A well-built man with deep-set gray eyes rounded the bar before I could answer. "Gorgeous!" the man shouted at Solace, then stalled at the sight of me. I looked behind me to be sure it was me he seemed stunned by.

"Pauly," Solace called back, making his way over. They were obviously pleased to see each other. Pauly opened his arms to embrace Solace while never taking his eyes off me. I slipped my thumbs into the front pockets of my jeans and sauntered over to their love fest. I wasn't jealous at all. Not one bit. *Who calls another man gorgeous? You do, you idiot,* I scolded myself. Hadn't I called Solace that as recently as the other night?

"Why are you looking at me like that?" he'd asked after glancing up from his book, as if he'd sensed my gaze on him. He'd been sitting in his favorite armchair, shirtless after a shower, droplets of water perched along his collarbone. I was supposed to be doing research for the photo shoot, but I couldn't stop staring at him.

"You're gorgeous," I'd said, then cursed my nonfunctioning filter. *"I mean, you look relaxed."*

He'd pursed his lips, taking what I'd said into consideration. *"I like gorgeous better."* Then he'd gone back to reading.

"Pauly, this is Noon. Noon, meet Pauly." Solace's introduction hauled me from my thoughts.

"Hey, there," Pauly said, extending a hand. I accepted it, smiling through the secret hand-squeezing contest that ensued. Pauly relented first. "Why don't you two sit at the bar?" he said before dropping his tone and staring down at Solace. "Then I can give you my undivided attention."

"I think undivided is a bit much," Solace said, his voice holding a subtle warning. "You do have other customers to take care of."

I scanned the place, counting only three frazzled servers taking orders.

"I have to agree with Solace," I said. "Just take our drink and food order, and I'll handle the rest."

Solace didn't need any of Pauly's damn attention because I planned on giving him all of mine.

"Oh, don't worry your pretty little head about that," Pauly said to me, smirking when I failed to suppress my bristle. "We've got a few girls clocking in as we speak." His eyes twinkled with unconcealed amusement. Pauly swaggered over to the two stools closest to the tap and patted the seat of one. "Come on, place that sexy little rump right here, sweetheart."

"Pauly," Solace cautioned again, his eyes narrowing on the large man.

"I'll be a good boy," he promised, holding his hands up as he made his way behind the bar.

"I'm sorry," Solace said once we were seated and Pauly was out of earshot. "Takes a while to get used to his brand of humor."

"Are you sure he doesn't have a thing for you?" I sized Pauly up from where he stood laughing with another patron at the other end of the bar. I was taller, broader, and better-looking in jeans. My lips curved into an egotistical smile that had Solace's brows lowering.

"I'm positive. Just ignore him. Actually," he said, looking around. "What do you say we go sit in the booth way in the back?"

"I say, what are we waiting for?"

Pauly still made it his business to serve our table, even with a now fully occupied bar. He also didn't miss any opportunity to take Solace's words out of context, or to drop a few double entendres of his own.

"I'll have the beef tenderloin and a bottle of still water," Solace ordered.

"Single serve bottle?" Pauly asked.

"I'll go with the large."

"*Someone's* thirsty tonight," Pauly said, wiggling his brows.

"We're going to share it," Solace replied, not bothering to hide his exasperation.

"That'll be all for now," I bit out after Pauly took my order and then stood there staring at Solace.

We were lucky enough to eat and drink in peace, but then Solace challenged me to a dart throwing contest.

"I've never thrown darts a day in my life," I said, finishing up my food and cleaning barbeque sauce off my fingers. Pauly was an asshole, but the food was exceptional.

"How do you know?" Solace leaned into the table. "For all you know you could be a dart throwing champion."

I laughed, moving a strand of hair hanging from his bun before it swung into the drops of steak sauce he'd spilled on the table. "I'm pretty sure Leland or my sister would have told me if I'd become some glorified dart champion within the two years I can't recall."

"When's the last time you spoke to your sister?" His tone turned subdued. Solace felt for the people in my life. For the people who missed me.

"It's been a while. We mostly text now, and when we do, I keep things brief. Thankfully, she's too busy with her twin boys to make too much of a fuss about it. It's not that I don't want to talk to her... It's more like I don't want to talk to anyone. No one gets it." *Except you.*

He nodded as if he'd heard those two unspoken words and agreed. "You have nephews."

"Yeah. Guess I do." I hadn't thought of them in that way until then. I'd been so preoccupied with keeping my distance from the people who cared about me that I hadn't accounted for the two infants who were growing up without their only uncle in their lives. I'd turned down every request for me to visit, and couldn't find it in me to even FaceTime. "I need to do better."

"You will," Solace assured me. "I used to daydream about raising twins."

"Before or after having Gavin?"

"After. For a while I'd sworn off the idea of ever becoming a father again. Kids are so fragile, and we're so imperfect. I couldn't afford to make another mistake."

"What changed your mind?" I asked, already guessing.

"*Who* changed my mind," he corrected. I glanced pointedly over to Pauly, who was animatedly talking to a trio of drunken men at the bar. He did everything with his whole body, and I found that characteristic annoying. I found everything about him annoying. Begrudgingly, I had to admit that it had little to do with the man himself, and a lot to do with his level of comfort around Solace. Was Pauly *the one*?

"What? No, absolutely not," he said after trailing my gaze. "I love Pauly, but I can only take him in small doses." He scooted out of the booth without putting an end to my curiosity, and something told me that was intentional. "Come on, master dart thrower. Let's see what you've got."

"My money's on the hot blond," Pauly drawled as we passed by the bar, winking when I scowled.

I was surprisingly good at it, but the hot blond did win, five-to-one. We headed back to our booth, laughing as I hounded Solace for a rematch.

"Now, why would I risk losing my trophy?" He held up a dart with a ribbon attached that read "winner." Apparently all the winners got one, and they took the honor seriously.

"Winning looks good on you, gorgeous," Pauly said, placing a glass of red wine in front of Solace and a juice box in front of me. "Apple juice for the designated driver," he explained.

"Can't you take a hint?" I asked.

"No, but I was hoping I could take him home with me."

"He's coming home with me," I snapped.

"Don't you mean that *you're* going home with *him*?"

"Same difference," I growled, feeling territorial when I

shouldn't have, feeling thrown off when Pauly's arrogant smile turned soft. How did he know where we were going anyway?

"Pauly," Solace said quietly, resting a hand on his friend's forearm. I tracked the touch, feeling even more confused when Pauly backed away from it.

"Just trying to help," he said, the crass act vanishing. For the first time, I understood he truly cared for Solace. Maybe it was in the shutter of sadness that fell over his eyes when he turned to his friend.

"You aren't helping," Solace said, not unkindly. I wondered what it was that Pauly thought he needed to help with. "We'll take the check," Solace added.

"The check?" Pauly scoffed. "Your meal is on the house, as always."

"The check," I enunciated in a tone that left no room for argument. My ego wouldn't allow for the man who'd so flagrantly flirted with Solace to cover our meal. A teasing smirk hit his lips. He left and returned with the bill.

"It was good seeing *both* of you," he said, before leaving again. I shrugged, chalking it up to him apologizing for screwing with our night out, and making it clear that the apology applied to the both of us.

We rode back in thoughtful silence, unloading the bags, then separating to shower before meeting up in the kitchen for our nightly tea.

"You're awfully quiet," Solace said, placing our empty mugs in the sink before leaning his lower back against the counter and folding his arms. I remained several feet away, seated at the island. "I'm sorry about Pauly. I should have taken you somewhere else."

"It's not about Pauly," I whispered. "It's about how he made me feel."

"How did he make you feel?"

"Jealous. Territorial. Possessive of you."

"Is that such a bad thing?" he asked in a tentative voice.

"Shouldn't it be?" I pushed up from my stool, pacing, trying to remember my purpose for being there in the first place. "I haven't thought about my wife in days. Not once. It's been even longer since I've dreamed about her. I came here hoping to regain the last two years I'd lost so I could remember that time spent with her. I want to remember everything, of course, like the time Leland and I snuck out at fifteen to attend our first house party, instead of struggling to bring the fuzzy memory of it into sharp focus as he recounts it to me. But most of all, I want to remember every second spent with her, because she was an amazing person. I want to remember every amazing thing she did. Our child would have been lucky to have her as a mom, and I'm starting to forget that."

Solace flinched at the mention of the child I never got to know, reminding me of his loss. I never dwelled on that specific part of my pain, because losing Stacey encompassed losing them both. But also, I hated to see the look that currently resided in Solace's eyes—unbearable heartache.

"My wife was amazing," I repeated, hating that it sounded rehearsed. I needed to hold on to that, to weaponize it to force distance between myself and the man in front of me. I grabbed hold of the wedding rings hanging around my neck. The rings that hung between my future and my past. The rings that hung between Solace and me now.

"Is that what you believe?" Solace asked, his expression closed off in a way it had never been. "That she was amazing? Or is that what you *want* to believe?"

"What's that supposed to mean?"

He shook his head, unfolding his arms to grip the edge of the counter. "Nothing. I guess I'm jealous too. You haven't mentioned her in a while, and now I have to share you with her again. I shouldn't feel this way, but I do."

He was right. He shouldn't have felt that way, and I shouldn't have enjoyed that he did.

I crowded his space, drawn to the pain in his eyes, hating that I'd put it there. "I didn't want to bring her up. I felt like I had to."

"Why?"

"Because I'm starting to forget her, starting to forget that I loved her, because now all I can think about is you. And that scares me." I grazed my fingers down his cheek, and he grabbed my wrist, flattening my palm along his soft skin so he could burrow into it.

"Why does it scare you?" He closed his eyes, as if drugged by my nearness, by my hand on him. He was captivating. Would it ever stop feeling like a betrayal to think so?

"Because I need to love her. Because I *do* love her."

"*Why?*" he asked again, but this time it felt like a test, like a push for me to dig deeper, to explore. It should have offended or alarmed me that he needed to ask in the first place. She was my wife. Why wouldn't I need to love her? Why wouldn't I *love* her? I didn't feel offended at all, though. I felt terrified, because what alarmed me instead was that I now had to think before answering, and that my answer somehow felt like a lie.

"Because loving her is the only part of me that I'm sure of, and without it, I'll be sure of nothing. Without it, I'll truly be lost."

"You'll never be lost as long as I'm around, Noon. I'll find you. Always."

"You've used that word more than once. Always. I never noticed it until now." We hadn't known each other long enough for him to wield that word in the way he sometimes did. Even if my soul felt like it had known him for an eternity.

"Feels like I've known you forever," he said.

"It does," I agreed.

"You can talk about her as much as you want, Noon. I'll... *always* be here to listen." He swallowed. "I can't expect you to *not* talk about her."

Those last words he'd spoken sounded hollow, and his shoulders hunched like he'd received a blow to the chest. He looked beautifully broken, and I would have done anything in that moment to fix him, even if it meant distracting the both of us.

I reached over for my camera, snapping shot after shot until he gave me a bashful smile and pushed the camera away. The atmosphere had lightened, the seriousness from a moment ago not forgotten but tucked away for now. I set my camera back on the counter, then idly twirled his hair around my finger.

"Why modeling?" I asked. "You said teaching was what you loved, so why not go back to that?"

"Maybe I just wanted you to take my pictures."

"I would have done that for you anyway."

"*Now* he tells me," he said with an eye roll.

"Seriously, why not go back to teaching?"

Solace flattened his palms against my chest, then removed them, as if realizing they didn't have a right to be there, not after all that we'd said minutes ago. I used my free hand to reaffix his, one at a time, to where they'd been. To where I wanted them. We were beyond decorum. And I decided to accept how contradictory that made me. I could love my wife and want Solace's hands on me too.

"I have this fear that being around children again will be a painful reminder."

"Maybe," I responded. "Or maybe it'll be a beautiful one."

"A beautiful reminder," he whispered hoarsely, dipping his head.

"Hey." I stroked his cheek until he looked at me again. "What just happened?"

"Nothing. It's just... Sometimes you say things that make me hopeful, that make me feel like all isn't lost, you know?"

"Yeah, I know, because sometimes you do the same." I thought about the guy he'd lost. The one I'd come to mentally refer to as 'the one who got away.' "How could anyone walk away from you? How could anyone move on and forget about you?"

"I-I don't know how to answer that," he breathed, shocked by my question.

"I want to say it couldn't have been willingly. That there had to be a force greater than him at play. But I can't think of anything that would make someone not hold on to you until their dying breath." I didn't have the details of what caused their separation, but I knew without a doubt that the blame wasn't on Solace. I knew it like I knew my own name.

"It wasn't his fault," he whispered, "and it wasn't mine."

I wasn't convinced about the former claim, but I let it go. We hugged, rocking from side to side for what seemed like forever, until I pulled back to place a kiss on his forehead. He sucked in a breath.

"What was that for?" He searched my gaze like he thought he might see something, or someone, there that he hadn't seen a second ago.

"I don't know. I just...thought it might make everything better," I said slowly, ransacking my brain for a better answer and coming up empty.

"It did," he said, his eyes flickering over my face from within their watery depths. "It did."

CHAPTER 12

Solace

Then

THE MOMENT NOON'S lips touched mine, my entire body went up in flames. And when his tongue dragged along the seam of my mouth, begging for entry, I nearly wept.

This kiss was nothing like the hundreds of kisses I'd shared with Patick throughout the years. This kiss was warm. This kiss held need and wanting. This kiss was all about exploration and patient—albeit domineering—passion.

Noon was overpowering from a distance. From this close, this intimately connected, he was paralyzing, and there wasn't much I could do besides hold on to him.

My towel fell to the floor, and with nothing holding my cock back, it bounced off my stomach.

"Noon," I moaned, inching away from his onslaught to address my need for air. He shoved his hair back, his own breathing loud and unsteady. Then he bent to pick up my towel, handing it to me. He never took his eyes off mine as he did so, choosing respect over ogling. He'd wanted a kiss, and he wouldn't push me for anything else.

I let the towel fall back to the floor, letting my arousal spur my courage as I repeated what I'd said to him minutes ago. "I want more. I *need* more."

Noon exhaled in what sounded like pained relief, still holding on to his control—barely. "How much more, Solace?" His jaw worked as he waited for me to be abundantly clear.

The heat of shyness spread over my skin. I didn't allow it to stop me from saying, "All of it."

Noon didn't waste either of our time by giving me a second to rethink. This kiss was rougher than the last. It held ownership, as though my request for all that he had came with phantom shackles and a collar. I'd gladly wear them.

"Oh no you don't," he said, voice low and raspy when I attempted to break away for air. He grabbed my hips and lifted me onto the edge of the sink. "Get used to being overwhelmed by me, Solace. Get used to it fast." He fisted my braid and snapped my head back, pulling a wince from me and urging pre-cum to my slit.

Noon muscled his way between my legs, fought his way back into my mouth, licking everywhere his tongue could reach. I did my best to keep up. My best couldn't rise to the occasion, though. It was either drown or surrender.

"You taste like mint and sin," he whispered, one hand still gripping my hair to the point of pain while the other twisted my pert nipple. I whimpered, an embarrassing sound made all the worse because I was the only one naked, the only one writhing on a bathroom sink as my cock leaked between us.

"Noon," I said again, needing *something*.

"Uh-uh," he warned with a salacious smile. "I'm going to take my time with you."

He dipped me back to gain access to my neck, my head bumping up against the mirror as his tall frame hunched over further. Noon sucked his mark into the spot next to my Adam's apple, vowing that it would be the first of many I'd receive that night. I wanted to tear his shirt open, to send buttons flying so I could get my hands on his skin. On every place I'd imagined but never had the privilege of seeing or touching before. I couldn't manage, his mouth and my invisible shackles stilled my hands.

"I-I need you naked, Noon."

He shut me up with another searing, life-stealing kiss, only offering me relief when his own lungs forced him to retreat for air. I dug my heels into the backs of his thighs.

He dove for my throat again, making me wait until he was done, until the flesh on my neck no longer belonged to me. Until it had been completely branded by him. His eyes were cloudy when he released me, lips swollen and red. His hooded gaze ran down my body, taking in every shiver, every tensed muscle, right down to the sticky mess my cock had made in my navel.

Noon licked his lips, his hand rubbing along his hard shaft that snaked down his inner thigh within his jeans. I swallowed, wondering how the hell I could take him inside of me, knowing I would die trying.

With him distracted by the pearls of pre-cum trickling down my cock and the smears of it along my stomach, I tore his shirt open. I'd intended to free his suffocating cock from the confines of his jeans, but my brain short-circuited after seeing the network of corded muscles along his shoulders, abs, and chest.

I sifted my fingers through the silky, dark hair covering his pectorals. He trembled as he ripped the shirt away from his hulking biceps, one of them the equivalent of two of mine. I'd never felt so small in all my life.

"Jesus, Noon," I breathed. I frantically tussled with the button and zipper of his jeans, my opening pulsing for him. He batted my hand away and lowered over my erection with an open mouth. I slapped a palm against the wall and grabbed hold of his hair to keep from falling off the pleasure cliff as he took my shaft to the back of his throat in one go.

Even knowing that Noon had been with men before, he'd been with Stacey for so long that I'd assumed his lack of recent experience would've left him rusty. The way he flattened his tongue along the underside of my cock as he bobbed up and down while moaning said he remembered everything from his prior experiences. It said he missed this.

"I-I'm gonna come," I panted as he buried his nose into the short hairs at my base while my cockhead tapped at his tonsils.

"No, you're not," he snarled, releasing me with an audible pop. "And that's an order. I need you to hold on a lot longer, beautiful." His lips glistened with saliva and pre-cum, and his eyes darkened as if he knew I wanted a taste of it and wasn't brazen enough to ask.

"Do you want to taste yourself?" he crooned as he jerked me off with languid movements.

My hands now gripped the sink's marble edge, the tips of my nails bending under the pressure. "Yes," I whispered, undulating in his huge fist, feeling the scorch of embarrassment climb the long expanse of my neck. I'd never done this before, never given voice to what I wanted sexually, had never been asked what I wanted. Had never so shamelessly participated. Or maybe not so shamelessly.

"Never be embarrassed to ask me for what you want," he said in a soft, lust-filled tone. "There's no judgment between us, no right or wrong, only what feels right. Only what we want to fucking do to each other. Do you hear me?"

"Y-yes," I said, so close to disobeying his order not to come.

"Good." His eyes narrowed to slits. "Now, tell me what you want."

I bit my lip, nostrils flaring as I focused on answering him and not spilling all over his hand. Noon groaned, a damp spot forming on his light blue jeans from where his own pre-cum had leaked through the material. "I-I want to taste your mouth."

"Why?" he asked, toying with me.

"Because..."

"I'm listening, beautiful."

"Because you look like you want to eat me alive, and I want to know why," I said boldly. Noon released my cock, melding his mouth to mine before the ache of being left bereft could make a sound. Unlike before, he didn't take the lead, didn't wrestle me into submission with his sheer mass and devastating ferocity.

He allowed me to savor him, to dip in and out of him, to indulge, to lick and lap up what remained at the corners. I tasted like salt and cream, smelled like cedarwood with a hint of masculine musk. I swayed as though intoxicated, hypnotized, and he held me still, held me together with a forceful squeeze of my nape as he trailed fingers up and down the leg I'd secured around him.

"Fuck me," I said crudely, so unlike myself. With more aggression than needed, I got his jeans undone, reaching in to withdraw his erection with building trepidation.

"Are you ready for me to fuck you, Solace?" He gave me time to weigh and measure the monster in my hand, time to understand what a challenge taking him would be, what a pleasure it would be too—if I could manage.

I thought about Stacey, instant jealousy burning, as I wondered if she'd been able to handle all of him. "Yes," I said firmly.

"Where?"

I looked through the open door into the bedroom, the bedroom I'd shared with my husband. A bedroom I hadn't slept in since shortly after Noon had arrived.

"Take me in the bed Patrick and I once shared, then take me everywhere in this house. Make everything ugly within it beautiful again. Make the last memory of this place be filled with something other than pain."

"Are you sure?" Noon unraveled my braid before slipping his hands under my ass and lifting me into his arms. My legs tightened around his hips, his cock sliding through my exposed cleft as he spread and then kneaded my ass cheeks.

"Yes," I said before capturing his lips in a kiss that we both shared control over this time.

Noon walked us into the darkened bedroom; the scant light spilling in from the bathroom and the hallway more than enough to see him by.

He placed me on my back near the foot of the bed, examining every inch of me, likely wondering which part he wanted to devour next. "Let me see you," he whispered, one hand gripping his testicles, the other working his cock. He looked lewd standing above me, his muscular thighs and arms flexing as he openly stroked himself to my modesty.

"*Please,*" he begged, and I lifted my hands from where they guarded my straining cock. He groaned, dropping his chin to his chest as he pumped his shaft harder and faster in a broken rhythm. "Now show me the other place, beautiful. That's it," he hissed as I spread my legs for him.

Patrick had never watched me this way, had always been too selfish about his own needs to appreciate me like this. I'd thought what we had was magical, at one point. I'd thought he loved me so much and wanted me so badly that he couldn't be bothered to wait. Thought being inside of me felt so good to him that waiting until I came before he did was out of his hands. How wrong I'd been. I was currently staring at the definition of magical, the epitome of want and need, and a body that would break worlds apart before it dared to climax ahead of me.

I clasped the backs of my thighs and spread my legs for him, the moment feeling symbolic, empowering, even, and I held my breath until I felt lightheaded, forcing the tears away.

Noon let go of his cock and balls to fall to his knees, tracing my ring of muscle with one shaky digit. My head dropped to the mattress as I gritted out something nonsensical.

"Just a taste," he whispered before driving his tongue toward my opening. I inhaled sharply in surprise, my heels dropping to the bed and pushing me away from his seeking mouth. Noon yanked me back onto his face, folding me in half, my knees nearly touching my ears.

"Oh God!" I panted as the initial shock wore off, gripping his hair and fisting the bedsheet. I peered down my chest to find his hungry eyes on me as he lapped at me, nostrils pumping furiously as he breathed my scent into his lungs.

"You taste so fucking good." His hair slipped from my fingers when he pulled away to drag the back of his hand over his wet mouth before plunging back in.

I shouted when he bit down on one cheek, strangling the root of my cock to keep from coming right then.

Noon stood unsteadily a few minutes later, his cock an angry shade of purple, the head wet, a milky teardrop running away from it. "I need you now." Arousal added a cutting edge to his words.

"The drawer," I said, pointing, voice dripping with desire.

"Do we need condoms?" he panted, destroying the nightstand to get to the bottle of lube.

"No," I said. "We don't."

"Good." He poured lube over his hardness, reclaiming his spot at the foot of the bed like a god looking down on his worshiper. He'd need a good amount to adequately cover his cock—the distended crown stretched well beyond his belly button.

"I hope you don't have plans for the foreseeable future," he said, the mattress sinking as he knelt between my legs and proceeded to drive me up the bed with his thighs, "because I'm going to fuck you every chance I get. I'm going to fuck you until all you taste and smell is my cum. Until my cum is seeping from your pores. I'm going to fuck you right here, until this bed is bathed in us. Until you can't even remember his name."

I groaned deep in my throat as he drenched his hand and my hole with lube before slipping his pinky finger in, all the way to the second knuckle. What should have been the smallest digit on his hand equaled the girth and length of two of mine combined. Nothing about Noon was normal, though. Not his hands, his cock, his mind, or his heart.

"Breathe," he instructed, relaxing onto his haunches and taking his time to loosen me up. He inserted a second finger, scissoring them and holding my hips down when my lower body lifted off the bed. By the time the third digit entered me, I was welcoming them in with enthusiasm. I didn't give a damn which one of us came first or when, and by the time I was ready to handle a fourth, my whole body was saturated with sweat.

"I'm ready," I said unevenly. He lowered to one forearm, and I wanted to kiss him but our height difference made it difficult in this position. I settled for kissing his collarbone while fucking his hand and begging for his cock. "*Please*, Noon. I'm ready."

"No, you're not."

"I. Am," I gritted out, tugging his hair. It had to have been an hour since we began kissing in the bathroom, maybe more. If his goal was to send me so far toward the edge that I was stripped of all decorum, he'd succeeded. This time, there wasn't a hint of doubt in my voice when I barked, "Fuck me already."

"Promise me you'll tell me if I'm hurting you," he said, but I was too busy salivating at the sight of him guiding his cock to my entrance to process the request. "Promise me, Solace."

"I promise," I said as he hooked one arm behind my knee before planting his fist into the mattress.

I fought for air as he took his time seating his tip inside of me, my nails digging into his back, pulling a wince from him.

"How does that feel?" he asked, letting go of his cock to grip the headboard for support, the wood groaning under his strength.

"Good," I moaned. Noon started up a rhythm of shallow thrusts, giving me an inch at a time. "More."

"Not...yet," he forced out between his teeth, sweat giving his body a glistening sheen. "You're fucking tight, Solace."

Even with all the preparation, it was still a challenge to accept him. The vein at the center of his forehead bulged from the effort it took to hold himself back, and my orgasm began tickling up my spine. He made it halfway in before picking up his pace. We moaned in unison.

"You feel so good," he said, thrusting and panting, no longer feeding me more of his cock, never graduating beyond the halfway point.

"I can take more," I panted, bearing down. Noon tested the waters, and I stiffened.

"It's still good just like this," he said, striking my prostate repeatedly until I couldn't remember my own goddamned name. "You're still the best thing I've ever felt."

Was that what he was used to? Had his wife not been able to handle all of him? Patrick wasn't even half his size.

"I want it all," I said, my conviction bigger than this moment. "No more settling for less." That went for the both of us.

Noon rolled us, and I gasped, my hands slapping onto his chest as this position made him feel impossibly larger, made me feel incapable.

"We go at your pace," he said, brushing my hair from my face as I caught my breath. He lay there trembling as I took my time rising and lowering onto his cock. I rode him at the speed necessary for me, until I had him fully sheathed within me. I felt stuffed beyond capacity, the pleasure too consuming, the sensation of him filling me so deeply the only thing I could spare brain power to focus on.

Noon sat up, catching me off guard, back bowing so that our faces aligned. He kissed me as if punishing me, and I slowly rocked on top of him. We were shaking the bed before we knew it, my ass crashing down onto his lap as my hole swallowed every impressive inch of him.

Noon repositioned my legs so they circled him, then lifted me by the hips until only his tip remained inside before slamming me back onto him. "Why wasn't it you?" he asked with surprising emotion. "Why wasn't it always you?"

His features warped through my burgeoning tears, because if it weren't for not regretting a single day that I got to love Gavin, I would have wished Noon had found me first too. That he'd gotten to me before Patrick. In a perfect world, I would have rewritten history, and Gavin would have been ours.

I kissed the corners of his wet eyes as we fucked, as we shared sweat and tears, as we realized that this moment was about more than just sex, much more than two lonely souls finding solace in one another. We were healing ourselves, making each other new. *This* was how it should have been. This was what I'd been missing.

"Come, Solace. Now."

My control snapped with his whispered permission, my hand seeking out my erection. Noon swooped in to devour my cry of orgasm, of freedom, of...*happiness*. He bucked into me twice more before stilling, his mouth opening and closing as his own release clawed through him and into me.

My heart was so full I thought it might explode from my chest, and all I could do was hug him tight, letting his rapidly beating heart connect with and speak to mine. The tremors started for the both of us soon after, and all we could do was touch, kiss, and cry together. I'd never felt this stripped down to my foundation before, this raw, and that had to do with never feeling safe enough to do so. Noon made me feel safe. I knew I could trust him with my heart, my most prized possession.

Because he'd handled it with such good care thus far, when he didn't have to.

We'd crawl out of this bed as blank canvases, and I couldn't wait to see how we'd reinvent ourselves. Together, if I was lucky. We hadn't spoken about, or looked, that far into the future, but I hoped.

He carried me to the shower, cleaning me under the hot spray after meticulously checking to make sure my body had survived him unscathed. Our wedding bands clinked as we entwined our hands while we kissed. I couldn't get enough of his lips, couldn't get enough of the way he seemed so desperate for me.

We peered down at our joined hands at the same time. Without prompting, we twisted and pulled, even adding soap, until we were free of the bands that chained us to a painful past. We watched them fall and roll toward the drain. We were ready now. Ready to see who and what we'd become.

"Let him have her," he said, smiling as the water cascaded down his face.

"Let her have him," I said, his happiness contagious. I caressed his smile, and he touched mine as he backed me into the shower wall.

The same shower where, just a few hours ago, I'd been trying to scrub away the insecurities caused by watching Patrick belittle me in our home videos. Noon, being Noon, read my thoughts before strolling over to the shower shelf for the bottle of lube there. We were about to make a new memory that would obliterate all the previous ones.

"How many more rooms do we have to go?" he asked as he hoisted me up. I wrapped my legs around him, holding on to his broad shoulders as I sank onto his cock.

"At least 7," I said, voice husky. "More if you count the garage, the front yard, the backyard…" I trailed off on a moan as we began moving.

"I say we count them all," he replied, pinning me to the tiled wall.

I handled him a bit easier now, but "easier" and "with ease" were not the same thing. I didn't think I'd ever be penetrated by him and not be aware that something sinfully intrusive had taken control of my body.

I welcomed the hard work of taking him, though, because I refused to believe that my body wasn't made for him, and because he deserved someone who would work hard for him. He deserved me, and I deserved him. I wanted him, wanted *all* of him. Every. Damn. Time.

CHAPTER 13

Noon

Now

THE LIGHTING FOR the photo shoot finally arrived, and Solace left me to get things set up in the living room while he went to change into the first look of the day. Photography came naturally to me, but staging for a shoot was a different realm. When I'd expressed my concerns to Solace, he'd told me in that Zen way of his to not take things too seriously. To have fun with it.

I started with a white backdrop and a tall wooden stool. Solace didn't need a lot of frills, he was captivating all on his own. Anything outside of him wouldn't hold anyone's attention anyway.

I'd just finished repositioning the soft-box lighting for the tenth time when Solace descended the stairs, his vintage black and white oxfords clicking against the hardwood.

"The setup looks great," he said.

"So do you," I replied, sweeping my gaze over him. He'd gone with a classic look. Black turtleneck and matching trousers that fell to the ankles. His abstract dress socks were nothing more than a tease. With his hair cinched into a braided bun at his nape, there was nothing to distract from his hypnotizing eyes. We were staring at each other, or rather, I was gawking at him while he observed me do it. I didn't care. I stopped caring weeks ago after being caught one too many times.

"Guess your crash course came in handy," he said absently, still watching me watch him.

I cleared my throat, willing some professionalism into it. "A little too soon to claim victory, don't you think?" The equipment being on backorder for three weeks had turned out to be a blessing. It'd given me the opportunity to study up on how to use it, and to work on my craft. Solace had also been a well of information, offering me tips and tricks of the trade.

"You've got this," he said. Those three words, and the sweet conviction behind them, elevated my confidence.

"How do you do that?"

"Do what?"

"I don't know. Make me believe I can do anything." I marveled at his skill to do so.

Solace shrugged. "Because you can. And because someone once helped me to believe the same thing about myself."

A rumbling growl escaped me. Solace chuckled, bowing his head with shyness. Prior to our conversation in the kitchen a few weeks ago, I would've berated myself for my reaction, for allowing him to witness it. But something had changed after my confession of feeling unjustifiably possessive of him. And after his admission of feeling jealous of Stacey. Jealous over sharing me with my memories of her. Our growing friendship had taken on an ease that allowed me to be myself—allowed me to discover my new self. I'd developed a crush on him, and although we had yet to discuss it, I knew he'd developed one for me too.

It was obvious in the way I stared at him, and in the way he blushed and stared back. Not to mention neither one of us had slept alone in weeks. Solace fell asleep with me on the couch every night, and held me protectively in his arms until dawn.

Some might've found it comical that he was the one protecting me, but I'd be lying if I said I didn't enjoy it, didn't give in to it. It felt good to let go, to let someone look after me after having resisted that from my friends and family since the accident.

It seemed as though Solace needed it too. Maybe being protective of me helped to heal something in him still bruised from losing his son. So I let him hold me each night. I let him find me whenever I drifted out of his arms to step outside and peer into the night sky. I let him curl his fingers around the hair at my nape as I explained the fragmented dream that had woken me up that time, what flash of memory had come back to me before abandoning me again. And then I let it go, knowing that I couldn't let it have control over me, knowing I would miss these new moments I was making if I did. It would all come back to me in time, and if it didn't, that was okay too. Solace had taught me that.

I would then allow him to lead me in from the cold and back to the couch where he'd draw the blanket over us and squeeze me even tighter while whispering, *"Sleep, Noon. I've got you."*

"Ready?" Solace asked, snatching me from my thoughts. He'd settled on the stool, one foot propped on the wooden foot rail.

"Ready," I answered, stealing another glance at him before turning on some background music and getting started.

We began with an intense stare into the camera lens, one hand gracefully hanging off his knee while the other tugged on the collar of his turtleneck.

"Raise your chin a little," I directed as I snapped away. "That's it. Now part your lips just a bit. There you go." I alternated between direction and praise, getting into it, stopping occasionally so we could review what we had so far and adjust the lighting. Once we were both satisfied, Solace left to swap looks while I staged for the next series.

He returned barefoot in fitted jeans and an equally fitted Henley. Solace had a way of appearing as if he'd rolled out of bed and grabbed the first article of clothing his hands landed on. Like he hadn't tried to look sexy, but he always did. T-shirt, jeans, cuffed khakis, sweats... It didn't matter. He wore the clothes; they never wore him.

He'd replaced the slicked-back hairstyle with a messy top-knot, inspiring my spontaneity.

"Follow me," I said, abandoning the living room for the kitchen. I set him up at the island with a book and a steaming cup of tea, handing him his glasses as an afterthought. The snowy backyard beyond the floor-to-ceiling glass doors created the perfect ambiance.

Time moved fast, and we hadn't even taken a second to eat. It'd been a race to get the daytime shots done before we lost sunlight. We'd accomplished it, and were both more relaxed once we moved to the last look of the day. Solace wanted to recreate the photo of himself in the oversized suit. He wanted the pictures grainy and dark, for him to be the only beacon of light in a world full of gray. I opted for a narrower lens.

"I want the final series to be my most vulnerable," he'd said during the planning phase.

With nothing left to do but wait for him to come downstairs, I dimmed the setting on the lights and changed the playlist to something haunting to help set the mood. Sunset had brought along a profound amount of icy rain. An added bonus. I made a mental note to get a few shots of Solace against the glass wall, to catch the deluge pouring down around him.

"Ready?" Solace whispered from behind me.

I pivoted around. "Yeah—" The rest of my words lodged in my throat.

Solace stood at the bottom of the landing wearing a tuxedo that had seen better days. The forest green jacket swallowed him, his fingertips struggling to appear through the sleeves, and the hem of the baggy pant legs pooled at his feet like a worshiping puddle. I suddenly wanted to worship at his altar too.

"You look...ethereal," I said softly, because beautiful was too tame of a word.

"Thank you." Solace's signature blush made an appearance. His hair tumbled down his back in loose waves, and that familiar tug I'd been experiencing more and more lately started up in my head.

I took a step toward him, pausing when the image of a dance floor packed with dancing bodies zapped like a strike of lightning through my mind.

I took another step and was met with another strike.

Tears streaming down a pale cheek.

Another step. Another strike.

A woman with mascara-smudged eyes peering at me. *Stacey*.

Another step. Another strike.

Pounding on a front door.

Another step. Another strike.

Heartache. *Extreme* heartache.

I reached for my rupturing heart just as Solace met me the rest of the way and steadied me.

"Are you remembering something?" he asked, and even through my flare of panic I could hear the hope in his voice, and see the matching expression light up his face.

"I...I..." I squeezed my eyes shut as the images grew distant, as they faded away into the tunnel I didn't have access to. That old, familiar rage stood poised to take their place. I snarled through clenched teeth, sinking to the floor.

"Look at me," Solace commanded, dropping to his knees and cupping my face. "It's okay. Let it go for now. If it doesn't want to stay, remember that it's okay to let it go." He repeated his orders on a loop, his voice softening each time as my breathing evened out and my aching teeth unclenched. "That's it. Let it go." He held my hands now, rubbing the pads of his thumbs across my skin while leading me through measured breaths.

"I'm good now," I said through a scratchy throat. "Crisis averted."

"Are you sure?" he asked, shaken up, as if I'd transferred my anxiety to him.

"I promise. I'm fine now." I touched my brow to his before getting us to our feet.

"Maybe this was a bad idea," he said, looking down at the suit.

"The photo shoot was a great idea. Don't let me ruin this for you."

"Yeah, the photo shoot," he said distractedly, taking in all the equipment.

I held my camera up with a smile I hoped he believed. "Ready whenever you are." Things weren't all the way fine yet. The atmosphere had shifted, and it would take more than a few seconds for it to right itself. I'd be damned if I wouldn't fake it for his sake, though. I wouldn't screw this up for him just because my brain picked that moment to glitch. A few minutes later we got started again.

These shots were broody, pensive, and unguarded as Solace transitioned through emotions with ease. I didn't have to direct him at all, and something inside me warned that it wasn't an act. His anguished gaze bore into my lens with a fragility that made me want to catch him before he shattered to the floor.

I stopped to make a few adjustments, and Solace took the opportunity to give me his back. To hide from me.

Moments later, I whispered his name, purposely giving no indication that I was ready to continue as I stood poised to capture him. Instead of turning his whole body, Solace peered over one shoulder, watery eyes wide like an animal snared as I clicked away.

We ended with him sitting on the floor, his arms wrapped around his bent legs as he lowered his head to his knees. When he gazed up, a solitary tear rolled down his cheek, his expression stoic.

I captured it all, even while wanting to scoop him into my lap and take his sadness away. That would come later.

Later came after we'd eaten and showered and were hanging out in the sitting area of his bedroom since the living room had been temporarily converted into a photo studio.

"Tell me what's wrong," I said after adding more kindling to the fire and taking a seat next to him. This couch was half the size of the one downstairs but still accommodating. He stared at me, eyes full of gloom, and said nothing. Maybe he didn't know where to start.

"Come here." I took his hand, giving in to my earlier urge to pull him onto my lap. There was a moment of surprise before he sat astride me, his hands lacing together at my nape as he relaxed.

"This is new," he said.

"Sorry." I lifted him at the hips, planning to set him down beside me. He dug his knees in, stopping me.

"No. It's fine."

"Are you sure?" I could be forward with my affection. Invasive even.

"I'm positive."

I slouched down, getting comfortable. "Now, talk to me."

"Can I ask you something first?"

"Sure."

Solace licked his lips. "What happened downstairs?"

I glanced to the side, my forehead tightening in concentration. "Weird flashes. Nothing solid. Nothing that told me anything. And they were gone before I could make sense of them." Even now I couldn't recall what they were.

Solace dropped his head back, peering up at the ceiling. I didn't push him. I watched his throat work as he mulled over what to say to me. "I struggle with not knowing if I'm helping or hurting you. Making you better or making you worse."

"What do you mean?"

"I told you to live in the moment. To not let your memories, or lack of memories, interfere with you living your life. What if... What if I should have said something else? *Done* something else?"

"I haven't had a panic attack in a while. I'm enjoying my time here with you. My time getting to know you. I feel better when I'm with you, and that's all that matters." How far I'd come.

"What if it's not all that matters? What if the truth matters more?" His frustration seemed internalized.

"The truth will come to me when it's ready. I'll get my memories back if I'm meant to. Okay?"

"Yeah, okay." He seemed more dejected than convinced.

I scooted forward so that his legs could circle me, working from instinct instead of my head. We embraced, hard enough that he grunted from the discomfort, hard enough that his cock pressed into my stomach. His rapidly swelling cock. My own cock stirred, pushing against the thin fabric of my lounge pants to slot between the covered crease of his ass.

Solace moaned, the sound reverberating against my skin from where his mouth and nose now rested against my throat. He rocked his hips, and it was my turn to moan from the friction.

"What are we doing, Solace?" I breathed as he continued to thrust in my lap.

"I don't know." He eased back to look at me. "But I want to do it, whatever it is."

This moment had been building for weeks, and I was done trying to outrun it. Done trying to live in my truth—in my physical attraction for him—while somehow also playing it safe.

He raised his arms, and I followed his lead, removing his t-shirt. He tore away the elastic keeping his hair up, and I caught some of the thick strands in my hand, holding it out of the way so my other hand could explore the lean muscles along his back. We didn't dare tear our gazes away from each other.

Solace continued to dry hump my cock while my fingers roamed his skin. Neither of us were in a hurry to move on to other things just yet. His eyes smoldered with passion, and his body warmed with the heat of the fire and exertion. Sweat slickened his back, a bead of it trickled down his spine to drip onto my hand, provoking another image. An image I'd seen several times before, one of a sweat-slicked back and hair wrapped around my fist.

I curled my fingers tighter around his locks and yanked him back. Solace sucked in a razor-edged breath, his hips stilling as we panted into the silence. A memory of a scent saturated my nose until I thought I might suffocate from it. My mouth then flooded with a flavor that was familiar yet out of reach of my memories.

"Noon? Wha-what's wrong?" The haze of arousal clouded his eyes.

I swallowed past the choking taste, eyes frantically darting over his features as I twisted my fist around the length of his hair. "Why do I know that you taste like mint with a dash of sin?" I asked accusingly, without knowing what the hell I was accusing him of. We were so close we shared breath, and not a hint of mint assaulted me. I couldn't recall ever smelling it on him. Still, the sudden surety that he would taste like it—or should taste like it—was something I would've gambled my life on. I needed to know why.

"I-I don't," he whispered, scrambling to climb off me. I flipped him to his back, unleashing my weight on him, searching for the truth through his fear.

"Prove it," I said through ragged breaths. Indecision and terror turned him to stone beneath me, and so I took his mouth with mine, stealing his option to refuse.

Nothing. There was nothing to substantiate my accusation. Solace tasted of chamomile and warmth, and kissing him felt like returning home, yet mint gorged itself on my body.

It overtook my mouth, then spread like wings throughout every part of me, embedding its flavor into every organ, every cell. I wanted more of it. Hating the taste while loving it. Hating it but loving that it came from him, yet didn't. I couldn't distinguish fact from fiction, memories from the here and now.

Solace's stone facade crumbled beneath me. I'd offered him no choice. It was either give in or be taken, even though both looked and felt the same.

We were like animals, the kiss turning bloody when one of us nipped the other's lip. I couldn't breathe. I didn't want to. All I wanted was to inhale the man currently fighting for air underneath me.

He squeezed my ass while I devoured him, urging me to move between his spread legs. I couldn't move, couldn't think, couldn't do anything but search for answers within our kiss. Once I could move, once I'd gained awareness when the tug in my mind gave way, I pulled back. The air was clear again, my tastebuds mint free.

I thought back on our exchange before the kiss began.

"Why do I know that you taste like mint with a dash of sin?"
"I-I don't."

Maybe he hadn't lied, but my gut told me that wasn't the whole truth. I glared down at him with accusing eyes again and whispered, "Liar."

CHAPTER 14

Solace

Then

WE HAD SEX everywhere and all the time. Baptizing the sins of this house away, even cleansing the walls. The only space we didn't touch was Gavin's room. He was innocent in all this.

I groaned from atop Patrick's desk as Noon thrust between my legs. It was the only thing in his office that hadn't been tossed into the fire pit. That and the desk chair I'd rode Noon on less than an hour ago. The broken pieces of the chair littered the floor, and I had a nice kneecap bruise to show what the force of our lovemaking could do. *Break and rebuild.*

"Oh God, right there, right there," I panted as he rotated his hips, striking my bundle of nerves with precision.

"Yeah? Right there, beautiful?" he asked huskily as the sound of our slicked skin slapping against each other filled the room.

"Yes," I hissed, then shouted as I orgasmed between us.

Noon slowed, giving me a moment to come down from my climax. A moment in which I both thanked and cursed God for making this degree of pleasure possible.

He braced his palms along the wooden desk in preparation for his own release. His gaze asked if I was ready. He began surging in and out of me without mercy before I nodded yes.

I cried out, unable to escape him as the desk screeched across the floor from the impact of his thrusts. I felt him everywhere. From the apex of my thighs to my fingertips. Noon gnashed his teeth, fighting his body's need for release.

"Come," I panted, holding on to him for dear life.

"It's too...soon," he said, neck straining as his cock expanded within me.

"There's always later," I reminded him, because Noon made love as if it were the last time every time, as if he needed to make it count. "I need your cum in me right now." My words were saturated in desperation. I wouldn't feel complete until he finished inside of me, until he gazed down at me in wonder, as if he hadn't experienced anything like me before. I craved it. Had become an insatiable creature because of it.

Noon barked a shout, crashing into me once more, the desk lifting then slamming to the floor again as he flooded my hole with his cum. He grunted, pressing his hips forward, ramming his cock into me again as I begged him not to pull out until I had it all.

"The things you say when I've got my dick inside of you," Noon whispered once he'd blinked back to awareness, his cock jerking with aftershocks. "Have I corrupted you?"

"That's one way of seeing it," I said, stretching my neck to meet his chaste kiss.

"What's the other way?"

"Maybe you've freed me."

"Possibly," he said. "But then how do you explain the heat that floods your cheeks as soon as we're done and my cum starts leaking out of you?"

"I don't know what you're talking about," I answered coyly. "You're a human furnace. Do you even know how hot you are?"

Noon's guttural laugh made my toes curl and my opening spasm. "Deflection and innuendo," he said, impressed, brushing his knuckles over my burning cheeks. "Don't ever change, beautiful. You're perfect just the way you are."

"Perfect for you, perhaps."

"Perfect all the same." He straightened, staring down at the hickeys and cum covering my chest. "God, how long has it been now?" He swirled a finger through the mess on me before licking the digit clean.

"Two weeks and one day," I answered. That was how long it'd been since we'd first made love.

"And I still can't get enough of you," he said, swirling and licking again.

"You say it like it's a problem. The feeling's mutual," I promised. Noon hauled me up with a firm grip to my neck before bending for a dirtier kiss. One that demanded I cede control to him. I did so willingly, drinking in his possession of me.

The kiss and mild strangulation left me devastated and slightly wheezing. My hair clung to my sweaty face and back, and my lips were swollen and sensitive. "Beautiful," he whispered, forcing my mouth open with a cum-slicked finger. I sucked on it as he fussed with my hair, turning me into the picture of perfect debauchery, something that had been deliciously tainted.

"Noon." I groaned in complaint when he strode to the windowsill for his camera. I shielded my face, and he struggled to take the photos one-handed while trying to drag my hands away.

"I'm going to hide that thing." I chuckled, giving in to him once he had me on my back again. He was too absorbed in what he was doing to reply, so I indulged his need to capture me like this for a minute longer before rolling away and vanishing through the door.

"I'm going take a bath," I said as he followed behind, the camera flash flickering.

"I'll join you."

"No cameras allowed," I replied over my shoulder, turning a corner. He continued to snap away. I'd created a monster.

"I can't help it," Noon said after we'd submerged ourselves into the soapy water. He took pictures of my scowl from his side of the freestanding tub. He'd worn me down until I agreed to let the camera into the bathroom. "Especially when you make those fake angry faces."

"Fake?"

He lowered the camera. "Was that one supposed to be real?"

I sent a splash of water his way, and he raised the camera above his head to spare it from any water damage.

"Okay, fine." He grinned, setting it down on the short stool next to the tub. "No more photos of your adorableness."

"Thank y—"

"For now," he interrupted, nudging me with his foot, his gaze soft and sweet. How could I be annoyed with him when he looked at me like that? It was all I'd ever wanted for so long, and now I had it. I had a feeling there'd be enough photos of me to fill ten galleries, and I'd let him take every last one.

Noon reached over to the stool again where his phone was. A chime indicated he'd synced it with the wireless speaker. Classical music echoed around us. He'd lit the pillar candles surrounding the tub before we'd gotten in. I'd purchased them with Patrick in mind. He hadn't cared about having a romantic night at the time. I swept that thought aside, deciding if I was going to dwell on something, it'd be the man in front of me.

"This is relaxing," I said, in reference to the music. "I played the piano for, like, five minutes when I was a kid. My parents couldn't afford to keep up with the lessons."

"It's an original," he said, reaching below the water to massage my foot. "My friend Cole is classically trained. He created this playlist for me. Some of his own original pieces are on here. I hadn't given classical music a thought until meeting him. He's responsible for my love of horses too."

"Horses?" I asked in surprise, moaning when his fingers worked a particularly tight spot. "This bath is going to end before it even begins if you keep that up."

Noon's smile was wicked, as though his evil plans were working. "He and his husband Jasper have an estate outside of the city. They have a few horses. One big enough to handle me." He paused, and I gazed at him with curiosity, wondering why he appeared to battle with whether or not to continue. Even his hands had stopped moving along my foot.

"It started with Stacey wanting to learn," he said carefully before stopping again.

"We can talk about them," I whispered. "That shouldn't change now that we are... Whatever we are." I didn't want to give it a label if he wasn't ready to.

"Together," he said firmly. "Now that we're together."

I smiled as joy filled my heart. "Does it seem like this is happening too fast?"

"Yes, but I don't care."

My smile broadened. "Together," I repeated in agreement. I wiggled my toes, causing his face to brighten with amusement before he lifted my foot above the bubbles to kiss it.

"You have the sexiest pair of feet I've ever seen," he mused, then proceeded with his sweet torture of them. "Where was I?"

"Horses," I prompted as his compliment spread over my body like a soothing balm.

"Ah, yes. Jasper began giving her lessons on the weekends. It was a great excuse to get away from the hustle and bustle of city life. Leland and his partner Franklin—who also happens to be Cole and Jasper's father—would come. Sometimes Jasper's best friend Sophia and her family would too. We'd laugh, eat, drink, and spend time out at the stables. Didn't take long for me to join in on the lessons. From there I grew pretty attached to Delores. That's my horse's name. Well, Jasper and Cole's horse, but, you know." He shrugged. "She's mine whenever I'm around. She takes care of me, if that makes sense. I feel safe with her. Maybe because she's a wildcard. Doesn't care too much for anyone else but me."

"You said Franklin is Cole *and* Jasper's father. That would make them—"

"That's a story for another time," Noon cut in wryly. I set my interest aside.

"Your friends sound amazing. Sounds like they're attached to Stacey." Would they welcome me into their lives? Or would I be seen as the person who fractured their circle?

"They'll accept you because you make me happy. That's all they'll care about."

"Do they know what's going on?"

"No. None of them know. Not even Leland."

"Where does he think you are?"

"On a work assignment."

I knew he worked as a property and estate manager, and that depending on the location of the job, work could take him away for a week or so. Never for this long, though. "You've been gone for a while."

"Yeah, well, with Stacey off on her planned trip, it isn't that far-fetched that I would accept a longer assignment. Not wanting to be away from home—away from *her*—had notoriously been my reason for declining contracts that would require me to be gone for too long."

"They'll be back in less than two months," I said, unsure of how that made me feel.

"I know." He moved on to my other foot. "And we'll deal with it. Together."

I sighed, closing my eyes and resting my head on the back of the tub. Noon worked his way up my calves, letting me have my silence for a while.

"Come here," he said. I cracked an eye open to make sure the tub hadn't grown in size while I'd been immersed in my thoughts.

"We barely fit in here together as it is. My legs are literally mashed between yours. No way can we both fit at the same end." He hitched his legs over the edges of the tub, sloshing water onto the floor and putting out one of the candles in the process. "You look ridiculous," I said, even while shuffling to lean back against his chest.

"Want to share what's on your mind?" he asked, kissing the side of my face as his fingers explored my shoulders and collarbone.

"You're so handsy," I complained, not-so-secretly loving it.

"You're starting to sound like Leland. He'll love you."

I tilted my head to one side, a subtle request for his lips to find their way to my neck. They did so as I worked out where to start. "Do you ever wonder what she sees in him?" It was a difficult question to voice because the same could be asked of me. This was different, though. I'd heard Patrick and Stacey together. *Seen* them together. The Patrick from the museum wasn't the same version of the man I knew, and part of me couldn't help but to be angry at that. I felt cheated, not good enough to have received that side of him. I felt all that even while being grateful to be free of him. *Almost* free of him.

"All the time," Noon said with a sigh. "Stacey and I had our problems, but I can honestly say she's never set out to dismantle my belief in myself. Not like Patrick did to you. An affair is one thing. And affair with *him* is another."

"Sometimes people can be different with other people," I argued. "They can change. Not *for* them, but *because* of them. That's what makes me so angry, because when I saw them together... He was different, Noon. Changed, almost. Or maybe he was himself in a way that he never was with me. Why couldn't he be that way for me? What does she have that I don't, to make him love her in a way that he never loved me?"

I craned my head to look at him, hoping he wasn't upset by my questions, hoping he didn't think I still wanted to be with my husband. There was still this need to work out why he'd treated me the way he did, and it had nothing to do with wanting him. Not anymore. I saw understanding in Noon's emerald eyes as he caressed my cheek. I saw the same need in him. A need to fully heal. A need to hear ourselves speak and release these toxic thoughts. To, hopefully, once and for all, be rid of them.

"He hasn't changed," Noon said. "And what you saw..." He turned away, his jaw tensing, as if he'd imagined what I'd seen. "What you saw wasn't either of them being themselves. They were two people high as a kite on the thrill of excitement. High on sex and secrets and betrayal. Being with each other was easy. They didn't have to fight through the messiness of life together. They got to leave their baggage with us and live like there's no tomorrow with each other. What do you think is gonna happen now that their secret is out? Now that the thrill is gone? Now that they're stuck together day in and day out in some third-world country?"

"I think now they're getting to really know each other," I whispered with understanding.

"Exactly," Noon said.

"And what about us?" I asked, turning and getting on my knees to face him. It was a tight squeeze, but I managed. "Are we high right now? Will we come crashing back to earth when they return?"

"No," he said, his tone adamant. He slid his wet palm around my throat, rubbing at the handprint there. "We're different."

"How do you know?" I dug my nails into his forearm, needing something to hold on to, something to keep me from sinking.

"Because this hasn't been fun and games for us, Solace. We've been to war together. We've been in the trenches, fighting alongside each other, looking out for each other, being the strong one in moments where the other is weak. We get closer each day, and I have no doubt that you'll be there for me when times get hard, because it can't get much harder than this, and you haven't wavered. Not once, beautiful. Not once. You want to know what you have that she doesn't?"

"Yes," I said, voice wavering in spite of what he'd said about me in that regard.

"You have honor, Solace. You are honorable."

"And so are you," I said, vision blurring. "And so are you."

Noon stood abruptly, catching me before I fell backward and lifting me into his arms. Bath water rippled, swashing out of the tub, dowsing more candles as the music continued to play. Our bodies were slippery, and we left a trail of water in our wake as he carried me to the dining room—the only room we hadn't made love in yet.

He spread me over the table, bringing me to climax with his mouth, neglecting himself until he'd touched and licked me in enough places to make me hard again. Noon kept it simple, spreading himself over me as his cock sought out my center, then tenderly moved in and out of me until he'd sent us both careening over the edge. Our hands and eyes remained locked on each other the whole time, and other than moans, and whimpers, and labored breathing, neither of us uttered a word.

"Let's not wait, beautiful," he said afterward. "Let's not wait for them to get back, for conversations of divorce, or to get over what they did to us. Let's start our new life now."

I understood what he meant. We had to get out of this house. We'd been punishing ourselves by being here, and now that we were done cleansing it of our pain, it was time to move on. Stacey and Patrick were on the other side of the world doing exactly that. Whether they would last or not didn't matter. They'd moved on from us.

Some may have said that this thing between Noon and I happened too soon and under the wrong circumstances. I didn't care. I'd spent enough time being emotionally abused for loving the wrong person. Noon helped me realize that I was worthy of a *good* person, worthy of someone who could look past their own pain to care about mine, no matter how difficult.

Noon was it for me, and if he was willing to let his heart guide him, then so would I.

"Where's a place that we can go that'll be just for us?" he asked, kissing the corner of my mouth. "A place that won't have any reminders of them?"

I shut my eyes, thinking long and hard, when suddenly the perfect place popped into my mind. I peered toward the hall that would lead me to Gavin's room, and my stomach ached.

Noon turned my face back to his and whispered, "We can take Gavin with us."

Knowing just what to say and when seemed to be his specialty, and my heart made more room for him in that moment. "I know the perfect place for the three of us," I said, dragging a finger across his burgeoning smile.

"Where to, beautiful?"

"Haley Cove."

CHAPTER 15

Now

"IT'S PERFECTLY NORMAL *to wake up disoriented, and head-aches are to be expected."*

I played back my doctor's words as I woke up both confused by my surroundings and with a migraine that threatened to split my skull down the middle. Even with the low embers burning in the fireplace, the room was cloaked in darkness, and I gripped the sides of my head, blinking until my vision adjusted.

Swinging my legs off the bed, my gaze landed on an open bottle of painkillers on the nightstand. I couldn't recall if I'd taken any before falling asleep. If I had, the effects of them had worn off, so I shook more than the prescribed dose into my palm and swallowed them dry. Noticing the glass of water too late, I downed that too.

Behind me, Solace lay shirtless and asleep, his features twitching with tension as though he didn't do so peacefully. We were in his bed. *How did I get here?*

Breathing through the pain, I thought back on the night, remembering the last thing we'd said, the last thing we'd done.

"Why do I know that you taste like mint with a dash of sin?" I'd asked, to which he insisted he didn't.

"Prove it," I'd demanded next.

We'd kissed, and although he hadn't tasted like mint then, I knew without a shadow of doubt that he used to. As I'd worked through what that had to mean, he'd managed to get from under me. I latched on to his thin sweats, attempting to hold him there, to hold on to the memory climbing the bottomless abyss in my mind. I'd ripped them clean off of him, which explained why he slept next to me naked, the translucent sheet covering his lower half.

A blinding headache had followed, one that made the flames of the fireplace too bright for my eyes. I was left shaking, the rolling nausea causing me to fold in on myself.

Solace had gotten me into his bed and held me until the pain subsided enough to fall asleep. He'd dabbed my neck and face with a cold, wet cloth while whispering that he...that he loved me.

Stumbling over to the sitting area, I shoved my hands between the couch cushions until I found my phone, then checked the time. Almost midnight. I'd been asleep for three hours.

Next stop was the guest bedroom where I kept my things. I struggled into a pair of jeans, stopping twice to cradle my aching head before gritting my teeth and getting it done.

I looked in on Solace once more, debating if I should slip back under the covers with him, remain ignorant, keep ignoring the signs, and continue to pretend I couldn't read between the lines. I couldn't do it. I needed answers, and while maybe he'd ultimately be the one to give me most of them, he wasn't where I wanted to start.

Downstairs, I laced into my boots and snatched up my coat. I took one last glance up the stairs before leaving, heading for my truck.

By the time I pulled into the parking lot of Pauly's Bar and Bistro, my migraine had begun to recede. The pain now pulsing instead of stabbing.

The sign on the glass door said "Open," but other than a few waitresses clearing tables, and a guy swaying in his seat at the bar, the place was empty. I hung my coat and took up a stool, deciding too late to ask the waitress passing behind me if Pauly was in. She was already disappearing down a hall in the back.

I spent a few minutes staring at my hands, fisting and releasing them, but whether curled tight or splayed out on the bar top, they shook.

"I'm cutting you off, Neil."

I snapped my head up to find Pauly talking to the drunk guy at the other end of the bar, the one still attempting to right himself. Pauly confiscated his beer, dumping the remaining dregs of it into the sink.

"I should've cut you off a long time ago. I'm calling Maggie to come get you."

The older man grumbled, but Pauly ignored him, turning for the phone near the register when he noticed me. "Hey," he said, peering around for Solace, I assumed.

"I'm alone."

"Alright," he drawled, clearly confused. "What can I get you?"

"You know me," I said. "You know who I am."

"Sure I do. You came in for dinner with Solace."

"Cut the crap," I bit out, short of patience. "You *know* who I am."

He observed me, as if weighing his options, before replying with unmistakable fondness in his tone. "I guess some things never change. You still have a low tolerance for bullshit. A low tolerance for anything that isn't Solace, I should say."

The sickness in my stomach returned, rising higher and higher. I swallowed past it, locking eyes with Pauly, letting him know I wasn't in the mood to be strung along or spoon-fed information.

"Yeah, I know you. Met you a little less than a year ago when you showed up in town with Solace. You helped him get things started again with the new house. He initially introduced you as the property manager—or was it construction overseer?" He shrugged as if the distinction didn't matter. "Anyway, within five minutes of being around you two, I knew that was a lie. Or that it wasn't the whole truth."

"When we were in here last, you'd said you were just trying to help. What did you mean by that?"

"We had a thing going, you and me. I'd harmlessly flirt with Solace, and you'd threaten to kill me if I so much as laid a finger on him. Almost nailed me in the eye with a dart once." He flicked his wrist, brushing it off as nothing. "Don't look so appalled. It was a typical night for us. I thought getting you riled up earlier might jog your memory."

I rubbed at my temple, my knee bouncing as I fought to not lose my shit while he asked the curly-haired waitress, Becca he'd called her, to have Maggie swing by for Neil.

"You really don't remember any of it, do you?" he asked after handing Becca the phone.

"No. Why would I lie about something like that?"

Pauly considered me, my bad temper rolling off his back. "Maybe you're not lying. That doesn't mean you're not afraid to remember."

"Why wouldn't I want to remember my life?" All I'd wanted to do since waking up in that hospital was remember every facet of my life, especially the time period Pauly spoke of now. I'd come to Haley Cove hoping to remember.

He tossed the towel he held over his shoulder and braced his palms on the bar, lowering his voice. "Look, Solace never told me whether you were single or not. He never told me more than I needed to know about you two. Hell, maybe he didn't even know. I knew *he* was married, though. I attended his wedding.

He'd sworn he'd be divorcing the douchebag the second he returned from that"—he fluttered a hand in the air as if in search of the right words—"that 'save the children mission' he was on. He said they hadn't been happy together in a long time. Said that Patrick had done something pretty terrible, and I believed him. All I cared about was that my oldest friend was happy, and Solace seemed downright euphoric with you." He straightened, assessing me.

"But maybe your situation was different from his. Maybe you were involved with someone at the time, and maybe that person was good to you, didn't deserve being cheated on. Maybe you don't want to remember that you may have hurt someone for completely selfish reasons. Or maybe this loss of memory thing is purely medical and has nothing to do with what you want or don't want. Like I said, I don't know your story. I knew you were in an accident that wiped a good deal of your memories. Solace was pretty tight-lipped about the rest."

"It *is* purely medical. I suffered a brain injury and had to be placed in an induced coma so that my split skull could heal. And I'm married. *Was* married," I corrected. "My wife didn't survive the crash." The wedding bands I wore around my neck now felt like an anchor of guilt instead of the buoy of hope they once were.

"I hadn't even suspected that I'd had an affair until a few hours ago," I said, unsure if that was true. "Hadn't received confirmation of it until now." That statement rang truer than my previous one.

"Okay, then. But why are you here talking to me? Why aren't you talking to Solace? Pretty sure he'd clear all this up for you real quick."

I opened my mouth to shoot him a defensive reply, but then stopped myself. Had I come here for answers to the more important questions—answers Pauly likely wouldn't have—because I was afraid of what I would learn about myself if I'd asked Solace directly? *Was* I afraid to learn about what I'd potentially done to my wife? My *pregnant* wife? And that I'd done it for no good reason?

He'd said that Solace was married, which I'd known. Had I participated in wrecking their marriage? A marriage that would've already been fragile due to the loss of their child. Had I lost my wife and child to the universe's laws of karma?

"All I know," Pauly said, slicing into my spiraling thoughts, "is that he loved the fuck out of you, and you loved him. There were months after your accident where he couldn't even get out of bed. Days when he couldn't get up off the floor. And now you're back, and his world is right again. Or *almost* right. Memory loss or not, I won't sit around and watch you put him on the floor again." He balled up the bar towel before pitching it somewhere out of sight. "Go talk to him. Figure this shit out." He stalked off.

"Why didn't he come looking for me?" I called at his back. "Why didn't he find me and tell me the truth?"

"You'd have to ask your BFF about that."

"What?" I asked, mouth going dry, heart punching at my sternum.

"Solace showed up to the hospital. More than once. I don't know the particulars, but I know your best friend put a stop to him seeing you."

"My...my best friend?"

"Yeah. Some guy named Leland." And with that he strode off.

I made for the parking lot on autopilot, shutting myself inside the cabin of my truck. Cranking the engine, I dropped the gear shift into reverse before shoving it into park again. "Fuck!" I barked, banging the back of my head against the headrest, the ache that hadn't fully subsided protesting.

Connecting my phone to the car's Bluetooth system, I dialed Leland. It was late, but this conversation couldn't be put off. He answered on the first ring.

"Noon?" he whispered, sounding worried. Shuffling could be heard in the background, then a door closing. "Are you okay?" He spoke a bit louder now.

"I'm fine. Did I wake you?"

"No. Franklin's asleep. I hadn't drifted off yet. Was up thinking about you, actually." The concern, though no longer urgent, was still palpable in his tone.

"Sorry I haven't kept in touch much. I'm calling with a question."

"Shoot," he said. "I'll do my best to answer it."

"Did someone come around the hospital claiming to know me after the accident?"

"No," he said. "Not that I can remember."

"Are you sure?"

There was a long pause as he thought about it. "As a matter of fact, there was a guy. Visiting hours were over, but I'd snuck back up hoping to peek in on you without being noticed. They'd brought you out of the coma earlier that day, and you hadn't handled the news well. I kind of thought you'd still be asleep from the heavy sedation they'd put you under, but when I got off the elevator you were awake and hysterical. Shouting the word "liar" in between asking for Stacey like you couldn't remember what had happened. You'd wake up really disoriented in the weeks after too. Each time, we'd have to break the news to you again." His tone held anguish, as if reliving it right then.

"Anyway, this guy was backing out of your room in a daze as the doctors and nurses piled in. He was pretty shaken up. After you'd been sedated again, I asked him how he knew you. He'd said you two were friends. I knew all your friends, and he wasn't one of them. He seemed unstable. Looked like he hadn't slept or changed his clothes in days, so I asked him to leave. One of the nurses told me later that she'd seen him hanging out in a stairwell a few times. I caught him the next day lurking outside your room, chewing his nails as he watched you sleep through the door window. I told him if he ever showed up again I'd have him arrested. We implemented a strict visitors list after that, and made sure every doctor and nurse on each shift knew about it. Security personnel too."

"I don't remember any of that," I said, my heart breaking for Solace.

"That's understandable."

"Why didn't you tell me any of this later on?"

"Honestly, it slipped my mind. There were far more important things to worry about, like breaking it to you that Stacey's parents had buried her while you were in a coma. We thought you'd never come back from that news," he whispered. "*Was* he a friend of yours?"

"No," I said quickly, then to myself thought: *He was more.* "Were Stacey and I having problems?"

"What, like marital problems?"

"Yeah."

"No way," he scoffed. "You two were the most solid couple I'd ever come across. She was your whole world, Noon."

"Thanks," I said, feeling weary.

"Are you remembering things?" he asked, the hope unmistakable.

"Not really. Just flashes occasionally, and dreams. More of the same. Nothing solid."

"Well, don't worry," he said. "It'll come back eventually."

We were quiet for a while. Me staring out the windshield, watching as the night breeze caught a few pieces of litter inside its current.

"You know," Leland started. "I've got some time on my hands. I could meet up with you."

"Now's not a good time," I said, hating to crush him. "Being away is helping. I don't want to get distracted. Wouldn't want any setbacks, you know."

"Yeah, I know," he said, letting me off the hook. "I'm here if you need me."

"Hey," I said hurriedly, hoping to catch him before he hung up.

"Yeah?"

I pressed back into the headrest again. "What I said about not remembering… That wasn't exactly true. There is something I remember." I hadn't wanted to give him false hope. Hadn't wanted him to believe this small kernel would amount to an entire crop. Telling him was the right thing to do, though. Telling him was equivalent to saying thank you. "It's nothing, really. Something small. May not even be worth mentioning," I said, minimizing it, attempting to manage his expectations.

"Nothing is too small," Leland said. "Tell me."

The memory came to me while in the shower after the photo shoot. I hadn't even told Solace. Maybe I'd been managing his expectations too, especially after he'd been visibly affected by my episode earlier that night. The one he'd had to talk me down from.

It was a split-second memory of Leland and me as boys. Of Leland being sad, of his sadness somehow having to do with his mother, and me trying to make that sadness go away. It was the one memory of us that came with a feeling, not just an image. We'd forged a bond that night huddled together in my tiny bedroom. I'd felt it in my heart, in real time.

"Noon?" he asked, checking to make sure I was still there.

"I'm here."

"What did you remember?"

I kept it simple, sticking to the thing that would mean the most to him, if I were going off the look on his tear-stained cheeks in the memory. "Forehead kisses…" I trailed off. "Do they make everything better?"

"Yeah," he said, voice tight, "they do."

I spoke through the emotion piercing my chest. "Thanks," I said. "For putting up with my shit. For waiting for me."

"Always," he promised, then we hung up.

I'd been about to pull off when I realized that in my dazed state I'd left my coat in the bistro. I jogged back inside, removing it from the hook when part of my conversation with Pauly came back to me.

"He'd sworn that he'd be divorcing the douchebag the second he returned from that 'save the children mission he was on.'"

Another memory came on the heels of that, from the night Solace told me about Gavin's death.

"Gavin's father is a doctor."

My coat slipped from my hand, and in a daze, I dragged myself over to the bar where Pauly worked on restocking the shelves. *"Pauly,"* I mouthed, then repeated it. This time with sound. "Pauly!"

"For fuck's sake," he breathed, wheeling around and clutching his chest. "I might not take a hint, but that doesn't mean I'm deaf, Noon. What the hell are you still doing here? I thought you left."

"The mission that Solace's husband was on," I began as my old friend Panic started working its way through my veins.

"Yeah," he said, waiting expectantly.

"Is it possible that it was called Doctors Beyond Borders?"

"Yes," he hissed, snapping his fingers and cracking my heart in two. "That was it."

◆ ◆ ◆

Solace was asleep in the same position I'd left him in, only now his back wasn't hidden by his hair, and I finally had to admit to myself what I hadn't wanted to acknowledge before.

The sweat-slicked spine I'd been dreaming about for months came into sharp focus then, and it was undoubtedly male. And the thick mass of hair I'd tangled around my fist like an endless spool of yarn in said dream was ashen blond, not golden. Not like Stacey's.

I think I knew. I always knew, or at least intrinsically from the moment I saw him, that he was the reason I'd felt such a strong pull toward Haley Cove. That the sensually moving body that haunted my dreams had been staring back at me every day since I'd arrived here. Pauly was right. I hadn't wanted to know the truth, which was why it had never seemed like the right time to kiss Solace. To do more than hold and be held by him, because that had felt safer.

Solace stirred after I sat on the bed, blinking up lazily until he noticed I was fully clothed. "Noon?" He scrambled up, catching the sheet at his waist. "Where are you going?"

"Nowhere," I said, wrapping my hand around his hair, closing my eyes and revisiting the ghost of my dream.

"You're scaring me," he said. "How does your head feel? And why are you dressed?"

There was no escaping the truth, even though I wanted to. If I wanted to know where I was going, I first needed to know where I'd been and why. It started with asking the right questions. It started with asking the hardest one first, the one that squeezed at my heart and clawed at my gut. I took the deepest breath I'd ever taken and then started where I knew it would hurt the most.

"The baby wasn't mine, was it?"

Solace sucked in a sharp breath, gaze darting across my face, over the pain he saw there. He inched closer, cradling my cheeks between his hands before whispering, "No, Care Bear. It wasn't."

CHAPTER 16

Solace

Then

I TOOK OVER the task of driving once we arrived in Haley Cove. Not only because Noon missed our exit twice, but because I wanted to play tour guide, and he wanted to capture every scene and every second of the place I dreamed of calling home one day.

"Can you close the window now?" I asked with a carefree laugh.

"The photos don't come out the same when a sheet of glass is in the way," he replied, face hanging out the window as he snapped photos of the mom-and-pop shops we passed along Main St. I shook my head as I cranked the heat up to compensate for the brisk air pouring in.

"Be careful you don't drop it," I said, lips twitching with the need to smile when he sat back in his seat, yanking the camera to his chest in a protective manner.

"Now you've gone and spooked me," he complained. "This place is beautiful, Solace. I can't believe a place like this exists outside of TV."

"Yeah," I said wistfully. "There's a lot of history here in Haley Cove, and the residents fight to maintain its authenticity, for the most part."

We turned down a cobblestone road almost too narrow for Noon's truck. He put his window up, content with using his eyes to record the charming brick and stone row homes lining both sides of the street.

"So you and your brother would spend summers up here," Noon said, gaze still glued out the window.

"Yeah. Gav and I lived in Lakeland with our dad. We were young when our mom died. It wasn't easy on my dad, raising the two of us on his own. My grandfather tried to convince him to move us out here where he could help, but we had friends and a life back in Lakeland, and Gav had his sights set on football. My dad got a nice break every summer, though. My grandfather made sure of it."

"So eventually your grandfather passed away and left you the farm? Why not leave it to Gav since he's the eldest? Or to the both of you?"

I made a left toward the parkway, leaving the tourism behind for another day. I was anxious to get to my grandfather's property. *My* property. "My ambitions were never lofty. I wanted to be a teacher and a father. I was the one suited for this type of life. For settling down. Planting roots. Gav couldn't even sit still long enough to finish a meal. If he hadn't blown his knee out sophomore year in college, he'd be living the fast life on someone's NFL team. My grandfather knew that.

"He sold off the livestock when he got sick. Gav and I were equal beneficiaries of those returns as well as his life savings and insurance payouts. Left me financially able to turn the farm into whatever I wanted. What I wanted was a home away from home for Gavin. I wanted him to enjoy summers here, like I had. I wanted a place Patrick and I could retire to, raise more kids in. Didn't end up working out that way. I'd been lucky enough to end up close to Haley Cove when Patrick accepted Columbia Medical School's offer after finishing up his undergraduate degree."

"You mentioned that Patrick's never been here. How is that possible?"

"Between medical school, his residency, and then Gavin, there never seemed to be any time. Homeschooling Gavin gave me the flexibility to move around. It didn't matter where he was, just that he learned. Haley Cove became our thing. Our place."

Noon squeezed my knee, and I covered his hand with mine, throwing him a glance before fixing my attention on the road again. "We're almost there."

"What made you name Gavin after your brother?"

"Mostly the threat of bodily harm if we didn't," I joked. "He was also the most important person in our lives at the time. Patrick and I had both lost our parents by then, and he didn't have any siblings. Then Gavin was born on Gav's birthday. We took it as a sign and gave in to the threats."

"Same name and birthday. Must be a painful reminder."

"Surprisingly not," I replied, with a reminiscent smile, before turning onto the private road leading to the property. "If anything, it's a beautiful reminder." Wishing my brother a happy birthday this year had been the one bright spot of that tragic day. It had felt like my son still lived on somehow.

The moment the partially constructed home came into view, along with the expanse of snow-covered trees and woodland surrounding the property, Noon began snapping away again.

"Jesus," he whispered as I eased to a stop. "How many acres does this sit on?"

"A lot." I chuckled at his gobsmacked expression.

He turned his attention back to the house, which was nothing more than an unfinished structure. I'd stopped all construction after Gavin's death. "Show me around," he said, already stepping out of the truck.

We were lucky; weather-wise it was a mild day, allowing us to take our time and not be turned into popsicles.

"Glass wall," he said appreciatively as we walked in, maneuvering around the disregarded supplies and debris.

"That was Gavin's special request. I have Iron Man to thank for the inspiration."

We made it through the lower level quickly, seeing as we only had the bones of it to explore, then headed upstairs.

"And this is the primary bedroom," I announced, looking back to see Noon bending to clear the top of the doorframe. "Sorry. When they asked if standard size was okay, I hadn't thought about having a giant over to the house. I can get them all adjusted."

"Adjusted? You've decided to move forward?"

"Well, I guess I hadn't thought about it until now, but yeah. I'd like to."

"And you'd adjust your doorframes for me?" He tugged me into him before stealing a kiss. I stretched up to make it easier for him.

"I think I'd do just about anything for you," I whispered breathlessly after he finished having his way with my lips.

"You're blushing," he said around the sweetest smile.

"I am," I confirmed, feeling the truth of it on my skin.

Noon stepped around me, taking in the nuts and bolts of the room. "I can fast-track whatever permits you'll need. Call in a few favors and have a crew out here in a couple weeks." He gripped one of the wooden beams, as if checking that the structure was sturdy. "Shouldn't take more than a few months, maybe four, to get everything done. You said your grandfather's farmhouse is still functional, right? We can live there in the interim. Or rent something in town. I can oversee it all—free of charge, of course. If you give me your budget I can make sure we remain within it," he went on, still moving as I trailed him.

"I can manage some of the work myself," he said from the bathroom now. "I'm licensed and certified to..." His words petered off as he took in my expression. If it matched what I felt in my heart, he had to have been overwhelmed by it.

"What?" he asked, crowding my space and cupping the back of my neck. He applied just the right amount of pressure. Enough to both let me know I wasn't going anywhere, and that I was free to leave if I wanted to. "Am I falling too hard for you, beautiful?"

I loved it when he called me that. I especially loved it when he made me *feel* that way.

"Am I moving too fast, Solace?" His toe-curling grin said he already had the answer to both questions. Likely because they were written all over my face.

"No," I said decisively. "I don't want either of us to hold back or waste precious time on trying to pace ourselves, trying to spread out our feelings over the course of months or years, or however long the outside world thinks is appropriate. I want you here. I want this to be *our* home. I'm ready to build *our* life."

"Are you sure?"

"When you know, you know, Care Bear. And trust me, I know that I want you."

He granted me one of his delectable forehead kisses. It was lingering, and reverent, and he inhaled like he was siphoning life from me, like he wanted to draw in the very essence of me too.

He eased away and stared down at me with stars in his eyes and joy settling at the corners of his lips.

"Don't give me that look," I warned, backing away.

"What look?" he asked, the picture of innocence, as I leaped out of his reach.

"Come on," I said, laughing at his displeased frown. "I've got a lot more to show you before we lose sunlight." I let him catch and drag me into his chest once more for a hot and heavy kiss. And when he finally released me before striding off with a triumphant huff, all I could think was: *This is what it means to be cherished. This is what it feels like to be loved.*

◆ ◆ ◆

"Dear, God," Noon said, rolling off of me and stretching out like a cat. "Where has this couch been all my life?"

"Gee, thanks," I retorted, sweaty and covered in his cum. "I thought I was the reason you're utterly satisfied right now."

"You are," he swore, rolling back to hover over me. "But anything this comfortable should be illegal, and I've never come across a couch that every part of me could fit on at once, let alone that a second person could fit on with me. Tell me we're taking it with us to the new house?"

I giggled at his pleading expression. Actually, giggled with pure happiness. "Saying I fit is a stretch. I guess since we sleep on top of each other anyway, it'll work. Do you think you can keep it clean?" I gestured to my chest, to how sloppy he'd been with me. "Seeing as how it'll be our bed for the foreseeable future."

We'd explored every inch of the property and made it to my grandfather's farmhouse right before sundown. It wasn't until we'd made it to my childhood bedroom that I remembered it contained a twin bed. Gav's room did too. Neither of us wanted to have sex in my grandfather's bed—the bed he'd taken his last breath in—so we'd made the living room our temporary bedroom.

"We'll just have to triple up on the sheets," Noon said, fingering the thin sheet we currently lay on. "And add a blanket beneath us. That should do."

"Are you going to insist we sleep on this thing even when the house is done and we have the gigantic, custom-made bed that your measurements require?"

"Maybe," he said before adding as an afterthought, "You act like you're not tall as well." He slid down my body to lick my chest and stomach clean before returning for my mouth, our tastes mingling to form a potent cocktail of cum.

"Not when standing next to you," I said, swiping my tongue over my lips once he backed off.

"Well, no one's tall when standing next to me." He arranged us onto our sides, draping one of my legs over his hip, one of his legs sliding along my other. "You had someone clean the place before we arrived," he said, playing with the wetness trickling from my hole—the place where he'd released the first half of his load.

"Pauly. He keeps an eye on the place for me. I told him I was coming, and he offered to have things ready."

"Pauly?" Noon asked, interest piqued.

"A childhood summer friend," I explained.

"I'm excited to meet one of your friends. Will I like him?"

"He's...an acquired taste."

"Uh-oh."

"We're complete opposites, but I think that's why we work. It also helped that I only had to deal with him for a couple months out of the year."

"Tell me something about him," he said, snuggling deeper into me.

"Why do I get the feeling you just want to hear me talk?"

"What makes you say that?" He smiled mischievously.

"Because for some odd reason you love to hear me talk, especially when you're sleepy."

Noon hummed. "You know me so well already."

"Because I'm obsessed with you. I study your every move, your every word... Your silences too." I pecked him on the lips once, then twice, then again. I peppered him with kisses until I had to stop myself or risk starting up a whole new round of lovemaking, and I wanted to talk to him. Loved talking to him.

"Pauly's a flirt," I started before he could protest the end to my onslaught of affection.

"Oh, I love him already," he groused, and I bopped him on the nose. He bit down on my finger faster than I could yank it to safety, then kissed the hurt away. "He'd get along with Leland. Well, the old Leland, I should say. He's a reformed flirt now that he's with Franklin."

"Can't wait to meet your friends," I whispered, refusing to let the idea scare me anymore than it already did.

"And my sister, Deb. She lives back home in Seattle, though. We'll visit."

"I'd love that."

"We don't get to see each other much, but we're close. Plus, she loves to give Leland hell. Always has. She's responsible for his ridiculous nickname."

"What is it? Can't be worse than Care Bear."

"Well, they both have the word "bear" in them..." He trailed off as his eyes enlarged comically. "Shit, he's never going to let me hear the end of it."

"Don't worry," I said, amused. "I'll defend you and your nickname." We lapsed into silence for a while, stroking and nibbling at one another.

"How will you introduce me to Pauly?" Noon's tone lost some of its lightness. We were still married to other people, and although that would change the moment Patrick and Stacey returned, we needed to decide how we were going to navigate the situation around the people we knew.

"I'll say I hired you to oversee the renovations."

"Think he'll believe it?"

"Think you can manage to keep your hands off me for five minutes?"

"No," he said without a trace of humor. He hugged me hard enough to leave bruises, and kissed me hard enough to do the same before causing my back to arch when he plunged the full length of his middle finger into me. "I don't think I can. And even if I could, I wouldn't want to." He didn't remove the digit, but he didn't move it within me either. Another sign of his exhaustion.

Noon liked to keep me plugged with one or more fingers as we slept.

I waited until my breathing had leveled, until the intensity of his stare simmered to burning embers. "You know I'm not hiding this because I'm ashamed of it, right?"

"I know," he assured me. "We can't live in our truth without sharing how we got here, and it's no one's business right now. We have a right to our privacy until we say otherwise." His eyes slowly closed and didn't reopen, and panic began to set in. I wasn't ready to lose him to eight hours of sleep. I wanted to stay awake with him forever.

"Tell me something about you," I said. His eyelids reopened at a snail's pace. "Tell me something from your childhood. Talk to me about your mother."

He gave me a sleepy grin but obliged. "My mother was an alcoholic. A mostly functioning one during the day. Nights were a different story, and nothing I ever did would make her stop drinking." His voice was a tired rasp, his gaze going distant. "If I hid the alcohol, she'd just buy more. If I replaced half the contents with water, she'd just drink double the amount. And if I stole her money so that she couldn't afford to buy more, she'd put on a pretty little dress and miraculously have more money by sunup. She'd stumble inside, reeking of cheap cologne and booze."

"Noon," I breathed, and he hummed in acknowledgement of my empathy.

"One night, she got so drunk that she fainted over the toilet bowl, banging her head on the edge of it. It scared the crap out of me," he whispered, his blank stare lighting up as if a movie reel had fired up in his mind. "I didn't know what to do. If I called the cops we'd be taken away from her—or I would. Deb primarily lived with her father. I wasn't so lucky. I didn't know who my father was. My mother didn't either."

My breathing turned unsteady with my mounting distress for him, so he removed his finger, immediately sending two back in, trading one heart pounding emotion for another.

"It was just the two of us that night, so I took care of her. I rolled her onto her back and placed my ear to her heart to make sure she was alive. Then I cleaned her up. Mopped up all the vomit, disinfected the cut on her forehead and put a bandage on it. The bandage was too small. It was the best I could do."

I tried to pull his hand away, to sink further into the pain in my heart rather than the pleasure overtaking the rest of my body. But Noon was an immovable slab of stone.

"Noon," I called again, but his fingers kept going, kept pumping, passively winding me up. I didn't want to be distracted. I wanted to live in this memory with him, wanted to suffer right alongside him. He wouldn't let me. Even now he was intent on putting me first.

"Normally, I'd shut myself in my room whenever she got plastered. Not that night," he continued, still stuck in the past. "She was too heavy for me to carry to bed, so I brought pillows and blankets in and slept next to her in the bathroom all night. She felt terrible about it the next day. Hated that I saw her like that, that I had to take care of her. She didn't drink for days afterward. Her guilt wouldn't let her. I never closed my bedroom door again." Noon's eyes went from distant to sorrowful as he dragged himself back from wherever the recollection had taken him. Probably to that cold, bathroom floor.

"Eventually the guilt wore off and she went back to drinking until she blacked out again. But now every time she woke up it was to a clean house, to breakfast on the table, to two pain tablets and a glass of water on her nightstand, to me sleeping next to her, holding her. Her guilt was the one thing I could use to keep her safe, if only for a little while. And then I met Leland. He'd help me with my mother whenever he spent the night. Sometimes his being there amplified her remorse."

I didn't know what I hated most or wanted more. Aiding in the cycle of him giving care to get love—if it meant that in this moment he'd be okay—or showing him that with the right kind of love, he could surrender to his needs, to his visceral pain. I chose the latter, because it was best for him and also true. He needed to know he could be selfish and trust that he would still be loved deeply.

"Please," I begged, reaching back to grab hold of his wrist. "Let me be here with you, Noon."

He kept going for a few seconds, then gave a deep sigh as he removed his fingers. The wet digits dampened my skin as he squeezed my hip, as I went from someone in need of his protection to his protector. His anchor.

"How old were you?" I asked, skirting my fingertips along his neck.

"Five," he said around a swallow, "when the habit started."

I knew he was referring to his habit and not his mother's. This was what shaped him. This trauma, this pain, this thing that no child should have to endure was what molded the most incredible person I'd ever known.

"Where's your mother now?"

"She died from alcohol-related liver disease."

I didn't have to ask to know that he'd taken care of her until the end. "Who takes care of the caretaker?" I needed to know that somewhere along the way someone had taken care of him. That he hadn't always had to put others first.

"No one," he said, bemused, as if he never expected anyone to. And that, most of all, made me sad.

"I promise to always take care of you when you need it, and even when you don't," I vowed. "And I'm hoping you'll let me, because you don't need to take care of me to be worthy of my love." *You have that already,* I thought, too much of a coward to say it.

Noon pushed me onto my back before bullying his way between my legs, tossing one over the back of the couch and growling for me to hold the other one open. He jammed a pillow under my hips, tweaking my position until he had me situated how he wanted me, never once apologizing for how urgently he seemed to need me. He didn't need to apologize. In this moment and all others, I would gladly be the vessel in which Noon needed to purge his pain.

He roughly lubed his obscene cock before launching three fingers into my hole with only a snarl as warning. I cried out, gripping the sheet-covered couch.

"Can you take me again?" he asked without inflection, as if it weren't a question at all, as though the answer didn't matter, like his barbarity was out of his control.

I peered down the length of his shaft to his heavy sack, already filled with cum after having released a load not too long ago.

"Yes," I whimpered, remembering to breathe, stomach muscles aching from the tension they held.

Noon leaned over me, hunching to whisper a warning against my lips. "This won't be gentle." He rose above me like a behemoth god, his body casting a dark shadow over me as he directed his crown to my entrance. He pressed his hips forward, breaching me with just the tip, staring at me as if waiting for my final words.

"I don't need gentle," I panted, dragging my nails down his chest as I let go of my leg to wrap it around him. "All I need is you, Noon." My heart exploded at the unguarded emotion in his eyes then, pieces of it rushing throughout my body before meeting back up again to form something new, something healthier and more whole. "I…" My mouth grew dry, my tongue absorbing my words.

"Say it," Noon ordered, both arms caging me in, thumbs brushing the tips of my ears. "Say it." The second time was a plea.

"I love you, Noon. God help me, I love you."

"God help us both, then," he whispered. "God help us both." He sank into me slowly, bottoming out and then waiting. I couldn't move. All I could do was suffocate on the air trapped in my lungs as his cock nailed me to the couch. Every ounce of his intimidating, muscular frame shook above me with the willpower it took for him to wait.

"I promise to always shower you with affection without making it feel like a reward, like something you need to earn," he gritted between clenched teeth as he began to work me. "I promise that my touch will always feel like something I want and need just as much as you do, because loving you will never be work, it will never be a chore. *Never.*"

Not like the way it had felt with Patrick, he didn't say. Didn't have to.

For all the brutishness he'd displayed moments ago, and the warning of his savage intentions, his movements—although no less devastating—were now measured. The light breeze before the cyclone-wind. The calm before the storm.

Noon had something to say, so he held himself in check to prove that his love outweighed his arousal. That it outweighed his need to be let off his leash, to prove that needing to let loose on me didn't come at the expense of the bigger moment we were sharing.

"I promise to always overwhelm you," he declared, "to keep you breathless with love and anticipation. I'm going to love you the way you deserve to be loved, Solace." His hips began to snap with every downward thrust now, with every grunted word of affection that slipped past his lips to be absorbed by my heart.

"I love you, Solace. So damn much." His hair fell onto his forehead, and at this point, at this velocity of speed, it should've been impossible for him to speak. Regardless of what it looked like, or what it felt like as he ruled my body with bared teeth and not an ounce of compassion, he was making it clear that even in this, even as he used his cock against me, it was done with love.

Through the increasing rapture taking over me, and the mind-blowing and near-violent fucking, his love smothered me as he promised it would. Still, I managed to make a vow of my own. "I promise to always find you when you get lost. I..." I paused to let loose a moan. "I promise to fall for you hard and fast every day, and I promise to appreciate all the big things, because nothing you say or do will *ever* be small."

Noon chiseled away at me, punctuating each promise with a hard drive of his hips. I wanted to come up with more, if only to see how much harder and faster he could go. To see if he could fuck me until we merged and became one.

We were at the end of a road paved in pain, the kind that came from not being loved properly, because with proper love and respect, all of life's other pains could be faced down and survived.

"Now comes the hard part, beautiful," he whispered before pulling out and forcing me onto my stomach. Noon sealed my legs together, the pillow beneath me keeping my ass propped in the air.

I scrambled to my elbows as he straddled me, straightening his legs until they bracketed mine, keeping them closed. His cock nudged at the tight crease of my ass. "Noon," I gasped. This would be more than I could handle.

Fisting my hair, he pulled my head up and to the side so I could see him. "You can take me," he said. "Relax your muscles and take me, beautiful." Noon encouraged me as he went, inch by inch and sweet word by sweet word, he surged through my snug opening. My cock strained between my abs and the pillow. One wrong move and I'd blow.

Noon still held me by my hair, his face close to mine as he held himself up on a flattened palm. Strangled breaths were the only sounds to leave our parted mouths as his cock dove deeper and deeper into my channel...and then I had all of him.

Cursing, Noon kissed me as he began a bloodthirsty pace. The kiss was awkward, with one half of our mouths being neglected due to our position, and sometimes we missed the mark altogether because of his height. We were mostly reaching tongues, animalistic grunts, and clashing breaths. We didn't care.

The couch scraped across the floor until it banged into the iron end table. The scattered pillows cushioned the porcelain lamp's fall. Noon let go of my hair, sending me crashing chest-first onto the couch before he released all two-hundred-plus pounds of muscle on top of me.

With me now completely pinned, and his cock plundering and conquering my hole, all I could do was pray I didn't splinter under the force of his brutal thrusts. The pleasure was almost too much for me to withstand, as it should've been.

He'd asked me to take him. To accept all of him. So I did, and I always would.

CHAPTER 17

Noon

Now

SOLACE REACHED FOR me from his spot in the middle of the bed. He resembled a porcelain doll, and the pain etching cracks along the corners of his eyes made him appear as fragile as one too.

"No," I mouthed, yanking my arm away as I stumbled from the bed. I'd sat immobile as he walked me through what he and I meant to each other; and while he'd explained what my wife had done to me. What she... What *they* had done to *us*. The two people who had promised to love us unconditionally, till death do us part. "Sh-she wouldn't do that to me."

"I know you want to believe that, Noon, but you don't remember the facts," he said in a gentle tone, but the truth of it still stung.

"And yet I'm supposed to believe *you,*" I shot back with disbelief in my voice, even while knowing I could. I withdrew further from him until my back met the wall. I'd prepared for this. I'd braced myself for it the whole ride back from Pauly's. Yet having a strong suspicion that my child—that my *wife's* unborn child—wasn't mine, and receiving confirmation were two different things. I'd fooled myself into thinking I was ready for this level of pain.

And the rest of it? This wasn't some one-night stand or a fling that led to an accidental pregnancy. Our spouses had been engaged in a prolonged affair with one another. Had been planning a life together and were prepared to step over our broken bodies without looking back.

The real strike to the chest came when Solace announced how little they'd thought about our feelings after the truth had come out. They'd dropped a bomb on our lives and then immediately rode off into the sunset together. *Cowards.*

Maybe Solace was the liar. Maybe he'd fed me nothing but lies all this time. Stacey wouldn't have done that to me. She couldn't have. Yet in my heart-of-hearts, I knew she had. I was angry and confused and hurt, and so clinging to denial seemed like the best solution. My grasp on it was slipping, though. It hadn't been a solid hold to begin with. Not when faced with the beautiful man in front of me.

"Yes, you're supposed to believe me," he said, voice brittle, "because you know me. The mind may not remember, but the heart *never* forgets. Your heart knows me, Noon. I'm its only source of solace in this world. Listen to it."

I couldn't move if I wanted to, because the love emanating from his blue gaze nailed me to the wall, even as it tugged my heart forward. It was that same tug I'd been experiencing for months now. That feeling of knowing, even while my mind kept me in the dark. I'd mistakenly attributed it to Stacey. The pull hadn't been toward her, though. I'd been drawn to Solace. That feeble tether to denial snapped, but there was still so much rage and pain in the way. Still so many unanswered questions. It was time to ask them.

"I've missed you," he said, fisting his hands in the sheet swathing his hips. "So much."

"Then why was I the one who had to find you?" I bit out. "Why have I been living my worst nightmare for months while you've been enjoying life on your own?" It wasn't true, and it was far from fair. I'd felt his despair since the day I arrived in Haley

Cove, but I needed an emotional punching bag and he was the only thing there. Solace nodded, as if he knew my reasoning and was willing to take whatever I tossed his way.

"I thought you'd taken her back," he admitted, his eyes a chasm of regret.

"What? Why?"

"We were so happy here," he said. "Too happy. We were making plans fast, and sometimes I asked myself if that was because we somehow knew we were on borrowed time." He dipped his head, and it took everything not to lunge for him, not to plead with him to never take those gorgeous baby-blues off of me again. They were the only thing keeping me glued to reality because everything they conveyed felt real. Felt like the only real thing in all of this. I was willing to admit that to myself now.

"Please look at me," I whispered.

"They'd reached out to us," he went on, holding my stare. "They were coming back and wanted to meet. To...talk."

The way he hesitated made me assume there was more to their request than that.

"We were both shaken up after hearing from them—for different reasons. We were happier than we'd ever been, and now we had to separate to face the people who'd hurt us." He huffed a cynical laugh, then pressed on. "It was supposed to be quick and easy. I mean, why wouldn't it be? They didn't want us anyway. They'd made their choice, right? Only thing left to do was legally sever ties." He shrugged. The casual gesture and his tone were at odds with each other, letting me know it hadn't been easy at all. This time when he looked away, I let him.

"I never came back," I said slowly, as realization dawned. "Solace," I whispered when more than a frenzied heartbeat passed and he hadn't responded. His gaze returned to mine, hauling me into the tidal wave cresting within it. I instantly understood that my not returning had been the single most devastating thing that had happened to him—next to losing Gavin.

"I thought you'd taken her back," he said again, in a strained whisper. The words weighed down by a lifetime's worth of pain. "I thought you took one look at her and realized that what we'd shared those three months was just a fantasy."

"Why would you think that?" I asked, my knees scarcely holding me upright. "If you and I were so in love, why would you think—"

"Because Patrick wanted me back."

An involuntary growl charged up from my core. I cut it off before any sound escaped my lips. Solace continued, oblivious to my lapse into possessiveness.

"Turns out the magic between them was only magical when they were sneaking around. He'd had an epiphany," he said in a mocking tone before swiping roughly at his cheeks. His tears would be my downfall. "And when you didn't show up or call, didn't respond to any of my calls and texts..." He shook his head sadly. "I thought you'd had one too."

"I'd never do that to you," I swore, sure of it. Positive that I'd never want to see him break the way he was breaking in front of me right now. He deserved better. Even with my memories of that time missing, I knew he deserved better, and that I wasn't the kind of man who could do something like that to him.

"I was frantic," he said. "And desperate. And *angry*. I didn't have contact information for anyone in your life. I'd camped outside your place for two whole days but neither of you ever came home. Your lights remained off. All sorts of scenarios ran through my head. I-I thought maybe you two had run away together. Maybe you had a second home somewhere that I didn't know about. I was sick, Noon. Sick without you. I just wanted you back. I would have *begged* you to come back to me." His words were a panicked rush of breath, and my own sort of wild panic began building momentum within me.

I wanted to reach for him, to grab him by his hair and tell him he didn't have to beg for anything, that I would find a way to travel back in time and remove all traces of every moment that he ever felt like he had to. But I was still angry, and I didn't know if some of that anger should be directed at him or not. Until I knew for sure, I'd remain sagging and barely breathing against the wall.

"How did you find out about the accident?"

"Patrick, of all people." He spoke his ex-husband's name as if it left a foul taste in his mouth. "He didn't know about us. He called because he didn't have anyone else to turn to after finding out about her. How ironic that after everything, he hoped that I would be there for him as he grieved for her. He had no idea what the news had done to me. Had no idea what you and I had come to mean to each other."

"How did *he* find out?"

"Word of Stacey's passing had made its way to her friends and colleagues at the hospital she and Patrick worked at together."

"I don't understand," I said, pushing off the wall only to realize I still needed the support. "She was pregnant with his child."

Solace explained to me that Stacey and I had struggled to have children, and that the problem was me. I remembered us trying, then the months spent trying a little harder. My memories must have cut off before the "struggling" phase.

"He didn't know," Solace said. "Or at least he never mentioned it to me between all his groveling. I don't know why she wouldn't have told him, even if they'd decided to end things before she got around to it." Solace grappled with his tears, the fight visibly wearing him down, and the need to be his pillar of strength was beginning to outweigh my anger. "Maybe she wanted the two of you to raise the baby together."

"I would have never agreed to that," I said, because it appeared that he needed me to, and because it was true.

Solace shivered, rubbing at his arms. Some primal instinct to take care of him bubbled up in me, conflicting with my need to keep my distance until I had all the answers. My legs began moving without the signal from my brain, taking me to the fireplace where I added logs to the pile burning out within the hearth. He watched me from the bed, attempting a grateful smile.

Removing the throw from the back of the couch, I made my way over to him, kneeling on the bed to drape it across his shoulders. My fingers grazed the smooth skin along his neck. We both shivered from the contact. I held my breath against drawing his distracting scent into my lungs. I didn't inhale until my back was once again against the wall.

"Do you know what I had to do to see you in the hospital?" he asked, holding the blanket around him.

"Tell me." Leland had told me his version of the events, but it didn't include the pain and suffering Solace had to have gone through. I needed to hear it all. I needed to know what loving me had cost him.

"Seeing you during normal visiting hours was impossible. Someone was always with you during the day. So I had to flirt with the head nurse who worked the night shift. Make promises I wasn't sure I'd have to keep in order to be let into your room when visiting hours were over." He stopped talking when his gaze fell to the fists I'd curled in preparation for tracking that nurse down. I still felt jealous, still felt like Solace was mine to protect, even while upset and confused. My emotions were all over the place.

"I'd sit in the stairwell, or somewhere else, waiting for him to arrive and let me in," he continued. "I dreaded opening his text messages, because what if he was ready to cash in? I feared

I would have done anything to keep seeing you. Leland got me banned before that could happen."

"Why didn't you just tell him the truth?"

"Because I didn't know if you'd left me for her. What good would it have done to expose your secrets if you no longer wanted me? If you were going to wake up and want her?"

He was protecting me. Even then. Even when telling the truth could have gotten him what he wanted. My chest warmed as my heart thawed.

"I had to know first," he whispered. "I had to talk to you first."

"And then I woke up."

"Yes,"

"And I didn't recognize you."

"No," he answered, his anguish clear.

"And then you told me the truth."

"And then you pushed me away."

"Because I...was in love..." The puzzle pieces began slotting into place then. I couldn't insert that last one, though. I couldn't say it, couldn't hurt him with it, so he said it for me.

"Because you were in love with her."

"I didn't remember... Solace... Leland said I would become disoriented after being brought out of the coma. He said I would forget where I was, forget what had happened. I-I don't remember you being there."

"I know. I was there when they woke you up. I was hiding in an empty patient room across the hall. You broke down when Leland and the doctors explained everything to you. The sound of your pain..." His features contorted with emotion. "Other patients and staff began filing into the hall to see what was going on. They had to sedate you. I nearly lost my mind.

"I just needed to get to you," Solace said hurriedly. "I just needed five minutes when no one else was around. I told myself that seeing me would fix everything. I got my chance when the sedation wore off, but you didn't know me. You didn't want me. You only wanted her."

"And I lost it again," I guessed. "I-I couldn't have wanted her. Not before the accident. Not after everything you've told me. I couldn't have."

"Not remembering me, and only remembering that you loved her, was just as bad as you leaving me for her, Noon. Don't you get that?"

"Yes," I breathed. "I do." Because either way, in the end, he'd lost me to her.

"I would have fought for you," I said. "I wouldn't have given up on us."

"I know." He nodded sadly. "You were always better than me in that respect. You have to understand, *everything* that I love, I lose. Maybe deep down inside, I'd always just been waiting to lose you. And then I did."

He was conditioned to expect the worst. He'd lost his mother, his father, his grandfather, his son, his marriage, and in some ways, the brother who he hardly ever got to see. And then he lost me. Now he was afraid that he'd lose me again. I inched toward the bed, surrendering to the need to be closer to him. I kept my hands at my sides, though.

"I tried showing up at your place again, after they released you. There was always someone around, going in and out. I spent most of my time licking my wounds at my grandfather's farmhouse," he admitted, letting the blanket fall from his shoulders now that the room had warmed up again.

His body was perfect, exquisite, as if parts of him were carved from the finest marble. His heart was supple, though, able to bend and endure without being indelibly broken. He was stronger than he gave himself credit for.

"Pauly convinced me that I could fight in other ways. He reminded me that memory loss wasn't always permanent, and that I could work on getting this place finished. Because if you came back to me, I wanted you to have a home to come back to."

He ran a hand through his hair, or tried to. It was a tangled mess, sticking up in some places and bunching together in others. He appeared debauched, as if someone had handled him roughly, as though they'd chosen not to take their time with him. I wanted that someone to be me.

"I didn't get your messages," I said. "Or your texts."

"I know that now. I'd hoped that was the case, but the part of me that thought you'd taken her back wasn't so sure."

"Why didn't you tell me?"

"I tried—"

"I'm talking about when I arrived in Haley Cove. You've had ample time to tell me the truth."

"You didn't want anyone telling you who you used to be—"

"Bullshit," I said, quieting him. "The first thing you'd said to me was that we'd never met. Don't give me a convenient truth, Solace. Give me the real reason."

He took a steadying breath, then whispered, "Because I didn't want you to push me away. Like..." He couldn't even bring himself to say it.

"Like I did that day in my hospital room."

He climbed to his knees, the sheet cascading to the mattress, his whole body revealed to me now. "My dreams had finally come true. You came back to me. But I hadn't accounted for you still not knowing me. When you asked if we'd met before, all I kept thinking about was that day in the hospital. That I didn't want it to happen again. That I couldn't survive it again, not when I hadn't really survived it the first time. I didn't want you screaming how much you loved her while branding me a liar. I didn't want you to run away." He crawled over to me on his knees, not stopping until they'd hit the edge of the bed, until I could feel his words just as much as I could hear them.

"What about since then?" I asked, my leftover anger now moving inward because I was too weak to fight him like this. Too weak to resist what he did to me, stirred to life in me, and damn it, I didn't want to. Not when the one thing of importance within me, the thing that beat ferociously now, belonged to him. There was more I needed him to explain, though. "I've been here for weeks. You could have told me what we meant to each other long before now. I wouldn't have run away. Not now. I wouldn't have." In a spur of passion, I'd gripped the sides of his head. Solace winced but didn't pull away, my reaction seeming to light a fuse to his own passion.

"How?" he asked too loudly for the sparse amount of space that separated us. His hands were in my hair now, his eyes wide and smoldering in the firelight. "How was I supposed to tell you what you meant to me when you were no longer *you*? When the man I loved more than life itself came back to me in love with someone else. When he's *still* in love with someone else." He said the words as if it had hurt him to, and my anger faltered completely, making room for an overflow of affection. I didn't fight it.

"Some days I'm so sad that it hurts to breathe, Noon. I have to stare at those wedding rings around your neck. I have to feel them pressing against my skin sometimes as we sleep, taunting me, reminding me that I don't have you. I have to hear you call her name with such longing while you dream," he said in sorrowful awe, like he wished that longing were directed at him. "And I have to smile when you tell me she was an amazing person. That isn't even what hurts the most, Care Bear."

"What hurts the most?" I asked, bracing for his answer to rip me to shreds.

"That with all the small, subtle things I do to help you remember me, to help you fall in love with me again...I'm not sure if I'm bringing you back to me—to where you want to be—or if I'm stealing you away from her, away from the place you'd chosen to be. And it *hurts*. It hurts so much to know I may be forcing you into something you'd already decided you no longer wanted."

"I did not decide that I wanted her," I said resolutely.

"You mean you don't remember deciding," he corrected, and that was the crux of it. But I didn't need to remember loving him in the past to know that I cared for him now. I'd felt drawn to him from the moment I saw him on my camera in that tavern. I hadn't been able to leave his side ever since. The mere idea of doing so came with an immeasurable ache deep in my soul.

I couldn't explain it, and therefore I couldn't make him believe it. All I knew for sure was, if given the option to have all my memories restored in exchange for losing what we had right now—even though what we had had barely gotten started—I wouldn't make the deal. Without question, I would sacrifice anything and everything to be with him, even if I couldn't remember why I should feel that way.

The truth of my feelings for him was complicated, but now that I had all the facts, I could no longer feel that suffocating love I'd had for Stacey. Almost as if I'd given it to her because it had sat so heavy on my heart and I didn't know where else to put it. Of course it had to be her, because I didn't remember *him*.

"Where do we go from here?" I asked with a sigh, brushing my nose against his.

"Do you think you could ever love me again?" he asked, almost childlike and hopeful, cracking my chest wide open. I couldn't crush him with a lie, so I told him the truth.

"Yes," I whispered. "I already do."

He pulled back, the ocean that had receded, crashing against the corners of his eyes again. It terrified me because I didn't want to hurt him any more than I already had.

I removed the chain from around my neck, giving the rings dangling from it one last look before marching over to the fireplace and chucking it into the flames. A weight had been lifted from me. The weight of many lies, to be more specific. And suddenly, I could see him more clearly. See *us* more clearly.

Returning to him and cupping his head again, I warned him, "My love for you is complicated, Solace. Please be patient with me."

"Complicated I can do, Noon. Never is the only thing that could break me."

I remembered something he'd said to me a little while ago.

"The mind may not remember, but the heart never *forgets."*

Truer words had never been spoken. "My heart knew," I said, tone overcome with emotion. "My heart *never* forgot."

He swept his thumbs over my cheekbones, smiling as he said, "I've missed you, Care Bear."

I smiled back, wondering at the odd nickname and whispered, "Our life starts now."

CHAPTER 18

Solace

Then

WHEN HAD I last raced through the woods? When last had my arms pumped at my sides as I leapt over fallen branches and dodged trees? Not since I was a child. I hadn't felt like a child in years, hadn't experienced that spark of wonder and excitement—until now.

I peered behind me in time to evade Noon's outstretched hand. My joy couldn't be contained, and I burst into the clearing with a winded whoop of victory and pure jubilation.

"The only…" Noon panted from behind, dropping the bundle of quilts he held to prop his palms on his knees. "The only reason you won is because I was carrying extra weight."

I unslung the backpack containing our lunch from my shoulders, holding it up with a meaningful hitch to my brows.

"And also because no matter how many morning walks I take to this clearing, I still can't find my way here—or back—without a damn compass or rescue team," he complained. "So, of course, I couldn't race ahead. I needed you to show me the way."

"I wish I'd known how much of a sore loser you were before I agreed to fall in love with you." I made my way to the patch of sunlight flaming through the break in the trees. It was the first day of spring, and although we hadn't completely left the cold weather behind, the temperature was warmer today. We wanted to take advantage of it.

I dropped the backpack near my feet so I could shrug out of my thin jacket, my back to Noon. "I'm the winner, and therefore—oomph."

Noon grabbed me around the waist, tackling me to the blanket he'd spread out.

"And I'm physically the strongest, so that means we do what I want, and you can't fight me on it." He had me out of my shirt and pants before I could chastise him for being a cheater.

"I get to choose the prize," I said, shoving at his face when he attempted to shut me up with a kiss. Between the running and my laughter, my strength flagged quickly, enabling him to have his way with my lips.

"It's not summertime yet, you brute," I said when he came up for air. "At least cover us with the other blanket."

Noon smiled, happy to be getting his way. He removed the lube from his pocket before stripping down to his socks. Suddenly, I no longer needed the blanket. One look at his naked body had turned my blood to molten lava. He fell to rest a forearm above me, covering us with the patchwork quilt anyway, before plucking a wildflower from over my head and handing it to me.

"A little romance before the plundering," he explained.

"Gee, thanks." I chuckled, then tensed when he tickled me for my sarcasm.

I tucked the flower behind his ear. "I thought you were hungry," I whispered, moaning when he wasted no time in slipping a slicked hand between us to work me open.

"I am *very* hungry," he said, the lust clouding his eyes speaking to exactly what he was starving for. "It's your fault for dressing so skimpily."

"Sk-skimpily?" I stammered as he inserted another finger. My hips began moving of their own accord. "I wore jeans and a thermal."

"*Tight* jeans and a thermal so fitted you might as well have just worn your muscles out here."

I couldn't quite master being amused and turned on at the same time, so I settled for rolling my eyes at him and pleading for a third digit.

"It's true," he said, removing his fingers for the sole purpose of hearing me cry out in displeasure. He waited for me to beg again before reinserting them, the addition of a fourth making me suck in a breath. "You've been getting quite the workout riding my cock lately. Your thighs are firmer from all the squats, and your upper body has benefited too. Takes a lot of strength to hold yourself upright when I fuck you long and hard from behind."

"So it's m-my fault," I breathed. "My body...and the way I dress makes you incapable of controlling yourself." I licked a stripe up my palm and slid my hand between us. Understanding what I wanted, Noon scooted up until his chin was above my head and our erections were aligned. Stroking us both as best I could one-handed—while my other hand clutched the blanket beneath us—I tipped my head back, straining to see him.

"Not only that," he said, peering down at me, nostrils flaring as I spread his pre-cum around and pumped him harder. "It's also that little bit of fear in your eyes right before I bottom out inside of you. Like maybe all the other times I've managed to sink all the way into you were a fluke, and this will be the time you can't handle me. Yesss," he hissed. "That look right there." His cock stiffened harder within my hand.

He was right. Intellectually, I understood my body could accept all of him without being harmed in the process. Still, I never trusted that it would until it did, no matter how many times we made love. Noon was wrong about the welcomed panic that often seized me, though. It didn't derive from fear only. It was a mix of excitement too.

Noon steered his cock to my hole, and my hand flew to his chest, pushing involuntarily, my body's self-preservation kicking in. "See," he said, tone soft with wonder, as he sank into me, pushing my right thigh out and up to make his journey easier.

"I wish you could see yourself. See how you gag no matter if my cock is entering your ass or your throat. I can't get enough of it, beautiful. You've got this," he encouraged quietly. "Yes, that's it." He let out a groan to rival all others once he'd stuffed me full of him. I couldn't see straight, couldn't think, couldn't work out the mechanics of breathing. "Hold on to me, Solace. This is gonna be fast and hard."

◆ ◆ ◆

With our lust dealt with for now, we'd finally gotten around to eating and discussing the renovations happening on the property.

"The stables should be done in a month, give or take," Noon said as I swallowed the last bite of my sandwich. "Could've been done sooner, but the stall guards you wanted are on backorder."

"You mean the ones *you* wanted," I corrected, bumping my knee against his.

Across from me, Noon smirked, chucking a celery stick my way. "The paddock's done, and the construction on the house is moving along as scheduled. Someone will be here tomorrow to test the soil and prepare the ground for the vegetable garden you wanted, and the blueprints for the remodeling of your grandfather's farmhouse are ready for you to review. Oh, and I was able to negotiate a better price on the security system upgrade."

"You're so good at your job," I said, pride evident in my tone. I'd told him as much when things got started, to which he'd arrogantly replied, *That's why they pay me the big bucks.* I hadn't had to lift a finger to do anything. All I'd had to do was say yes or no to his suggestions and provide alternatives of my own on occasion. Noon had taken it from there. Things were running smoothly and efficiently, and when someone wasn't doing their job, Noon didn't hesitate to replace them with someone who would.

"Would you be willing to leave a Google review?"

"Maybe. It'll cost you, though," I teased, leaning back on my palms.

"Fine," he said in feigned exasperation, "I'll fuck you again." He launched himself at me, sending us rolling half off the blanket, as I laughed until it physically hurt to do so. We came to a stop with me on his chest, and he reached over for the discarded blanket, wrapping us up in it. We'd been in the clearing for over an hour now and the temperature had begun to drop.

I stacked my palms and rested my chin on top of them, staring at him as he tucked one arm behind his head and plucked a blade of grass from my hair. "How many horses should we get? Two?" I'd never had the desire to ride a horse, but the prospect of riding the trails we were putting in, with Noon by my side, made me eager to learn.

"Or three. Maybe even four," he said with a shrug.

"Three or four?" I asked. "For guests?" I knew his friends Cole and Jasper rode, so maybe he wanted more horses for when they visited.

"Yeah," he said, trying a little too hard for nonchalance. "Or in case we one day decide to have kids."

"Kids?" I breathed, my senses immediately diving into that hole left inside of me after Gavin died.

"Is that something you would want?" he asked, his gaze tender and reassuring. If I said no, I knew he'd be okay with it, and would never pressure me or bring the subject up again. I went back to that place inside me, to that deep cavernous pit, and thought about how it would feel to fill some of that space up. There was no getting over Gavin, but maybe I could add a bit of happiness in there.

"With you?" I asked rhetorically. "Definitely."

Noon pulled me higher up his body to kiss my forehead and then my cheeks before settling me into the crook of his neck.

"Feels like we've crammed years into these three months," I whispered against his skin, kissing and biting at him gently.

"That's how life should be," he replied. "We should never waste a minute of it."

Three months. Patrick and Stacey would be returning next week, and although we'd done our best not to let the anxiety of facing them get to us, there wasn't a call or text that had come through on either of our phones that hadn't filled our stomachs with dread. They'd reach out, or we would, because we needed to sever that part of our lives to move forward with creating a new one.

"I can't believe all this time neither of them has called. Not once has Patrick called or sent a text to check if I was still alive after what he did to me and how he left things. My brother is his best friend. If he couldn't give two shits about me, he could've at least had the decency to give a damn about how Gav would feel once he found out what he did to me." I'd spoken to my brother last week, and he didn't know anything. I'd have to tell him eventually. I shot up, suddenly enraged. "And Stacey, what have you ever done but love her? This is how she repays you? Isn't the fact that you've shared so much of your life with someone worth them caring about how you were getting through the worst time of it?"

"Hey," Noon whispered, sitting up to take my throat between his hands, squeezing gently until I'd calmed, until I'd submitted. "How about we be grateful for all of it? Look at what we have here." He peered around the forest teeming with life, at the small family of deer peeking at us from beyond the trees. "We need to be thanking them, not hating them."

I sighed. It wasn't hate that drove my reaction, though. It was my anxiety about their return. "You're right."

"I know I am."

I rolled my eyes at him for the second time that day. "I wish I would've picked up on your nasty habit of thinking you know it all a lot sooner," I said. I found myself on my back again because of it.

"We are not having sex out here again," I said sternly, fighting against his hold on the zipper of my jeans. "It's getting cold, and we promised Pauly we'd come by the bistro for dinner."

Noon grumbled about not being in the mood to have to chuck another dart at Pauly's head for flirting with me tonight.

"You secretly love when he pushes your buttons," I said, watching him stand and zip into his jacket. "You get to pound on your chest and claim me as yours like some caveman. Then, you're so worked up by the time we get home that you can't even take the time to remove your clothes—or mine—before bending me over the nearest surface and taking your unspent jealousy out on me."

"You're right," he mused, stepping out of my line of sight as I began stuffing our trash into the backpack. "I do enjoy it, but that's our little secret. Anyway, let's go to the tavern instead. We haven't been there yet, and I'm dying to take photos of the place."

Because of Noon, the words "photo," "picture," and "camera" had been added to the list of words that triggered me. I stood with a groan, spinning toward him only to be greeted by his damn camera lens. He managed to snap a few before I snatched it from him, hiding it behind my back when he reached for it. I hadn't even known he'd brought it with us. I'd have to start frisking him before we left the house.

"Other than Pauly's, we haven't been anywhere but the farmhouse," I said. "You won't keep your hands off of me long enough to actually do anything in Haley Cove. I thought you wanted to see the museum. Check out the cultural center. We haven't even been to the supermarket."

Noon grabbed me by a belt loop, hauling me into him. "Your food delivery app has gotten us by just fine. We'll do all that other stuff next week. I promise."

"Let me guess," I said dryly. "This week you want to lie naked on the couch all day."

"Is that so bad?" he asked, frowning. I scratched at the stubble lining his jaw. It took me shaving him and trimming his hair for either to get done nowadays.

"No, it's not," I said, pulling his head down and lifting up onto my toes to kiss him. "I'll never complain about how obsessed you are with me." That earned me a swat to the ass. He helped me into my jacket before scooping up the blankets, and then we were off, racing through the woods again. What Noon gave me was all I'd ever wanted, and the feelings of love and devotion and obsession were mutual. We were completely infatuated with each other, and I loved it. I'd never take any of it for granted.

We ended up at the Haley Cove Tavern that evening—after I'd convinced him to go to both the museum and cultural center beforehand. Noon loved it all, and I even allowed him to pay for dinner after he'd complained that I hadn't let him pay for anything since arriving there. Aside from materials and labor for the renovations—which I insisted on covering the cost for—there really hadn't been much to pay for. When we ate out, we did so for free at Pauly's.

He'd signed and stuffed the dinner receipt in his pocket for the scrapbook idea he'd come up with.

"It's for the kids," he'd said. *"I'm going to chronicle our lives here for them. Starting with the best restaurant in town."*

"I think that's a great idea," I'd said, letting him blind me with his camera's flash as he pleaded with me to say cheese for the kids.

We didn't hurry to make love when we got back to the farm-house. We showered and cuddled up on the couch in front of the fire, giving voice to our dreams for the future.

"Would you want another boy?" Noon asked.

"It doesn't matter. As long as they're happy and healthy. What about you?" I dragged a finger along his collarbone as he combed his fingers through my damp hair. He normally braided it for me after a shower. Tonight he wanted it free. He'd said it was easier to fist and tug when the strands were unbound.

"A girl. And I'd want her to have your big blue eyes and long, ashen-colored hair. I'd want her to have your kindness too. And your sweetness. Oh, and I'd want her to be mild-mannered like you too."

"So essentially, you'd like a clone of me," I deadpanned.

"It sounds creepy when you say it like that." He wrinkled his nose. "I just think the world needs more of you."

In terms of the sweetest thing he'd ever said, that might have topped the list.

"So that's the solution to world peace?" I asked. "More of me?"

"And don't forget world hunger."

"Because we'll make mini-mes and feed them to the population," I shot back, matching his seriousness.

"Fertilize the earth with the likes of you."

"Cabbages will sprout with my face."

"How about potatoes?" he added swiftly.

"And broccoli?" I asked without breaking my verbal stride.

"And radishes!" He licked his lips as if tasting them now.

"Why stop at food?"

"Because there's nothing better than tasting you, that's why," he said, stumping me. His eyes danced as I fumbled for a quick response to keep our game of who-could-be-more-ridicu-lous going.

"I win!" he exclaimed while I sputtered. "Nope, I win." He slapped a hand over my mouth and rolled us off the couch onto the floor, sprinkling kisses over my face as I laughed, surrendering to his barrage of affection.

The sound of an incoming text rang out, silencing us. "That's your phone," Noon said, shifting so I could get out from under him. He watched me from his spot on the floor, the fire crackling behind him.

"It's Patrick," I said, heart thundering. "He moved his flight up. He arrives tomorrow and wants to talk. What do you think that means? That he's coming back early?" Granted, it was only by a week, but after all this time, why not finish out the remainder of the trip? Why go through the trouble of switching up your itinerary this late in the game? "It feels urgent." Or maybe that was me projecting my own urgency to remain uninterrupted in my bubble with Noon. I felt conflicted. Patrick returning meant we could get the dissolution of our marriage underway, but I didn't want anything interfering with what I now held dear: my relationship with Noon.

"I don't know," Noon snarled, getting to his feet, "but I'm coming with you."

"I don't think that's the best idea."

"I've spent the last three months watching you dig yourself out of the hole he put you in, and if he didn't put you there, he damn sure never extended a hand to help you out of it." He grasped the sides of my face, rage pulsing at his fingertips. "You're lighter here. Happier. More confident. You've come out of your shell, and I'm terrified that a few minutes alone with him might change you... Might break you."

"Nothing can break me, Noon. Not as long as I have you." I trailed a finger from his widow's peak to his jawline, the tension in it easing as I went. "I don't think it's wise to share what we have with them so soon." I wanted to protect it for as long as possible. "Let's meet with them to discuss officially ending things, to say our last words and ask our final questions. We'll see where it goes from there."

Seeing Patrick would be like cutting open an old wound. It needed to be done, though. We'd shared a child together and, at one time, we had loved one another. If we could disentangle ourselves from each other amicably, if we could wish each other well instead of having bad blood between us, that would be preferable. Especially since I now understood that the problem had never been me, it was always him.

"You're right," he said grudgingly. "If he tries to gaslight or manipulate you, if he so much as makes you think twice about your innocence in all this, I'm getting out of my truck—from where I'll be parked down the street without you knowing—and I'm laying him the fuck out."

"Noon." I groaned, whacking his arm when he squished my cheeks together until my lips puckered.

"I'm kidding," he said. "Kind of." He received his own text then, and I clutched at his arms before loosening my grip and allowing him to check it.

"Is she flying in tomorrow too?" I asked, not even needing to confirm if it was her. The blanching of his skin had said it all.

"Yeah," he answered. "And she wants to know if we can meet."

"Did she say why?" I crossed my arms with the instinct to protect myself, digging my fingers into my sides.

"No, but I'm sure she wants to tell me the same thing Patrick wants to tell you. They want to end this, and so do we, so let's not waste any time in getting it done. Okay?"

"Yeah. Of course. Okay."

"I'm going to pick her up from the airport," he said, typing a reply before sliding his phone onto the coffee table.

"Is that really necessary?"

"With any luck, we can sort shit out on the drive into the city, and I can leave her on the curb in front of our... In front of *her* home, and beat you back here for dinner."

"I bet you won't."

"Bet I won't what?"

"Beat me back here," I whispered. Noon tucked my hair behind my ear, his gaze knowing. If I had to resort to a childish bet to make sure he got back to Haley Cove as fast as he could, I'd do it. I didn't want him lingering around her too long.

"What do I get if I win?" His question was a seductive purr.

"You get to have me in your favorite position," I said, voice affected by the hand skirting my hip to cup my backside possessively.

An exaggerated gasp escaped his mouth. "You mean the one where you—"

"Mmhmm," I said, stopping him before he embarrassed me with the details.

"And then your legs go—"

"That's the one," I cut in as his arms went wide in demonstration.

"And then your pretty little ass—"

"Yes!" I exclaimed, pinching his mouth shut and looking around to make sure the walls hadn't picked up on what he was implying. "That one, you idiot."

He peeled my fingers away. "And what do you get if you win?"

"Just make sure I don't win, okay?"

"Deal," he said, hugging me. "I'll be waiting for you at the tavern in our favorite booth at the back."

"We've only been there one time, which happened to be tonight, and we already have a favorite seat? And more importantly, you already want to go back?"

"Yes," he said unapologetically. "I mean, I can always meet you at your old home—"

"No," I said, not wanting my meetup with Patrick to end in violence. "I love that you call it my old home, though."

"Because it is," he said, swaying us from side to side, as if music only he could hear played. "Your home is here now. Your home is with me and Gavin."

I squeezed him tight, quietly speaking my part of what had become our nightly ritual. "You belong to me."

Noon lifted me off my feet, his words sounding like a prayer as his lips brushed the shell of my ear. "And you are mine."

He made love to me repeatedly, only allowing us sporadic catnaps in between before making love to me in a number of ways again. I'd even been woken up to his thrusts before my mind had fully engaged.

He loved me. He wanted me. Only me. He'd drilled it into my mind and body all night as he did whatever he wanted to with me. I believed him. I did. I wanted to. But no amount of orgasmic bliss could remove the sense of foreboding competing for my attention.

The next evening I arrived at the tavern, and Noon wasn't there. I refused to be seated until our "favorite booth" became available, because that's what we'd agreed upon, and I didn't want to tempt fate.

I waited and I called and I texted. And then I ordered our food and drinks after being told I'd need to give up the booth otherwise. Then I waited and called and texted a whole lot more, my gaze cemented to the front door. I waited so long that the manager had to politely tell me they were closing for the night, and that I had to leave. So then I waited in the parking lot before hurrying through the streets to get home because maybe Noon's phone had died, and maybe we'd gotten our wires crossed. Maybe he was waiting for me on his favorite couch.

I blasted through the front door of the aged farmhouse, checking every room. He wasn't there. And so I waited by the window for his truck headlights to come into view on the road. They never did. I waited until the sun rose, still calling and texting. He never came. He...he never came back.

CHAPTER 19

Noon

Now

RECALLING THAT HE was naked, Solace slid off the bed to disappear into the closet. He reemerged in a pair of loose sweats. "I want to show you something," he said, tying the drawstring. I followed him out of the bedroom and down the hall. He piled his hair atop his head as he walked, securing the disheveled knot with the elastic band he kept around his wrist.

He turned the corner, stopping at the narrow set of stairs leading to the attic door. The place he'd said he kept Gavin's things. He took a deep, bracing breath before glancing over his bare shoulder at me, then ascended the steps.

From the width of the landing and the size of the door, I'd expected the space to be small. It expanded the entire length of the second floor. "The view must be beautiful in the daytime," I mused, transfixed by the deluge of rain hitting the double-pitched skylight.

"I like to sleep up here when it rains," he said. "On nights like tonight. It's comforting."

In one corner stood a bed with matching nightstands and lampshade-covered wall sconces. Off to the side, Solace watched me with his hands pushed into his pockets. The action tugged the waistband of his thin sweats lower, exposing the tapering V between his hips. With some effort, I tore my gaze away from him and noticed an abundance of picture frames hung on the opposite side of the loft. He'd been waiting for me to notice them, I assumed.

I crept over there, Solace not far behind. "What's all this?" I breathed, my heart fluttering. "I thought you said Gavin's things were up here."

"I've donated most of his things. What's left fits into a drawer in our closet. A few keepsakes. His photos are in an album, and a few are sprinkled around the house," he explained. I hadn't missed that he'd called the closet *ours*.

"You forgot your camera," he whispered. "The morning you left for the airport. That should've been my first clue that things weren't going to go as planned. You never forget your camera." He pointed to the wall... To the *walls* covered in framed photographs. Some were of us. Most were photos of him. "I printed everything out."

None of the images struck a chord, but the pictures of Solace stole my breath away just the same. "Where were we here?" I pointed to a profile shot of him. Tears streaked his cheek, and tendrils of his hair billowed away from him as if carried by the wind.

"That was before we came to Haley Cove. You'd only recently developed a love for photography. I was standing outside in the snow, thinking, I guess. I don't remember you taking it."

"And this one?" I asked. Solace wore a gray t-shirt at least four sizes too big. The collar hung off one shoulder, and the hem reached mid-thigh. All his sacred parts were covered, but with his damp hair framing his face, and his mouth slightly parted as if surprised, he appeared indecent, erotic.

"We'd taken a shower together," he said. "I'd scooped your discarded t-shirt off the bedroom floor and had just slipped it on when you sneak-attacked me. Typical of you to do so."

"What were we doing before showering? Or during it?" I didn't know why I had the urge to ask. Likely because he'd become bashful while explaining, and bashful looked good on him.

"I'm sure you can imagine," he said, gaze falling to his bare feet.

I moved on, my steps faltering on a photo one row below. There were no overhead lights in the attic, only the motion-sensor sconces positioned around. They provided a dim, sultry ambience to our surroundings. This shot I needed to see clearly, so I removed it from the wall, bringing it close. Solace lay sprawled in the center of a ruffled bed, looking completely spent and defiled. His lips were swollen, and a deeper shade of pink than they normally were.

Color sat high on his cheeks, hickeys spanned the expanse of his neck, and his eyes were glassy. His hair was also a mangled mess. The best way to describe him would've been the aftermath of a sensual storm. An aftermath that had been documented.

"I did this to you?" I asked, knowing I had and hating that I couldn't recall it.

"It's what you always did to me," he replied in a demure tone, and although I didn't remember taking the picture, I regretted not removing the sheet from around his hips first.

I placed the frame back on its hook, making a mental note to come back to it.

The next photo held me as equally enthralled as the last. Solace perched at the edge of a couch, his hands draped casually over his knees, legs spread wide. He wore a cropped football jersey and eye-black strips on his face. His hair fell in waves, like maybe he'd loosened it from a tight braid. The highlight of the photo, though, was the white lace jockstrap he wore. I could see the outline of his cock in the lace.

"You love football," he said. "Your team had made it to the Super Bowl, and so we threw a two-man party." He cleared his throat. "I might have had a little too much wine that night. For once I didn't give you a hard time for wanting to take excessive photos of me."

I peered around, and he was right. There was a whole series of shots from that day. Different poses and locations. Standing, sitting, hands and knees... The couch, the floor, the bed...

"Do you still have this outfit?" I asked, still scanning as he watched me.

"I'm sure I can dig it up from somewhere." His voice had deepened, and I turned to see him flush, his cock swelling behind his sweats.

My own pants grew tight around the crotch. I ignored it for the moment and went back to perusing the photos.

I'd been with men before. I remembered that much. But, for me at least, this would be my first time with Solace. I'd have to live up to what he remembered. I'd need to relearn what he wanted and needed from me. What he could handle, and what went beyond his limits. He'd have to teach me, and I'd have to get it right. What if I didn't? What if in this I was no longer the same either? The thought of not pleasing him, of not being worth the trouble he'd gone through to get here, terrified me. I worried about all of that as I scanned the photographs.

"Peppermint," I said, pointing to one where he laughed while holding up a handful of red and white striped candy. I thought back to our kiss in his bedroom. To the scent that hadn't been there, yet had consumed me anyway. "Mint is connected to our past."

"You hated it, I loved it," Solace said. "It doesn't agree with my stomach anymore. Had I known it would trigger your memories I would have risked the reflux."

I turned to the wall again. The pictures of me were the hardest to look at. Hard to see and not remember the look of total adoration and love in my eyes as I smiled into the camera, knowing the person I smiled for was him.

We were together in one photo. We'd likely set a timer on the camera before hurrying to get into place. We were mid-laugh, hugging while nude on the couch from downstairs. We couldn't appear more opposite of each other lying amongst the heap of throw pillows. My bare chest was broad, darkened by hair. My arms were packed with muscle, and I was in need of a shave.

Solace nearly vanished beneath my mass, his body smooth and pale. We were darkness and light, gruff and refined, uninhibited and reserved.

"You look so young and carefree," I said.

"I haven't felt like either for a long while," he admitted.

There were more shots of me, of us. Hugging, kissing, feeding each other, playing in the snow.

The final shot showcased Solace with his head thrown back, eyes closed and mouth open, my hand wrapped around the slender column of his neck. My hand was too large. Too big to have any business being around him like that. He didn't seem to mind. Didn't even seem to notice, caught up in rapture as he was.

"That was my third orgasm of the night," he said, coming up next to me. "It was a long night. I didn't even know you'd captured it until I printed the photos out."

"Was this our last night together?" I didn't know how I knew that, but everything in me screamed that I was right. Maybe it was the way the veins in my forearms bulged, as if I were straining to hold on to him. To not lose him.

"Yes. Do you remember?" His breathing went shallow, as if excited that my answer might be yes, or maybe it was fear he felt. Fear that my answer would be no.

"Not yet," I said instead of a flat-out no, trying my best not to hurt him.

"Oh," he said. "That's alright."

I moved closer to him, resting my hands along the side of his throat with total awareness of the precious thing I held between them.

"Don't be careful with me," he said. "You don't have to be."

I loosened a bit of my restraint, feeling the soft flesh compress beneath my palms. Solace tipped his head back, giving me permission to do as I pleased while his own hands reacquainted themselves with my chest.

"Why didn't you show me all this?" I asked. "The photos could have helped."

Solace looked at me as if to say they weren't even helping now. I conceded with a sigh.

"Still, you couldn't have known that they wouldn't." I said it without judgment, without blame. We were past picking apart what had been done wrong, what could have been done differently, but the fighter in me had to say it. I swept my thumb over the pulsing vein at his neck.

"I thought about showing you. That first day you came here, and so many days afterward. I was torn, for all the reasons I've already mentioned. I also didn't want you to feel obligated to fall in love with me simply because these photos proved that you were in love with me before. I wanted you to remember me on your own. And if not, I wanted you to fall in love with me again, without being swayed or pressured to. That's not what I wanted for you. That's not what I wanted for *us*."

I thought back on all he'd done to help me to remember. The places he'd taken me to that we'd likely visited before. The things he'd said that I now knew were said to me in the past. *The photo shoot.*

Something else popped into my head, something he'd said to me after my near mental breakdown at his grandfather's farmhouse.

"I'd like to believe that every time I share something with you, it's helping, or will help, in some way. That's my way of fighting in return."

He'd been fighting for me. For us.

"You called me Care Bear."

"Yes." He laughed, the sound a mix of nostalgia, sadness, and hope. "That was my nickname for you, because you care so damn much."

"Did I have a nickname for you?"

"More like a term of endearment, but I'm not going to tell you what it is."

"Why not?"

"You get to come up with something on your own now, because if I tell you, I'll always wonder if you're saying it because you think you're supposed to or if it's because you mean it. Because you feel it."

I nodded, taking in his eyes, his hair, his lips...anything I could use to come up with something fitting for him. That could wait until later. We had time. "Am I everything I used to be?" I asked, breath hitching, the backs of my eyes stinging.

"No," he said, angling his head at me. "You're so much more."

"Tell me how you like to be kissed, Solace. How you like to be touched by me."

"You can kiss and touch me however you want—"

"No," I said. "That answer doesn't work for me, and it doesn't work for you either. Help me remember. *Remind* me."

"What if it doesn't work?" he asked, in a voice that even when devastated sounded sensual. "What if you still don't remember?"

"Remind me anyway. Never stop reminding me of the life we shared before I forgot you." I backed us up slowly until we'd made it to the foot of the bed. I released the band holding his hair up as he unbuttoned my shirt. Once we were naked, I circled my arm around his waist, hauling him with me as I crawled to the top of the bed. I then switched our positions so he sat astride me, my hard cock cradled between his ass cheeks.

"I haven't been with anyone since you," he said, kissing along my clavicle.

"And I haven't been with anyone since you," I repeated back to him. That much I was sure of.

"No?" he asked, and I shook my head. "I'd hoped, but..." His voice trembled now.

"No," I said, smoothing my hands down his arms. "I've been too preoccupied with trying to remember you, with trying to find you." I hadn't known it at the time, but Solace was the one my heart searched for. Solace had been the one haunting my dreams and my every waking hour. "My love for you, however unknowing that it was, has kept me consumed these last nine months. There was never a thought of being with anyone else. Not even as a means of distraction, to pass the long and painful hours spent without you. Never."

Lifting his gaze, he blinked rapidly at the ceiling, then reached into the nightstand for a bottle of lube.

"Do you touch yourself a lot when you're up here?" I asked, my gaze drifting to the walls lined with photos.

"Too much," he whispered, color staining his cheeks.

"Did I always love how shy you'd get?"

"Yes," he said, his flush deepening.

Solace was graceful and submissive, and displayed just the right amount of hesitancy to make having him feel forbidden, to make what we were embarking on stray close to the side of wrong. Everything about him screamed off-limits, first-times, and handle-with-care, even though all of those things couldn't be further from the truth. Still, I wondered if I would split him in two. Strangely, the combination of it all made me want to.

"You'll fit," he said, as if reading my thoughts. "You always do."

His cock was as magnificent as the rest of him. Long, slightly curved, and with a gorgeous pink crown. I locked my fingers around it, the vein that stretched underneath pulsating against my palm.

"God," he breathed, his head rolling on his shoulders. He bit his lip, and I licked mine in response. As if again sensing the direction of my thoughts, he inched closer, the heat from his ass settling over my navel, my rigid length slipping from his cleft.

Solace lowered over me to whisper into my parted mouth. "You kissed me like you had a point to prove. Like I was a prize you hadn't already won."

I kissed him, just like that. Holding him to me with a hand at the back of his head, my other hand still gripping his shaft, spreading his pre-cum over the tip.

Solace moaned into the kiss, chest rising and falling as he fought to keep up, to not be consumed by me. I eventually let him go, my teeth tugging at his bottom lip until it slipped free. He held on to my shoulders to keep from falling over, and his eyes widened, almost in disbelief. He looked undone, and I hadn't even gotten my cock inside of him yet.

"Like that?"

"Y-yes," he said. "Like that."

"What else?" The question rumbled through me, lust guiding me now.

He hesitated, then said, "When I sucked your cock, you didn't expect me to take it all, but you loved to see me try."

"Show me," I whispered. "Let me see you try, Solace."

He scooted back, his dick slipping from my hand. I spread my legs so he could kneel between them, my cock throbbing and getting harder as he stared it down with equal parts awe and trepidation. I gathered his hair up, holding it aloft as he first tongued away the creamy wetness emerging through my slit, then sucked me to the halfway point where my tip settled at the back of his throat.

"Damn it," I hissed, stomach muscles bunching as he bobbed and gagged on my cock, attempting to take a little more of me with each downward plunge. His tongue worked my shaft in tandem with the suction of his lips, amping up the friction. And when he dared to breach my hole with his pinky, I almost detonated on the spot.

"Fuck!" I yanked him off me, fisting my base and digging my heels into the bed as I willed the orgasm away.

Solace heaved, as if he'd run miles, my hand in his hair the only thing keeping him steady. His lips were shiny with a mix of saliva and pre-cum, his face covered in tears from the exertion of trying to swallow a big cock and choking on it.

I dragged him up my chest and forced him into a kiss before he knew what had hit him. He struggled to straddle me again, but I was a whirling mass of wind, my current tossing him around.

I took pity on him, gripping his hips and planting him on top of me as my tongue reached and swept inside of him, searching for more of my taste.

"Get us ready," I ordered. "I need to fuck you now."

"My fingers won't do," he panted, using his reprieve to gulp down gasps of air. I snatched his wrist, inspecting his fingers. They were half the size of mine.

Solace pressed his palms to the headboard behind me, now hovering over my lap as he arched his spine. "Open me," he said softly, pushing his ass backward while widening his legs as far as he could take them from his position.

With a lubed hand, I reached behind him, my long fingers making the journey to his opening. I began the arduous task of readying him for my cock.

Three fingers deep, and his breaths heaved in and out of him, pelting my own parted lips as he fucked my hand. My balls drew close to my body, begging for release.

"Get on top of me," I demanded, dislodging my hand to slick my cock and hold it centered for him. Solace hurried to obey.

"Careful," I warned, holding him in place by the hip when he tried to take too much of me at once. "Fuck, you're so tight, Solace."

"That's always been our problem," he breathed, licking the pearls of sweat from his top lip.

"That's..." I paused to grunt, eyes screwed shut. "That's a good problem to have. What else do you like?"

"Pinch my nipples," he said, only able to ride the top half of me. He'd need to get adjusted before tackling the rest because my girth widened closer to the base.

The harder I pinched, the more cock he took, as if the pert pebbles were connected to his asshole somehow.

"What else?" I growled, and Solace arched his neck in offering. I lurched forward, biting down, nearly coming when he cried out. I licked at the marks my teeth left behind before sucking a bruise onto the patch of skin.

Solace raked his nails across my back as his ass crashed onto my lap, forcing me to hunch now that my cock was fully buried inside of him. I grunted at the sting of broken flesh.

I left hickey after hickey as he rode me slowly, whimpering my name as he did so.

"Noon," he moaned when I fisted his erection.

Rain pounded onto the pitched windows as he bounced on my cock, and not even the sudden clap of thunder could drown out the sound of his ass slapping against my lap.

"Did it feel this good before?" The bed squeaked in protest of our hard lovemaking.

"Yes," he whimpered. "Always s-so good."

I couldn't sit still anymore, couldn't remain a passive participant. I scrambled to get us off the bed, his legs tightening around me as I aimed for a bare wall, dragging him up and down my dick as I went.

"How does it feel now?" I asked, manipulating his body as if he weighed nothing.

"It's too much," he rasped.

"Good," I hissed, nailing his prostate and claiming his cry of pleasure with my mouth.

His shoulder blades met the wall, and with his fingers attempting to burrow into the skin of my nape, I fucked him ruthlessly. I watched with rapt fascination. Watched as his body jerked within my arms, as sweat dripped down the center of his chest, as his eyes shone with renewed tears. Through it all, my cock showed no mercy.

"How is it possible that I could miss something that I don't remember so damn much?" I asked, my own eyes watering. I kissed him, the softness of which I did so a juxtaposition to the way I fucked him.

"Please," he breathed once I'd allowed him to. His hair clung to every part of us; his body ablaze with heat, cheeks fiery red, lips hot to the point of searing my skin.

"What do you need, Solace?"

"I-I need t-to come."

"This doesn't end here," I gritted out, my own orgasm already a building vortex. "We'll get no sleep tonight, do you hear me?"

"Yes," he whimpered, his eyes rolling back. "Do what you want with me." It was that desperate submission in his tone, his acknowledgement of who held the power in this, his willingness to bend to my demands, that sent me tumbling over the edge.

"I'm coming," I bit out. "Grab your cock. Now, Solace!" I came, emptying deep inside his ass before he'd even touched his erection. Cum dripped from his hole as I pumped my hips furiously.

Solace shouted my name, then shuddered as his own cum shot between us like fireworks. I snaked my tongue out to swipe up a string of it from his chin, then sank to the floor with him once our shared release passed.

"Noon," he moaned, shoving at my shoulders when I kissed him savagely. "I can't breathe." I swatted his hands away, kissing him for a few seconds longer before allowing him the oxygen he needed.

He looked used and abused. My marks covered one side of his throat, his cum covered his chest, and my cum trickled from his asshole. There was so much I still wanted to do with him—do *to* him—and I didn't know where to start first.

I licked his body clean, swallowing down as much of our cum as possible. He peered down his chest at me, eyes going wide at the sight of my reinvigorated erection.

"I told you. No sleep tonight." I hauled him off the floor, then tossed him over my shoulder, grabbing the lube from the bed as I made my way down from the attic. I'd intended to carry him to the living room. Intended to take him on the couch I loved. We never made it there. We were fucking again as soon as we reached the bottom landing.

Solace was just as fevered as me, lowering his chest to the hallway floor, his ass high in the air as I fell to my knees behind him.

I pulled his ass cheeks apart, shoving my cock into him, loving the squelching sounds that came from me hurtling like a battering ram through his sticky, wet hole.

Solace whined at the back of his throat, the sound delicate and pretty. I flattened one foot on the floor for more leverage as I cursed and thrust into him non-stop.

He chanted my name as I began dreaming up what to do to him next. We had nine months of lost time to make up for, and I planned on reclaiming every second of it.

CHAPTER 20

Noon

Now

"I'VE SLEPT ON this couch before," I said, skimming my hands over Solace's body, getting reacquainted with him. Dawn approached, and we hadn't slept a wink yet. The couch pillows littering the floor and the overturned armchairs hinted at how we'd made use of our time since the truth had come out last night. I hadn't been kind in my handling of him. I'd needed to release my pent-up pain and lust and love, and I'd taken everything out on him, the true object of my affection. His body had bloomed for me every time, confirming that the edge of brutality imposed was not only welcomed but needed by him too.

"You remember that?" he asked from the crook of my arm.

"No," I answered around a sigh. "But it doesn't feel like the first time. A lot of things about this place, about you, don't feel new. I'd thought I was going crazy half the time, or that the familiarity wasn't specifically about you or this farm, but that maybe it all reminded me of something else. I thought that "something else" was what I couldn't remember. If that makes sense."

"Makes perfect sense," he replied, then frowned. "I'm sorry. I'm sorry I didn't tell you sooner. I'm sorry I lied to you, that I made you feel worse—"

"Shh," I said, quieting his guilty rant. "You don't have anything to be sorry for. You were right. Had you told me from the start, I would have pushed you away. I'm glad I had the chance to get to know you again first. To fall for you again on my own. You needed that. If I never remember our time together, at least you can be sure that what I feel for you now is real."

Solace nodded. "I can tell you everything you want to know. Maybe it'll help bring some of the fuzziness of your younger years into focus. I can share the stories you once shared with me."

"They tried that. Leland and Deb. It never worked."

"Yeah, but you're not angry now. And maybe your mind will be more receptive to it if it came from me."

"Maybe," I said. "We could try."

He slung his arm around me, kissing the scar tissue over my right pectoral. He'd found and kissed every scar I'd obtained in the accident. Solace cuddled closer. "And yes, you've slept on this couch before. We had a lot of sex on it. And we've danced to 'Tears in Heaven' too many times to count. We danced until doing so no longer made me sad."

I raised my gaze to the mantel, to the photo of Gavin holding the vinyl record. The record that had pulled such a visceral reaction from me. "And the clearing? Why do I need to walk there every morning?"

"We made love there too."

"Where haven't we made love?" I grinned down at him.

"In the canopy bed I had customized to fit at least three of you," he joked. "Most of this house, actually. It was still a work in progress at the time."

I hummed thoughtfully, watching the sun rise beyond the glass wall as I imagined everything he'd said, then letting it go when my imagination didn't spark an actual memory.

"Your last name..." I started, knowing I didn't need to say more.

"Cunningham," he replied, as if he'd known this conversation was coming.

"Is that Patrick's too?"

"It is. Outside of getting the divorce finalized, I didn't have the mental capacity to do anything else. I was too preoccupied with losing you."

"That changes now," I said, my voice clear that it wasn't a request. Solace's answering smile said he approved of my reaction.

"I'll get started on the name change petition tomorrow."

"Today," I corrected, twisting the braid I'd given him around my fist.

"Today," he whispered, kissing the corners of my scowl.

"Does your brother know?"

"I told him everything."

"How did he take it?" I wondered if his brother and Patrick were still friends. Solace's answer would greatly affect my opinion of his only living relative.

"He took a short leave of absence after everything happened. He stayed with me for a few weeks. I'd found it odd that Patrick hadn't contested the divorce. Then we met with our attorneys to sign the paperwork and I immediately understood why. *Gav* was responsible for how quick and painless our separation was. I sometimes wonder," he mused in a faraway tone, "if Patrick will ever regain full use of his right eye." He tried his damnedest not to smile.

"Nice," I replied, in approval. "I think Gav and I will get along just fine."

The warmth of his laugh tickled my skin. "I knew you'd appreciate that."

"I'm only sad I didn't get to deck him myself for everything he did to you."

He smoothed a thumb over my bunched brow, and I relaxed again. We held each other in silence, exhaustion creeping over us.

"Are you ready to meet everyone?" I asked. Now that I held the most important piece of my past within my arms, I felt ready to take on everything else. Ready to move forward in a way I hadn't before, and that started with letting everyone who loved me in. It meant knocking down the walls I'd put up to keep them all at bay.

"Yeah," Solace said as we hugged in preparation for falling asleep that way.

"Not for a while, though," I said through a yawn. "I want to be alone here with you for as long as possible before letting the outside world in." I wanted to soak in my complicated love for him. I wanted to make it uncomplicated. I wanted my heart completely full of him, and I wanted his heart, and his body, saturated with me. I wanted us to live like we had nowhere to be, and had no one's expectations to meet. I just wanted to love him, and be loved by him.

Solace hummed sleepily. "I'm more than okay with that, Care Bear. More than okay with it."

◆ ◆ ◆

We spent the last month of winter, and the first couple weeks of spring, locked away in Haley Cove. That was all the time we'd been afforded before Leland threatened to hunt me down. To buy us more time, I'd tasked him with getting everyone together for a family meeting of sorts, fully expecting my sister to join in remotely over Zoom.

I instantly regretted giving him the assignment when he called back a week later stating that my sister, nephews, and brother-in-law would be flying in the following weekend, and that Cole and Jasper would be hosting everyone at their estate.

"Are you nervous?" Solace asked as we drove there.

"I should be asking you that," I huffed. He was the one entering as a total stranger, the one looking to be accepted by a group of people who knew and loved my ex-wife. And those people had no idea who he was or that he was coming. I'd decided not to tell them beforehand. They deserved to hear the truth face-to-face.

"I'm here to support and protect you, first and foremost. To protect *us*. It'll be great if they accept me, but as long as I have your acceptance, I'm okay."

I brought our intertwined hands to my lips, kissing the back of his. "I love you."

I professed my love way too often, but I knew him better than I had a month ago. Knew that deep down he harbored some insecurity behind me not remembering our past. The kernel of doubt was small, thanks to me falling for him before finding out about us. I'd forever be grateful for that, would forever believe he'd made the right decision in not telling me until he had to. But because of that deeply planted doubt, my daily mission had become to prove that my love for him was unshakable and unbreakable, even if it had been disassembled and rearranged.

"I know," he whispered. "I love you too."

"I'm a little nervous," I admitted. "Mostly because I hate that look they all give me when I'm around. Like they believe I have the key to unlocking their happiness, except I don't remember what I did with the damn key."

"When you were thirteen," Solace began, "you started walking your neighbor's dog for pocket change before and after school. Mrs. Baker would greet you every morning with a kiss on the cheek, and Skippy, her Cocker Spaniel, would rush through the door and try to climb your legs. And in the evenings, she'd give you cookies and tell you to share with Deb. Skippy would whine when it was time to go inside—but only in the evenings," he clarified. "Things were going great until you turned fourteen and got a job at the library. Your free time was limited then. You avoided Mrs. Baker and Skippy after that, going so far as to wait out of sight across the street for them to go inside.

"Then one day you bumped into them in the hall, and Mrs. Baker said, *'Noon! Where have you been? It's been so long since we've seen you!'* You bowed your head, apologizing—again—for not being able to walk Skippy anymore. And do you know what she said?" he asked, pausing purely for dramatic effect. He knew I didn't remember that particular story. His dramatics worked like a charm every time, keeping me more focused on his retelling than my not remembering.

"What did she say?" I infused my tone with excitement.

"She said, *'That's okay, we'd just be happy to see you.'* And Skippy barked in agreement. You thought you were useless to them because you no longer had anything to offer, but they never saw you for what you did for them. They just saw *you*, Noon."

"Yeah?"

"Yeah. And I'm betting you're projecting that on your friends and your sister. My guess is you bring them joy simply by being around, and that look you're seeing on their faces, is their happiness to see you. Their gratitude for you being alive. Try not to read too much into it. Take the pressure off yourself."

Solace was my trusted guide into the past, the hand leading me down memory lane. He knew everything about me, a testament to how close and how in love we'd been during those months I couldn't get back. And as we weaved our way through our new reality, he took every opportunity to remind me why every moment was precious. He reminded me why I loved chamomile tea, that my favorite color was blue because I loved his eyes, and that the reason I enjoyed football so much was because my fourth-grade teacher did, and he'd been the closest thing I'd had to a father for a few years.

I'd fall asleep to stories of me, and wake up asking for more. Solace never grew tired of my requests to hear the same story more than once, and he told them in the most patient and theatrical way, as if he was there when it all happened.

The best parts were when I could jump in and add details of my own, when the fuzzy memories became clear. The more he filled me in on my past, the clearer things became, until I now not only recalled some pivotal moments of my adolescence, but I remembered how they made me feel.

Solace had been right. My anger and grief hadn't allowed room for Leland's and Deb's help after the accident. Now armed with the truth—armed with Solace—I was ready to listen in a way I hadn't been. Ready to accept what I was being told in a way I wasn't before.

"We're here," I said, turning onto the private drive of Cole and Jasper's property. Solace squeezed my hand as I continued to the front of the house. By the time I'd hopped out of the truck and rounded to his side, Cole and Jasper's front doors were thrown open.

Cheers of joy greeted us—or me. They hadn't noticed Solace yet. Listening to his advice, I told myself they were happy to see me, that they weren't waiting with anticipation for me to do some song and dance that the old Noon would have done.

They approached the truck. Deb with a baby on each hip, and Leland at the front of the procession. "How was traffic?" he asked, his smile faltering when I stepped out of the way so Solace could climb out. Everyone stopped to stare at him, even the babies, who'd been squirming and whining to be put down.

"Everyone, this is Solace. Solace, this is...everyone."

Solace came to stand at my side, and no one missed when he took my hand in his. He'd chosen the side that put him close to my sister with the babies now reaching for him with grabby hands. He shook a meaty little paw of the one closest, nearly losing a finger when he tried to extract them. "I forgot how strong they can be," he said before saying hello to the rest of the group.

They stood open-mouthed until I cleared my throat, shaking them out of their stunned silence. Simultaneously, they offered varying greetings of hi, hello, how's it going, and nice to meet you.

"Not awkward at all," I murmured for Solace's ears only. Cole ushered everyone inside, and the crowd dispersed.

My sister and brother-in-law went off to change the babies as they opened and closed their fists toward Solace, as if begging him to rescue them. Franklin headed for the kitchen to check on the food he was preparing for lunch, which seemed to make Leland nervous.

"We'll make sure he doesn't burn the place down," Cole said before he and Jasper disappeared, leaving Solace and me with my best friend.

"Well," Leland said, scratching his head in confusion. "I'm guessing this has something to do with why you've been gone for so long."

"Yeah," I said, unsure of where to start.

"And I'm also guessing I owe you an apology for sending you packing at the hospital," he said to Solace. Then to me he said, "Our phone conversation makes sense now."

The conversation about the unstable guy at the hospital. The conversation about Solace.

"It's okay," Solace said, waving him off. "Everything worked out how it was supposed to." He took my hand again, something he did a lot, something I was beyond grateful for.

"What's going on, Noon?" Leland asked, his brown eyes drifting between both Solace and me. There was an ache behind his gentle tone. He had to have felt left out of my life, even more so than usual. Maybe blindsiding him with Solace wasn't such a great idea.

"We'll explain everything soon," I promised. First, I needed a moment to regroup.

"Okay," he said, combing a hand through his cropped hair. "I'll show you guys to your room."

I grabbed up our bags and followed.

♦♦♦

We made pleasant conversation as we all ate together, temporarily ignoring the herd of elephants in the room. It gave Solace time to win everyone over without even trying, especially Deb. Every time Solace offered to take a fussy baby off her hands, she thanked heaven for him, then whispered to me that she'd take him if I ever decided I didn't want him anymore.

"That'll never happen," I said. She hid her grin behind the lip of her wine glass.

Sorrow and anger were the leading emotions expressed once we'd told everyone the truth. Mostly anger. Some of it directed at Stacey—who wasn't there to defend herself or to feel their wrath. I was surprised, though, to see some of that anger directed at me.

"Why didn't you tell me what was going on?" Leland asked, that ache from earlier still present.

"I don't know," I said honestly. "I...can't remember." Why hadn't I told my best friend about the problems Stacey and I were having? Or about the affair long before the accident occurred? Maybe Solace had the answer to those questions. We'd been so caught up this last month in renewing our love and filling in my past, that I hadn't thought to ask.

Leland wanted to be upset with me, wanted to be upset with the man he knew prior to the event that had cost me so much. I watched that battle play out on his expression until neither of us could take the tension any longer.

"Wait," he said when I stood to leave the table. "I'll go and cool off. You stay." He stormed from the dining room. Franklin smiled at me encouragingly before following him.

The rest of us took the party onto the patio, where heated lamps kept us warm from the cool spring breeze. The boys eventually grew bored of listening to adults do small talk, and Solace offered to take them to the play area that had been set up for them in the living room. Deb thanked everything holy for him again.

"Hey," Deb whispered as my brother-in-law chatted up Cole and Jasper. "Leelee Bear will get over himself. And if not, I'll give him a noogie for you."

I huffed a laugh for her benefit, vaguely recalling an incident when she did give Leland a noogie on my behalf. "He'd eaten the last of the strawberry cake you'd made. That last slice had been for me, right?" I asked, a bit hesitant. Her eyes, green like my own, shimmered. The noogie and the cake had been clear before. I'd been missing what connected the two. It was her love for me. I'd always been bigger than her, but it never mattered. Not when it came to defending me against others. I gave my heart a moment to absorb that.

"Yeah," she said fondly. She didn't push for more, and I appreciated that. It made me relax in a way I hadn't been able to since arriving here. Maybe Solace was right. Maybe all they expected, all they'd wanted for me was to be happy.

"I can't say I understand why he's so upset." I spoke low enough to not interrupt the conversation happening around us. "Some people don't discuss what's going on in their marriage. Not even to their best friend."

"I don't think that's the problem," she said, elaborating at my bemusement. "You and Leland had lost contact for some time after you and Stacey moved to New York."

"Yeah," I said, waiting for her to continue. That part I knew. It was why I had no recent memories of him. Our reunion, and the family we all created afterward, happened within the last couple of years before the accident. The years I was still missing.

"I think how he feels might go back to the state of your friendship before you left Seattle."

"What do you mean?" I sat up straighter, keeping my voice low.

"I get the impression, from little things he's said here and there, that there was a time when he didn't feel worthy of your friendship. That maybe you two might have grown apart because of it."

I had no recollection of that as it pertained to our childhood, so I thought hard about my young adult years. That point in time was relatively clear to me. I could recall spending less time with Leland after Stacey and I began dating. At that point she and I were ready to start a new life together, and had begun planning for it. I'd encouraged Leland to come to New York with us, to pursue his artistic dreams. He hadn't wanted to do either at the time.

Then I moved, and we lost contact after life and thousands of miles got in the way. But him not feeling worthy of our friendship was news to me. I'd been about to ask Deb for more context when Leland and Franklin returned. The former held a case of Stella in his hand.

I readied myself to make the first move in smoothing things over with him, but he beat me to it, popping the cap on two bottles before falling into Solace's vacated seat and handing one over to me. He clinked his bottle against mine before leaping into the ongoing debate over the lack of art programs in schools, a subject he was passionate about.

Leland nudged me with an elbow when all I did was stare at him in confusion. "We're okay," he said, his smile reassuring. I nodded, taking a swig of my beer.

Solace eventually returned, informing Deb that the boys were asleep in their playpen.

"You don't have to get up," he told Leland before taking a seat in my lap.

"I missed you," I whispered into his ear when he settled against my chest.

"I'm here now," he replied, stealing and finishing off the rest of my beer before scrunching up his nose in distaste.

"We'll raid Cole's wine cellar tomorrow," I said. He kissed my forehead in thanks. "Hey, that's my move."

"It's ours now," he said before the discussion turned to him. He answered every question directed at him with ease. I sat and watched as, over the course of the night, everyone fell in love with him.

When stories involving me came up, I didn't resist them like I normally did. I listened with fascination and acceptance, even asking an abundance of questions. There were moments when I got to be part of the story telling. Moments when something mentioned lined up with something I remembered, some detail I hadn't forgotten. The whole night provided missing puzzle pieces, but what mattered most were the new memories we were making together.

I'd taken the pressure off myself, like Solace suggested, and before I knew it, the people surrounding me didn't feel like burdens of expectation anymore. They felt like family.

CHAPTER 21

Noon

Now

THE FOLLOWING AFTERNOON, I slipped from the patio dining table after a parenting discussion over lunch segued into a spirited argument about alternative rock and classical music. Cole believed the latter to be more stimulating to a child's creative mind, and Deb snorted, calling his opinion snobbish.

Their voices grew distant the deeper into the house I went, until all I could hear were the soft snores of a congested baby as I neared the living room. I stopped on the threshold, observing Solace sleeping on the couch with two dozing ten-month-olds sprawled haphazardly across his chest.

The smaller of the two, Jackson, sucked on his thumb as he slept, while Nigel held the end of Solace's French braid.

"He got them to nap," Deb said in a hushed tone, startling me.

"Make a little noise next time," I grumbled, pressing a hand to my racing heart. "I didn't hear you coming."

"You were too busy drooling over him," Leland whispered, flanking my other side and scaring me to death. He motioned to Solace, and I couldn't help my smile.

Both he and Deb backed away from the archway with me. We didn't go too far. I didn't want to wake them, but I also didn't want to take my eyes off of Solace.

"He's good with kids," Deb noted, keeping our conversation hushed.

"Yeah, he used to be a teacher." I didn't mention Gavin. That was Solace's story to tell.

They both studied me as I continued to ogle Solace.

"The way you are with him," she started thoughtfully. "You were never like that with Stacey."

"No?" I asked, turning to her.

"Never," Leland chimed in.

"How am I with him?" We stood in a semi-circle now, and I alternated my gaze between the two of them, curious about their perspective.

"Vulnerable," he said after much thought. "And you never looked at her the way you look at him."

"How do I look at him?"

"Like he makes the world go round," Deb said, tackling that answer. "And he gazes at you like nothing else matters but you."

I glanced over to Solace again and thought she was right. He did make the world go round. My world, at least.

Deb kept going, as if she knew I needed to hear her next words. "Your love for each other is so visible and raw. It's nause-ating, if I'm being honest."

I chuckled low enough to not be heard by the three sleeping beauties. "Nauseating?"

"Yeah," Leland said. "Nobody wants to see that. It's like you two are sitting there naked with all your manly bits exposed." He feigned disgust. "I've seen enough of your big bits over the years."

I elbowed him in the side, then slapped a hand over his mouth to cover his grunt. Deb got in on the action, pinching my nipple. *"Ouch,"* I mouthed, batting her hand away and yanking on her ponytail in retribution.

She smiled like a goofball, and I did the same.

Putting our inner children away, Leland turned serious. "You never allowed anyone to show up for you, you know. You always shouldered whatever bothered you. It made me feel useless. Like you were perfect and had it all figured out. Like I could never measure up."

"I made you feel that way?" I asked, heart constricting. He hadn't said that *I* made him feel useless, but I couldn't help feeling like the problem had been me anyway. Deb rested a hand on my shoulder, letting me know she was there for me.

"No," he said. "I used to think it was you, or partly you. I eventually realized it was my own insecurities making me feel that way. It doesn't change the fact that you suck at letting people care for you. That's why I got so upset yesterday. You're a great friend, and I just want to return the favor."

Maybe that was why I hadn't told him about what Stacey and I had been going through or, at the very least, the affair. I thought about Patrick then. He'd lost his son, and hadn't turned to Solace for support through his grief. Maybe he'd turned to Stacey in a way I hadn't during our failed attempts at getting pregnant. According to Solace, I'd been everything she could have needed during that hard time. Maybe I hadn't allowed her to be everything I'd needed. It didn't excuse the affair, but it helped to understand how it could have happened.

Things were different with Solace. I leaned on him when I wasn't strong enough to hold myself up. And from what he'd told me, I'd been open to him in that way from the start, even during the moments when I'd put his pain first.

"I'm sorry," I said, because regardless of his assurances, I wasn't blameless. If he was willing to take ownership of his shortcomings, then I would own mine too.

"It wasn't intentional," Leland said, "and I could've done a better job at telling you how I felt. Being the strong one was where you found your value, it's what gave your life meaning.

But you let Solace take care of you. You let him hold your hand when the rest of us start to overwhelm you. You tell him the truth when he asks if you're okay. You allow him to see you weak, and you're stronger because of it."

"I love him," I said, squeezing the words past the emotion blocking my airway. "It's this wild, intense kind of love that I'm powerless to explain. I know I'm going to be okay when I'm with him."

"I know it too," Deb said, taking my hand. "Hang on to him."

"I'll be a better brother," I swore to her, then addressed Leland. "And a better friend."

"You're already the best, Noon." He shoulder-checked me. "Just be sure to lean on me sometimes too."

"I will," I promised, then leaned into him, giving him a taste of what it would be like from then on. We stayed like that for a while, me letting Leland support me and Deb holding my hand.

"Okay, maybe not lean on me literally," he croaked, straining to not tip over. "What have you been eating while you were gone?"

I straightened, giving him a ghost of a smile, which he returned.

Deb nudged her head in the direction of the couch. "Should I save him?"

One of the twins chose that moment to toss an arm out in his sleep, catching Solace in the chin. He didn't even stir. He was tired. I'd kept him up late last night, using his body to anchor myself after the day we'd had.

"Nah," I said. "Trust me, he's enjoying this."

We turned to leave, and I stopped her halfway down the hall. Leland continued out to the patio to rejoin the others. "Back in high school, I used to give your boyfriends hell," I said to her.

She scoffed. "That's putting it mildly. You were a prick. Threatened to reach into their bodies and rip out their guts. Who says shit like that?" she asked incredulously.

"I didn't threaten Gabe, though." The fog veiling the particulars of that memory had cleared in the middle of the night, revealing a tall, geeky guy trembling as he asked if he could date my sister. I'd given him my blessing.

Deb looked to her boys again, both the spitting images of their father. "No," she said. "Gabe you liked from the beginning."

"That's it," I said. "That's all I've got for now."

"And that's okay," she replied with a soft smile.

"Yeah. I'm gonna walk the grounds, get some fresh air. In case anyone's looking for me."

"Okay, just don't get lost," she said, giggling at my unimpressed expression. "Too bad you recalled your shitty sense of direction." She patted my cheek before heading for the patio.

◆ ◆ ◆

"I knew I'd find you here," Solace said, stepping into the stables an hour later.

I dropped the brush I held and marched toward him with purpose, crushing my lips against his in a jaw-aching kiss.

I'd come to the stables because I needed space, needed some alone time to think. But I never needed space from Solace, and if he'd been awake, I'd have taken him with me. Instead, I'd settled for missing him.

"I missed you too," he panted once I let him go. We lived in a constant state of longing for each other. If we weren't kissing, we missed each other's lips. If we weren't talking, we missed the sound of the other's voice. And if we weren't making love, we missed how life-altering it felt when our bodies came together in that way.

"I'm officially obsessed with you," I said, kissing his smiling mouth. "Thank you for being here with me."

"Of course." He wrapped his arms around me. "Never apart, never again."

That was our promise, our new pact.

"Jasper told me to tell you that Sophia's on her way."

Sophia was Jasper's best friend. She, her husband and their two boys were a part of the family we'd all apparently created. "Are you ready to have all these new people in your life?"

"With you by my side, I'm ready to take on anything." He peeked around me to the chestnut mare. "Is this Delores?"

"The one and only." I walked him over to her, then resumed brushing her thick mane as we spoke. "She remembers me. I wish it was a mutual remembrance."

"Your heart remembers," Solace said. "It's written all over you."

I nodded. "She's beautiful, isn't she?"

Sadness suddenly eclipsed the joy that had filled Solace's gaze, but then I blinked and it was gone. What had I said wrong?

"It's nothing," he said, holding up a hand. I hadn't realized I'd stepped closer to him. I

eyed him for a moment, then decided to let it go.

"Cole said we can take her to Haley Cove whenever we're ready."

"That's nice of him." Solace laid a hand on Delores's flank. "Think you can ride her?"

"I don't know. I mean, I want to. I'm assuming it's like riding a bike. I'm nervous about testing out that assumption."

The stablehand appeared up ahead, and Solace waved him over. "I guess we're about to find out."

"Solace," I started. "I don't think I—"

"Sure you can," he said. "You can do anything."

I'd been ready to change my mind, but one trusting look from him and I'd gained the courage I needed to try. "Will you ride with me?"

"Did you think I was going to let you have all the fun?"

I took Delores for a test ride inside the paddock alone. No way would I have risked Solace's life without first being sure I could at least manage the basics. For the most part, how to ride came back to me. With the assistance of the stablehand, Delores and I worked up to a nice trot in no time, then a canter once Solace was in the saddle with me.

Solace hugged me from behind, burying his nose into my back as we rode. "What's the matter?" he asked when I stiffened. "Noon?"

I slowed Delores to a walk.

"What are you remembering?"

"Wind in my hair," I whispered. "Feeling free, and... And a stream not too far beyond that path." I pointed in the direction. "I used to ride Delores down there. I remember that. Solace...I-I remember that."

"Take me there," he whispered, gripping me tighter.

Solace had never shown resentment for the clarity I'd been gaining about my adolescent years. Then again, those memories weren't the ones completely eradicated from my mind. This was the first time I'd remembered something from the two years I'd fully lost, and the memory wasn't of him. Wasn't of us. I could only be grateful that it wasn't of Stacey either.

I expected him to be sad, maybe even a little jealous. I might have felt those things if our roles had been reversed. Instead, he hugged me tighter, hugged me so close I could feel his heart leaping against my back. And when his lips lingered on my shoulder blade, and his next words contained nothing but the benevolence I'd come to expect from him, I was reminded of the magic of love.

"Your wins are my wins, Care Bear, and this is a win. To feel any differently wouldn't be loving you. Now, come on," he said, urging me on. "I want to see what's made you so happy right now."

"That would be you," I said, craning my head to look at him. "You make me happy, Solace. It's *always* you." Those glistening blue eyes cut straight to my heart, straight to the part of me that would forever belong to him.

The stablehand opened the gate for us, then mounted one of the other horses to follow behind. He remained a healthy distance away, giving us privacy, but I appreciated knowing he was there. Knowing we had a guide if we ended up lost on Cole and Jasper's estate.

"Tell me a story," I said as we moved along the trail, the warmth of the sun making the cool breeze bearable.

"Let's see..." He feigned thoughtfulness. "Are you in the mood for something you've heard before or something new?"

"Tell me about the time I lost my virginity."

"Ohhh," he said, extending the syllable. "I see someone's in the mood for a good laugh."

A burst of laughter escaped me right then, so loud and mighty that the birds within the trees we passed cleared their branches. "Don't forget that I remember all the details to that story now, so you won't get away with making me believe it ended with my tears of embarrassment."

"The downside to you remembering," he said wryly. Solace began the ancient story, and I listened and laughed, even stepping in a few times to keep him honest—to which he complained about me ruining all the fun.

We found the stream, and the stablehand made himself scarce as Solace and I forged new memories there—more than once, and in more ways than one.

Did it matter to him if I ever remembered the forgotten time we shared? Did it matter to me? Yes. It did, and it always would, if we were being honest. But we'd decided not to wait for my memories to return before starting our lives together. We'd decided it without ever speaking the words. Because one thing I knew for certain, one of the many things Solace had taught me, was that my heart remembered. My heart remembered every ounce of love we'd shared, every tear we'd cried together, every mountain of pain we'd climbed while holding each other's hand.

My heart had fought its way back to him, not even allowing me to stand in its way. My heart had claimed him. My heart knew him. And my heart always would.

EPILOGUE

Noon

Four Years Later

FOR ONCE I couldn't blame the hens for waking me up. I didn't know why I'd agreed to letting Solace set up the coop in the backyard anyway. Between the horses, the chickens, the goat, the three cats, the dog, the puppies, and the parrots we now had, the place would either soon be a working farm again or a petting zoo.

Shielding my eyes from the summer sunlight pouring through the bedroom windows, I sat up with a groan. Gone were the days when I awoke before sunrise. Nowadays, with all the animals taking over, I was lucky if I got any sleep at all. Today, waking before achieving a full eight hours wasn't anyone's fault but mine.

Dreaming wasn't new to me, but this dream felt too real to be classified as such. I remembered something. Remembered a few somethings.

I needed a moment to savor this. A moment to be sure before hunting Solace down with the news. Deciding I couldn't do any of those things with the cloud of sleep deprivation clogging up my head, I dashed for the shower.

With the steam clearing the fog from my brain, and the water masking the proof of my emotions, I cried and laughed into my hands.

I reached a shaky palm out to touch the phantom image of my now husband dressed in a tuxedo at a hospital charity ball.

He was devastatingly handsome, even while being shattered by betrayal.

My breath caught at the vision of him opening the door to his and Patrick's home. I'd thought he was the one Stacey had been having the affair with, but one good look at him and I knew he'd been broken by it, just like me. One look and I knew I had to be there for him.

I groaned, shuffling forward to press my forehead against the shower wall once I'd reached the memory of us making love for the first time. That lost look on his face that had made me want to take control of the moment. The shy blush of someone untrained in the art of seduction while his body moved with practiced experience. I was a goner. If I hadn't been before then, *that* had sealed my fate.

I'd remembered some of our initial time together throughout the recent years. Bits and pieces that had come to me in fits and shades of gray. Nothing ever worth mentioning, though. Nothing ever worth disturbing the life we'd come to accept. The life we loved. I remembered actual moments now, though. Full-blooded moments from start to finish. I still didn't have it all, but what I held now was a miracle.

I dried off and dressed quickly, dashing down the stairs and heading for the backyard where I knew I'd find Solace.

"Take my cock! Take my cock!" Igor chirped from his cage as soon as I entered the kitchen.

"Fuck me harder! Fuck me harder!" Elenor piped in, wings flapping. I muttered a curse. Solace and I should have never had sex in the same room as them. Maybe now he'd agree to get rid of them.

"Good morning to you too," I said dryly to them both, aiming for the open glass doors.

The insolent birds were forgotten when I laid eyes on my husband's tight rear end as he bent to collect eggs from the nesting boxes. My options were to get my mind out of the gutter fast or be the cause of Igor and Elenor's raunchy vocabulary expanding further.

Solace thanked each hen by name as he filled his basket.

"Maybe we should reconsider the location of this coop," I said, leaning casually against the doorframe. "They're a loud bunch."

"They're only noisy when they lay eggs," Solace said, chuckling as he worked.

"They lay eggs every day, beautiful."

"But not all day—" He whirled around, dropping today's batch at his feet. "Wh-what did you say?"

"I said they lay eggs every day, so by your logic, they're noisy daily."

"Don't make me strangle you, Noon." He approached me as if he meant to do just that, his breathing ragged. "You know what I mean. Say it again." His voice cracked as he gathered my t-shirt between his fists.

"I said, they lay eggs every day, *beautiful*." I spun a strand of his loose hair around my finger.

"Beautiful," he whispered. "You called me beautiful." He'd stuck to his word, never telling me the term of endearment I'd taken to using for him before the accident. I'd refused to start using a new one. I was glad for it now, because "beautiful" fit him perfectly.

"Yes, beautiful," I said. He'd get sick of me saying it now.

"You remember."

I kissed his forehead with significance, pulling back and looking directly into his eyes.

"You remember that too," he breathed.

"I remember."

Solace's eyes searched mine, seemingly asking if I recalled anything else.

"No," I said. "Not everything."

"Oh," he responded, smiling anyway. "You called me beautiful. That's enough for me."

If this were some romantic movie, or even four years ago, we would have fallen into each other's arms. I would have ravished him right where we stood. As parents, we didn't often get that type of luxury anymore. We wouldn't have had it any other way, though.

Activity sounded on the baby monitor perched near the coop, and then Pete the bulldog barked from in the kitchen, signaling princess Penelope's arrival. The other cats and dogs—who hardly ever left her side—trailed her as she padded her way from the downstairs guest bedroom. Solace normally carried her sleeping form in there while he dealt with the chickens. It gave him easier access to her if she woke up, allowing me to sleep in whenever possible.

She held a bunny in her arms. A bunny she *hadn't* owned twenty-four hours ago.

"Gav stopped by after you fell asleep last night," Solace explained with an apologetic shrug. "He wanted her to have it when she woke up. It's what she wanted for her birthday." His brother was in town for the party but had opted to stay at the farmhouse because we had too many animals for his liking. How ironic.

Our daughter loved animals, insects, and bugs. The last two were technically the same but worth mentioning twice.

"The birthday girl is awake!" I exclaimed, scooping her up and kissing her chubby cheeks until she squealed. Solace extracted the bunny from between us.

"I'm tree!" She struggled to get that third digit up.

"You don't look like a tree to me," I said, tugging lightly on one of her pigtails.

"I'm tree with a H." She nodded decisively.

"It's the best Gav and I could do," Solace murmured.

Our girl was beautiful, just like her daddy. And like Solace, she was kind and sweet and had the prettiest set of blue eyes. Penelope was our blessing, and the reason we would soon outgrow our home, because Solace didn't know how to tell her no.

"Girls are different," he'd said after bringing home the second rescue kitten.

"What's your bunny's name?" I asked when she reached for it. I set her on her feet so Solace could hand the fluffy animal over.

"Penelope," she answered, stroking the white fur.

"Perfect," I responded sarcastically, because two cats already being named after her wasn't enough. Solace coughed to camouflage his laugh.

"Uncle Yasper is getting me a turtle," she said, mispronouncing Jasper's name.

"A turtle?" I said with a tight smile. "How nice of Uncle Jasper."

"Animal Planet said turtles are low maymanants," she informed me, botching the last word.

"Animal Planet lied, honey. Turtles are *extremely* high maintenance."

"Daddy said calling people a liar is not nice," she said in a firm tone with a shake of her head.

"Of course he did." I glared up at him from my stooped position. My gaze promised retribution for this. The kind that would leave me collecting the eggs the next day because he wouldn't be able to move from our bed.

The cats spread out at her feet as Pete panted with his tongue hanging out from close by. The two pups barked their hellos at the coop.

"Jasper and Cole are taking her home with them after the party. She'll be gone the whole weekend," Solace said as I stood, letting me know we'd have the house to ourselves for a couple of days.

He and Jasper had become close after meeting. They were the most similar of our friends, in looks and temperament. We'd even crowned him Penelope's godfather. Leland too.

"A whole weekend?" I asked, then said pointedly, "I'll have to pace myself, then."

Solace backed away before I could grab for him, his bottom lip tucked between his teeth as he picked up his felled basket. "Come on," he said for everyone to hear—cats and dogs included. "We've got..." He stopped to count what had survived the fall. "Five eggs. Let's go make breakfast. I'll call Uncle Gav to come over."

"Can Baby Brother come too?" Penelope asked.

"Yes, Melanie is on her way," Solace replied, brushing a few blond tendrils out of her face.

Melanie was our surrogate. We were one month away from welcoming a baby boy into our tribe. Baby Brother attended every function, even if he wasn't here yet.

"Where's your camera, Papa?" Penelope asked. "We need to take pictures of P." She held up the bunny.

Solace's shoulders sagged. "Not the camera," he complained. In my rush to track him down I'd forgotten it on the nightstand.

"I'll run up and get it now, honey," I said, sticking my tongue out at Solace. Penelope loved when I took pictures of her and the animals.

With a shout of glee, she raced inside ahead of us, saying good morning to Igor and Elenor.

"Take my cock! Take my cock!" Igor replied. Solace and I winced.

"Daddy," Penelope called, confused. "What's a cock?"

"A boy chicken, sweetie," Solace answered, then turned to me. "It's your fault," he accused in a hushed tone. "Always wanting me to take your cock."

"Only because you take it so good, beautiful." I swatted his ass as we went inside, then I made the biggest stack of pancakes ever, topping it with birthday candles. The party didn't stop there. More people joined as the day progressed, and by the end of the evening, Jasper had to carry her exhausted, snoring body to the car. We sent Pete and the puppies home with them too.

We cleaned the house, showered, then slipped into bed, both too tired to hold me to my promise.

"We've got the whole weekend," Solace said, yawning as he rested his head on my chest.

"I'll make up for it tomorrow," I replied, stifling my own yawn.

He peered up at me then, tiredness and a burning need for answers flashing in his eyes. "How much do you remember?" he asked, sounding tentative, as if afraid the question might feel like pressure.

"A few things," I said vaguely. "We can talk about that tomorrow too." We'd eat s'mores by the fire pit, serve each other adjectives, and see who could win a game of fast-talk. We'd reminisce. We'd relive every moment that had returned to me today.

"Okay. Tomorrow," he agreed, still watching me, still waiting. He inched higher until our mouths were lined up, but he didn't kiss me. He needed something else from me first. In a voice that sounded almost like a desperate plea, he whispered, "You belong to me."

Solace spoke those words often. Every night, in fact, without fail. And I always repeated the sentiment verbatim. I hadn't realized I'd been getting it wrong until today. Hadn't realized it was more than a claim, it was a ritual. I hadn't remembered.

He'd never told me. Likely waiting... Likely *praying* for this moment.

"You belong to me," he said again with less hesitancy and more fire. This time I'd get it right.

I slid my hand along his neck, cupping his nape possessively before growling, "And you are mine."

The End

Bonus Scene
For a SWOONY bonus scene, other works by CP,
social media links, and to subscribe to C.P.'s Patrons
for EXCLUSIVE content, visit: www.cpharrisauthor.com

Pinterest Board
The Caretaker - Pinterest Board
https://www.pinterest.com/authorcpharris/caretaker/

OTHER WORKS BY C.P.

Visit here for all books by C.P. Harris
www.cpharrisauthor.com

FIND C.P. HERE

Website

http://www.cpharrisauthor.com

Newsletter

https://cpharrisauthor.com/#newsletter-signup

C.P.'s Patrons & Stalkers Reader Group

https://www.cpharrisauthor.com/subscriber-access

Amazon

https://www.amazon.com/stores/C.P.-Harris/
author/B088P988MF

BookBub

https://www.bookbub.com/authors/c-p-harris

Goodreads

https://www.goodreads.com/author/show/20305771.C_P_Harris

Instagram

https://www.instagram.com/authorcharris_?igsh=MWtjN-
Go1aDdiajcyOA==&utm_source=qr

ACKNOWLEDGEMENTS

To my cheerleaders and readers—who are often one and the same. Thank you.